# "Dear Friends," Letters from Abroad

## Ann Brady

 Pen and Ink Designs

"Dear Friends,"
Letters From Abroad

© 2019 Ann Brady
Cover images supplied by Adobe Stock

British Library Cataloguing in Publication Data.
A catalogue record for this book is available from the British Library.

Published in the United Kingdom by Pen & Ink Designs.

First Edition: 2012
Second Edition: 2019

Print edition ISBN: 9781912472628
Ebook edition ISBN: 9781912472635

Category: Historical Romance

# Chapters

# One

'The day has been a strange one!' thought Mary as she walked slowly up the steep gangplank of the ship. Her long skirt made it difficult to climb easily. Reaching the halfway point, she stopped. Turning to face the dockside her eyes searched, finally settling on the carriage she had just alighted from. Happy to see it still waiting she raised her hand and gently waved. A small gloved hand appeared from within, slowly waving back. No face appeared. It was unnecessary as Mary knew whose hand it was. Watching for a few seconds she raised her hand once more and waved. Dropping her arm, she turned and continued up the gangplank to finish boarding the ship.

The journey she was to undertake was a long and arduous one, which would hopefully lead her to a new and exciting life. She was filled with trepidation and sadness, having said goodbye to the only people she knew. Thinking of her predicament Mary was pleased Lizzie had come to see her leave. Even though they had spent so little time together it had helped settle her mind.

While Mary waited to meet the Captain, she looked at the vessel. It was large, about 200 feet in length. Originally built to carry goods it had room for six passengers plus the Captain and crew; a contingent of 25 men and boys. As a carrier for assorted goods it also acted as passenger liner and postal carrier, sailing between Britain and the British Colonies in the Americas. The ship would remain at sea for some fifteen weeks before docking once more in its home port.

Captain Morrison was welcoming, personally greeting each passenger. Mary gave her name and was introduced to Adam, a young cabin boy, who would be her attendant during the journey. Following him she was shown to her cabin. Upon entering Mary was pleased to discover a small, clean room. 'I think I shall be quite comfortable,' she thought. Looking around she was pleased to note her luggage had arrived but decided to leave unpacking until after the ship had sailed. It would occupy both her time and thoughts. Examining further she was glad to see a chest of drawers which would suffice her needs. As well as a small table and chair.

Happy with her quarters Mary returned to the deck and once more searched out the carriage. She waved one last time. The small gloved hand reappeared at the window and gently waved before finally withdrawing forever. The driver then took up the reins and Mary watched with sadness as the carriage disappeared from view. After it had left Mary wiped a small tear from her eye and leaving the ship's side she returned to her cabin.

Back in her room Mary chided herself for being silly and set her mind to more practical things, starting with sorting her luggage out. Placing her clothes inside the drawers she left what wouldn't fit inside the trunk and pushed it beneath the bunk bed. Then taking up her valise she sat at the small table. From it she took a small book covered in lavender silk. The book was a gift from Lizzie. She had given it to Mary just before she left the carriage. It was beautiful and was perfect for her to use as a journal. She decided to while away the hours at sea by writing about her life and then her adventures as they happened.

Picking up her pen she began:

*I was born in July 1861 in the small country village of Marston set in the heart of Hertfordshire. My parents were in the employ of the Lord of the Manor. Father as head gardener and Mother as a sewing mistress. My early life was settled and uneventful. I believe I had a joyful childhood living with my parents in the small tied cottage on His Lordship's estate. My maternal Grandmother moved into the cottage after I was born. She had lost her husband some years earlier, so didn't hesitate when Father suggested she come to help look after me. I grew up in a happy and carefree atmosphere.*

Mary stopped writing and sighed, thinking, 'I was

happy back then. We all were.'

*We were fortunate we always had plenty to eat. Life seemed idyllic and I was lucky in being able to attend school. It was run by His Lordship's spinster cousin Miss Catherine and taught both boys and girls.*

'Being taught to read and write at such a young age certainly proved to be to my advantage,' thought Mary. 'One I have found invaluable in recent years.'

*On Sundays we attended the local church and after the service I would play with the other children while my parents chatted with friends and acquaintances. My Grandmother often told me how the village people thought me a charming little girl. Whether this was true or not, I don't know. I was certainly dearly loved by my family and appeared to be liked by the villagers I spent time with. Family life was happy and carefree for a number of years. At least until tragedy struck.*

*It was June 1875. Father had gone to work early as we were to celebrate Grandma's birthday. Mother followed not long after, leaving me to do my chores before setting off for school. The morning was bright and sunny, promising to be a good day for the celebrations. I remember finishing my special gift for Grandma, a picture made from dried flowers and foliage. Wrapping it in some tissue Miss Catherine had given me and tying it with dried reeds. It looked very pretty and I was pleased with it.*

Mary stopped writing, recalling the joy she had felt at the memory of the picture she had made. She had kept it for a long time afterwards, only throwing it away recently as it had disintegrated.

*Father was working in the garden at the front of the big house when there was a commotion in the backyard. Someone had left one of the stable doors unlocked and His Lordship's stallion had escaped. It was a big fiery creature; black as coal, and difficult to handle. No-one could control him but His Lordship. People ran around, trying to catch the horse or urging him back into the stable but with little success. Their efforts frightened the horse more, causing it to turn and stampede towards the front of the house. Galloping around*

3

*the corner, it ran full pelt into a footman, knocking him to the ground, striking the man's head with its flaying hooves and seriously injuring him.*

*Unfortunately, his screams excited the horse more and before anyone could stop him, the beast charged across the front lawn straight into my Father. Being a little deaf he didn't hear the warning shouts until it was too late. By the time he looked the horse was galloping straight at him. Being on his knees he hadn't been able to move out of the way quick enough. He was killed instantly.*

Mary stopped writing. Taking out her handkerchief she wiped the tears which had sprung to her eyes at the memories of her poor Father. Finally, calming herself she began writing again.

*Everyone was overcome with grief at the accident, especially His Lordship. It had been a terrible tragedy. The shock of losing two of his staff in such a horrible way devastated him. He had the horse shot at once. Mother took the loss of her sweetheart extremely badly. Little was I to know how badly?*

Once again Mary stopped writing. Wiping the tears from her face she stood up to look out of the porthole. Even now, after so long, the memories still hurt her deeply. Only when she felt easier did she take up her pen again.

*My Grandmother proved to be a strong woman. Supporting my Mother and me, and encouraging us to keep going. His Lordship and Grandma organised the funeral, with His Lordship paying all the expenses. Mother was inconsolable. I often returned home to find her sitting by the fire having done nothing all day, ignoring all endeavours to help her. Fortunately, Grandma and I coped. I do believe Grandma kept reminding Mother she still had me to look after.*

The thought of her Grandmother and the strength she had at that sad time made Mary smile. 'Perhaps that is where I get my strength of character from,' she mused?

*The next few months passed slowly and before long Christmas arrived. The weather turned bad and the little cottage became draughty. Normally Father would have done some repairs but Mother had no thought for doing anything, other than pushing old rags into the cracks. Snow fell, the temperature dropped and it became colder. Grandma contracted pneumonia, with a fever taking hold of her. Before winter had passed Mother and I were alone. Grandma had, I was told, gone to join her husband in heaven.*

Once again tears filled Mary's eyes at the sadness she had felt at her loss. She had often wondered if her Grandparent had been so sad at her Fathers loss that she didn't want to celebrate another birthday. Perhaps it would always remind her of that terrible day. 'I know losing both her husband and parent affected my Mother deeply and though she tried her best to carry on it was obviously difficult. I honestly don't think she ever fully recovered from the loss?' thought Mary to herself. 'Nor did she realise just how much I suffered as well?'

*Being an only child meant I had to take on some of the jobs Father had done. Looking after the vegetable patch, feeding what few chickens we had, collecting the eggs and bringing in the firewood. I kept busy, but there were moments when I too felt lost. I had no-one to turn to, or talk to about my loss. The villagers rallied around us but still Christmas and New Year were quiet affairs. We coped. Until Mother became ill.*

*As her health worsened Mother could no longer work, having to give up her position at the big house. With the cottage being tied to the job it meant we had no alternative but to leave the village. The decision was a hard one for Mother. After all, her heart was here.*

*Finally accepting there was little choice, we went south to stay with relatives. Packing as much as we could carry, we set off for London to stay with my Father's relatives whom I had never met. Having often overheard my father talk about his brother, his comments had not always been good ones. I had never really understood why Father called him a layabout. Often saying the man couldn't hold a job down long because of the drink. To me my Uncle didn't sound very nice*

*but Mother hoped he might have changed. In a way I was*
*excited at the forthcoming journey for I had never travelled*
*far from our village before. The furthest distance being to the*
*annual market three miles away.*

Suddenly, Mary was disturbed by a knock at the door.
Calling 'enter', the door opened to reveal the ship's Doctor.
Greeting her affably he enquired after her general health.

"I must tell you Miss Watson, should you require the
services of a doctor while onboard I shall be available to
you."

"Why, thank you, Sir, for your kindness and
forethought. I am hoping I will not have cause to worry you
as I trust, once we sail, I will quickly find my sea legs."

Acknowledging her positive response, the doctor left.
As he did, Adam entered. "Miss Watson, the Captain would
be pleased if you could join him and the senior crew at dinner
this evening."

Delighted, Mary accepted the invitation and after the
boy had gone, she began preparing for the evening meal.

When the bell rang to announce dinner, Mary opened
the cabin door to find Adam waiting to escort her to the dining
room. The Captain welcomed her warmly and introduced her
to the other passengers joining in the meal that evening. The
food served was basic but tasty and fulfilling. Conversation
flowed freely and there was much laughter helping her to
relax.

After dinner the passengers took a short stroll around
the deck. As they walked Mary noticed lanterns strung along
the ships side helping to light their way. The sound of a fiddle
playing and men singing rose from the crew's quarters. They
listened to the happy music for a short while before
continuing. Reaching the end of the deck Mary found Adam
waiting with a lantern to escort her back to the cabin. Once
they were below, he entered the cabin first, making sure the
lantern was lit.

# Two

As Mary wasn't feeling tired, she decided to continue writing her journal. Having got to the part where they set off for London she smiled, remembering her girlish excitement. But also, how tired she had felt at the end of the journey and how frightening London had seemed to her.

*We arrived in London and I was shocked by the hustle and bustle of the place. Keeping a tight hold of Mothers hand, I didn't want to get lost as the dirty, busy streets all seemed never ending. Finally, turning into a side street in the poorer part of town we stopped outside a dull brown door with the number 36 painted on it. Raising her hand, Mother knocked loudly. A few seconds later the door flew open and a portly man with rosy cheeks stood looking at us. He was so like my Father I stared open-mouthed. And, for a moment I thought Mother would faint from the shock of seeing him.*

*Before she could speak the man grabbed hold and hugged her, all the while shouting a hearty welcome. Letting her go he held out his arms towards me. Reluctantly I let him hug me. He smelt of ale. Then drawing us inside we were greeted by the rest of the family. My Aunt gave us both warm, welcoming hugs, before making us some hot tea and toast which we sorely needed as we hadn't eaten since breakfast. Once we had finished our refreshments, we were shown around the house, which was fairly large. Uncle worked at the local hostelry and my Aunt 'did' for a lady living in a large house some streets away. I understood this to mean that she cleaned for her.*

*Unfortunately, the house was damp. Not the ideal place for Mother but, having no other choice, we made the best of it and quickly settled in. Mother and I were to share the second bedroom and my three cousins the large attic room. Within a matter of weeks, we were settled in to a regular routine.*

*I found the noise of London, and a house full of people, not an easy thing. Especially after living a quiet life in the country. London air was not to my liking, sometimes being so smoggy I often couldn't see my way through the streets clearly. But we couldn't complain as we were grateful to have a roof over our heads. Eventually Mother and I got used to living there. Each day I helped Mother get dressed before doing some chores for my Aunt. When she felt strong enough, Mother taught me my lessons or helped me to sew.*

Mary stopped writing, thinking back to those days. At the time they were as contented as they could be. 'Happy, without being happy' and she laughed at her thoughts.

*By August 1878 we had been living in London for eighteen months. One day my Uncle declared that two extra mouths to feed was putting pressure on the family's resources. Unfortunately, with Mother's poor health she wasn't able to work. Later confessing to me, "What little money we have is nearly gone. You are growing fast Mary and need new clothes." Sighing she continued, "Where is the money to come from, I know not?"*

*After much discussion it was decided I was old enough to contribute to the household income. My problem was, being slightly built it would have to be light work. When my Aunt learnt I could read and write she asked her 'lady' if she knew of anyone who might need a companion. A Mrs Maberley, who lived in a better part of the city, was found. It meant my leaving home early each morning so I arrived on time but, having now become familiar with the streets, I no longer feared getting lost. I started a week later.*

Remembering Mrs Maberley caused Mary to smile. She had been such a warm, generous, thoughtful employer whom she had enjoyed working for. 'I would arrive in time to have breakfast with her and leave after afternoon tea,' thought Mary smiling. She sighed at her memories.

*My days were spent doing light chores. Sewing, mending clothes or the linen. I would read to her or write the letters she dictated. Her eyesight was deteriorating, so my being able to read and write proved to be a godsend. Occasionally we went into town together, shopping or to visit her friends. As we walked Mrs Maberley always took my arm for, she was wary of tripping on the rough walkways. I was happy with my lot. And the additional money helped pay for a doctor for Mother. But, even with the medicine she remained pale and I became concerned for her. The little house being damp didn't help in her recovery.*

*Winter came. The weather proving to be particularly bad. Mother contracted a cold. My fear was that it would turn to pneumonia as she was finding it difficult to shake the illness off and her breathing was laboured. She spent much of her time in bed trying to keep warm. I did my best to encourage her to eat. Making hot broth with fresh vegetables which should have built up her strength. But I fear she did not improve.*

Shivers ran down Mary's spine as she recalled those bad winter months and the fears which had possessed her for her Mother. How she wished she could have done more. But it was not to be.

*Returning home one day I discovered Mother had a fever. The doctor was sent for and after examining her he announced he held out little hope. The illness was taking its toll on her already weakened state. Fear gripped me. What more could I do? Making the decision to stay home and nurse her, I sent a message to my employer. Mrs Maberley was most understanding and I was truly grateful to receive a basket of fruit from her to aid Mother in her recovery.*

*Christmas passed but, by the New Year I found myself alone. Mother was with me no more. Her health, having deteriorated so badly, meant she passed away in her sleep two days into the New Year. I was totally bereft. Not knowing what to do, for I had lost the last of my closest family.*

Mary placed her pen down, taking up her handkerchief once again. The tears coursed down her face as she recalled that saddest of times. Her dearest Mother had left her alone. 'I didn't know what I was to do. I was too young to be on my

9

own. And yet, I am on my own now, having lost another one close to me, my dear Lizzie.' And bowing her head Mary silently prayed for guidance. 'Dear God, please give me strength to go on? Why do you put me through this misery? There has to be a reason for your actions.'

Eventually calming down, Mary sat and took up her pen once more. She felt that she needed to finish this part of her writing. Perhaps to put England behind her. However, her thoughts are disturbed by a knock at the door. Calling 'enter' she watched as Adam entered carrying extra coals.

"I want to be sure the brazier remains lit Miss. It gets cold at night onboard so I will build it up to ensure you stay warm." Once satisfied he bade her goodnight and left.

The disruption, having broken her thoughts, made Mary put her journal away. Satisfying herself the door was securely fastened she readied herself for bed and climbed into the bunk. The thought hit her that she was now all alone and the idea caused her to shudder violently. Chiding herself for such gloomy thoughts she blew out the lantern and settled down. Pulling the covers up around her she felt the soft muted warmth of the hot brazier envelope the room. Listening to the sound of the waves gently lapping against the side of the boat she drifted off into a deep, untroubled sleep.

The next morning Mary woke to the tolling of the ship's bell. The morning sun was sneaking its way through the porthole, lighting up the cabin and giving it a warm glow. Rising from the bunk she looked out at the calm sea. A knock at the door brought her back to the present. Putting on her dressing-gown, she quickly went to open the door, finding Adam waiting outside with a breakfast tray.

"The Captain requests that you please take breakfast in your room this morning Miss. The ship is being readied to sail so there will be no time to serve the meal in the dining room."

Mary thanked him. "But of course, I understand perfectly, thank you."

Before leaving Adam said, "I will return shortly with

some fresh water for washing. Is there anything else you require Miss?"

"No thank you. I believe I have everything I need." And she smiled at the formality of the young man.

The boy smiled back before quickly leaving the room, returning not long afterwards to deliver the promised jug of hot water. As the cabin door opened Mary heard the sounds of activity coming from above, obvious evidence that the ship was being readied for departure.

The previous evening, she had learnt much about Adam, discovering he was thirteen years old. The Captain was his Uncle and he had been given the cabin boys job, so that he could earn money to help support his family.

During their conversation he told Mary, "My pay, along with the money my eldest sister earns from sewing adds to my Mothers who takes in washing. It means we are able to keep a good roof over our heads. Otherwise we would end up in the workhouse." Taking a breath, he went on. "My father was killed in an accident aboard a ship, three years ago, so now I'm the man of the house." Mary had smiled at his comment, for he seemed so young to be making such a mature statement.

Having finished her breakfast, washed and dressed, Mary tidied the cabin and sorted her possessions, before going up on deck where she met two of her fellow passengers. The Reverend and Miss Jayne Morgain, who had been introduced to her the previous evening. The three of them stood in silent companionship watching the activity of the seamen with interest. Mary had discovered the brother and sister were travelling to the same island as herself. The Reverend to take on the role of religious advisor to the islands people. Miss Morgain did not seem to be looking forward to the venture. It appeared the move, for some unexplained reason, had been forced upon her brother by his superiors. Mary had been surprised by the young woman's confession, deciding to befriend Jayne as she appeared to be a most personable young woman. Her brother however, was different, being arrogant and overbearing in manner. Something Mary found unusual in a man of God. She chose, however, to reserve judgement until she knew him better.

There seemed to be a lot of movement on deck as the crew ran here and there so Mary was not surprised when Adam arrived. "The Captain requests the ladies please retire below decks until after the ship has left port. There are many men running around and he does not wish either of you to be accidently knocked over."

Mary and Jayne acknowledged the request, taking their leave they retired to Mary's cabin. As they left the Reverend declared, "I will remain on deck as I wish to watch the crew at work." His comment brought some relief to the ladies. If they were honest, they both found his sour demeanour a little off-putting. Besides, in his absence they could talk more freely. The retiring of the two young women would occur often throughout the voyage, thus aiding and strengthening their future friendship.

Within the hour the ship had left the dockside. The ladies took turns to look through the porthole, observing the ships progress as it slowly crossed the water of the harbour towards open sea. As the ship left the protection of the port, the feeling of movement became more pronounced forcing the two ladies to steady themselves. A few moments later a knock on the door heralded the arrival of Adam.

"Miss Morgain, your brother is asking for you. I believe he is feeling slightly under the weather and requires you to attend him."

With an apology Jayne rushed from the cabin. This would not be the last time the poor creature was summoned to attend her brother's needs.

# Three

After Jayne left, and being confined to her cabin Mary took the opportunity to continue writing in her journal.

*The day after Mother's passing, I sent a message to Mrs Maberley. What kindness she showed me. Insisting I take as long as I needed to organise and attend my Mother's funeral. They were sad days for me. However, four days after the funeral I returned to my workplace and was surprised when Mrs Maberley offered me a home. I must confess to being relieved as I no longer felt able to continue living with my relations. My Uncle's drinking had worsened. He often wandered around at night in a drunken stupor, sometimes coming into my bedroom. When Mother was alive there was no problem, but now I slept alone, and I worried at the intrusion. My Aunt and Uncle were always warm and caring towards me but, I no longer felt comfortable, sleeping in the bed where I lost my dear Mother. And so, gathering my few possessions together I made my goodbyes and left their little house without a backward glance.*

Mary remembered that day clearly. The relief she had felt as she walked away from her relatives' house. She would always be grateful for their kindness showed in her time of need but, it was time to move on and she felt blessed to know Mrs Maberley.

*By the beginning of February 1879, I had been working for Mrs. Maberley for over a year. She proved to be full of kindness towards me. Upon returning to my duties I found myself allocated a small bedroom. So warm was my welcome I felt as if I belonged in her home. I was overawed and full of gratitude at the lady's thoughtfulness. My work was light and not taxing even though my days were filled in attending to all her needs. I sewed, did my lessons and learnt to speak French. I was a slow learner, finding it a little difficult to get my tongue around the strange vowels. However, I persisted in my endeavours to master the language.*

*One day Mrs Maberley and I spent time inspecting my clothes. She declared I must have a new wardrobe, one more befitting a lady's companion. It was, therefore, one very excited young woman (me) who left with Mrs Maberley on a trip to the dressmakers. Feelings of gratitude and affection filled me for I knew not how I could ever repay her generosity. My life had improved and I had so much to look forward to and be grateful for.*

*My days became settled as my relationship with Mrs Maberley became closer and closer. Time passed. I was nearly nineteen. Each day I met new people and was amazed at how readily they accepted me. Although a heady experience it was one which made me extremely happy. During a recent outing I had met a new acquaintance. A delightful young woman. The Honourable Miss Elizabeth Mountford, the only daughter of Lord and Lady Mountford. Though we come from different backgrounds we found ourselves becoming the closest of friends. She asked me to call her Lizzie (her father's pet name for her). Life was good and I often prayed it would last forever.*

'They were happy days,' thought Mary sighing, as she thought of her dear friend Lizzie. How she wished they could have gone on and on.

*Joining Mrs Maberley for breakfast one morning I was asked to run a couple of errands. I was to go to Dobson's to exchange some books and then the haberdashers to collect a yard of lace for a dress I was altering. The day, being Wednesday, was market day, so the area was busy but the weather was good and I enjoyed strolling to the shops. Outside the air was clear, with no smog. Which is good for walking. I met at least three people I was acquainted with. The town seemed busy.*

*It was an hour later I heard my name being called. Looking up I saw one of our footmen hurrying towards me. He was running fast and panting heavily. Instructing him to calm down he insisted on talking, telling me I had to return to the house immediately. He was quite distressed so I was*

14

*unable to get anything further from him. He just kept repeating that I had to return to the house. Realising something was dreadfully wrong I quickly gathered up my skirts and ran as fast as I could back to the house. The footman following closely behind me.*

'Never had I run so fast in my life,' thought Mary recalling that terrible day.

*At the house I found utter turmoil. The servants were standing around crying or pacing up and down. Upon entering the hallway, I met Jackson the butler who looked exceedingly distressed. He told, that Mrs Maberley had had an accident. She had been coming downstairs but missed her footing and fell. The Doctor was called and was with her. I was shocked. Wanting to know if she was alright but he couldn't tell me. With a cry I had dropped my packages, thrown my coat at the footman, turned and mounted the stairs two at a time. Racing up I dare not look back at the sad faces below.*

*Reaching the landing I had dashed to Mrs Maberley's room. Bursting through the bedroom door without knocking, what greeted me shook me to the core. Poor Mrs Maberley was lying on the bed, looking lost, pale and wan. The doctor, standing by the bed, moved away as I went forward. I knelt down, and gently took hold of my lady's hand as tears welled in my eyes. As I turned to look at the doctor, he slowly shook his head as if understanding my unspoken question. His response made me take in a sharp breath as I realised it was not good news. My heart was saddened as I realised, was I going to lose my dearest companion and friend?*

*Turning back, I watched Mrs Maberley slowly open her eyes. A small smile had crossed her pale face as she gently squeezed my hand. Just the once, before her eyes closed and she let out her last breath. My heart was broken. I couldn't move. A sob was torn from me. Tears streamed down my face as I found myself begging her not to leave.*

Once again Mary stopped writing as tears flowed down her face at the memory. Rising she fetched a fresh handkerchief and gently blew her nose. 'How I miss you, my dear Mrs Maberley. You were so good to me,' she thought. Once calm she continued.

*A few moments later the Doctor gently placed a warm hand on my shoulder and, in a kind voice, encouraged me to leave the room. Reluctantly I took one last look at my dear departed friend. One who had replaced my lost Mother. As I left the bedroom, I walked along the landing in a stupefied daze, before descending the stairs, with the Doctor following behind. As we reached the hall the Doctor took a deep breath before gently breaking the sad news that Mrs Maberley had passed away. The sound of shock and horror filled the hallway. There were tears all-round. Even Jackson wiped a tear from the corner of his eye for, in his opinion, Mrs Maberley had been the most generous and caring of employers.*

*The following days were a blur. Fortunately, Jackson was strong enough to take charge, running the household and assisting the Solicitor in making the necessary arrangements. I did little but spend my time sat hour after hour in the drawing room, wrapped in my deep sorrow. The room gave me solace, as it brought me closer to my dear departed friend. After suffering for a few days, I decided to send a message to Mountford House. I had no-one else to turn to in my sorrow. Dear Lizzie quickly arrived and I found myself breaking down as I explained what has happened. Bless her. She took charge, instructing the maid to pack some of my clothes before quickly removing me from the house. Taking me to her home, I was promptly put to bed, with Lady Mountford insisting a doctor be called to issue me a sedative. Within minutes of him leaving I was fast asleep.*

'Bless Dear Lizzie. Such a caring, thoughtful girl. I love her as a sister and could not have coped without her during that woeful time', Mary thought.

*The days passed quickly. I stayed with the Mountford's until I finally felt well enough to return to the Maberley house. Which I did not long after. Entering the house Jackson was there to greet me. There was also a lady I had never seen before, who was introduced as Lady Perryman. Apparently, she was Mrs Maberley's daughter.*

*The lady quickly took charge, asking me who I was? I was flabbergasted for in all the years I worked and lived with Mrs Maberley she had never once mentioned a daughter.*

*Shakily I had explained. Whereupon I was instructed to follow her into the drawing room. Once there she informed quite coldly that my services were no longer required and I should leave. To say I was astounded is an understatement. In fact, I was shocked. It appeared so quick and...., and calculating. She further informed me that Jackson was to remain as caretaker until the house was sold. The news had left me speechless. What was I going to do?*

'How uncaring her attitude had been,' thought Mary. 'Such a cold, hearted person. Oh, I am bad for such wicked thoughts.' But still, she couldn't help but smile.

*Gathering my thoughts, I had finally managed to explain that as an orphan Mrs Maberley had given me a home and that I had nowhere else to go. Reluctantly Her Ladyship allowed me to stay one more night but I was to leave in the morning. What could I do? I had no choice but to agree to her demands. Leaving the drawing room Jackson was waiting in the hallway. While he had been sympathetic, I knew the poor man was in the same position so there was little he could do to help me.*

'I remember to this day how kind Jackson was and I am pleased to call him a friend.' Mary smiled as she recalled the gentleman for in her mind's eye that is what he is.

*Retiring that night, I lay in bed sobbing for both the loss of my dear friend and my life as I knew it. The following morning, I looked pale and wan having not slept well worrying about the future. Jackson has shown some sympathy, offering what aid he could but I must have appeared lost as he took it upon himself to lead me below stairs, where we joined the rest of the household staff. Looking around I had felt distress for those gathered. They too were being put out of the only home they had known for many years. It all seemed unfair and cruel.*

*When Mrs Steadman, the cook, had asked me what I*

*would do or where I would go? I hadn't been able to answer her. It was obvious I was as bewildered by the whole affair as they were. It was at this point that Jackson had suggested that maybe Lizzie could help me. The idea that she might began to grow in my mind. So, I had quickly written her a short note which one of the footmen kindly delivered to Mountford House. After that all I could do was sit and wait.*

*But I needn't have worried for within the hour a loud urgent knocking was heard at the front door. When Jackson answered it, he found a very agitated Lizzie demanding to see me. Lady Perryman, hearing the noise, had gone into the hallway, being in time to overhear Lizzie stating most profusely, "I wish to see Mary, Miss Watson. It is my intention to remove her from a place where she is no longer welcome."*

Mary laughed out loud as she recalled the scene. Not sure who was more shocked. Jackson or Lady Perryman? "Bless Lizzie, for her actions," she said out loud laughingly.

*I am sure Her Ladyship didn't know what to say for as soon as Lizzie saw her, she commenced haranguing the lady. Telling her that her parents, Lord and Lady Mountford were astounded. Finding it a sorry state of affairs when a good person is put onto the street without a moment's notice. I had to turn my face away at Lizzie's audacity and bravado. This proved to me what a true friend she was. As for poor Lady Perryman she was so taken aback by the forcefulness of Lizzie's outburst, she was unable to speak. I confess it took all my self-control not to laugh out loud at the look of sheer horror on Her Ladyships face. Quickly packing my belongings, I obtained the wages due me and made my goodbyes to everyone. I then followed Lizzie from the house.*

'It was a sad moment for I knew I would never again set foot in the one place where, other than my country home, I had been truly happy,' thought Mary.

*Before mounting the carriage, I remember stopping, turning and looking back one more time at what had been my home for so long. As my eyes had wandered across the front of the house, I had spotted Lady Perryman watching me from behind the curtain. There was a look of relief etched across her face. It was most comical. With my head held high, I turned towards the carriage and climbed in, resisting the temptation to look back.*

The ship's movement was now more prominent, causing Mary to realise that time had passed. Wanting some fresh air, she decided to take the opportunity to go up on deck as she wanted one last look at England. She realised it would probably be some time before she saw her homeland again. The thought caused a strong feeling of sadness to envelope her. For a moment Mary had been tempted to shout it was all a mistake. That she did not want to leave. Fortunately, sense prevailed as she told herself not be so foolish. Straightening her back she resolved to be brave and strong, and to look forward to all she was to gain from the adventure she was now undertaking.

Mary had been standing looking towards England for some time when she heard footsteps approaching. It was Captain Morrison. He bowed slightly, smiling. "Good-evening Miss Watson."

Curtsying Mary responded likewise. "Good-evening Captain. I was enjoying a moment's reflection, as well as saying my adieus to England. Does that seem strange to you?"

The Captain was an astute man. "Not at all Miss Watson. It is only natural to want to soak up as much of the homeland as possible. Especially if you are to be away for some time. I often take the opportunity to say goodbye as we sail," and he smiled warmly to show he was not teasing her.

Standing in companionable silence Mary studied the Captain. Finally plucking up courage she asked, "May I be so bold as to ask how long you have been sailing Captain?"

Hesitating only slightly he answered her. "Well Miss Watson, I have been going to sea since I was a boy, much the same age as young Adam is now." He paused before continuing laughingly. "I have been most fortunate in my life. Both with my position and my dear wife who has great patience as she stoically tolerates my long absences."

"You are indeed a fortunate man, Captain," Mary stated with a smile. "And do you have a family?"

"Oh yes. I have three sons and a daughter. All three boys are sailors and my daughter has recently become betrothed. She will be wed upon my return from this voyage."

Taking a breath Mary hesitated, before asking, "Do you ever feel lonely while at sea?"

Looking down at her the Captain realised just how young Miss Watson was. Not much older than his own daughter Cassie.

He thought before answering her truthfully. "Yes, there are times when I feel alone. When I am away from my family. But I have the responsibility of this ship, and the men who sail with me, so I must not allow myself to be distracted too much." Mary nodded her head in understanding.

After a short pause he asked, "Tell me Miss Watson, have you ever been to the islands before?"

She shook her head. "No Captain. This is my first time aboard a ship. But I am not ungrateful for the opportunity I have been given. I was just thinking back to my childhood. Remembering my parents."

"They are not alive?"

Mary shook her head and before she realised it, she began telling him about her family. A short time later she apologised for delaying him and quickly wishing him goodnight she retired to her cabin.

# Four

Back in her cabin Mary wondered if she had been too forward in talking to the Captain. But, something in his demeanour reassured her that he would not be offended or put out by her confidences. She liked the man and believed he would prove to be a good person in her life.

With her mind easier she took up her pen once again remembering the feelings as she left Mrs Maberley's house. 'What a momentous day that was. The start of another aspect in my young life,' she thought. 'But how welcoming Lizzie's parents had been.'

*Arriving at Mountford House I quickly settled in. Lord and Lady Mountford were charming and welcoming. I knew from the start I could not stay there forever but for the moment it gave me a safe haven. As well as a respite from thinking about my predicament. It also meant I could grieve the loss of my dear friend. I found Lizzie and her Mother proved to be considerate and caring hosts. Aware of my delicate state of mind they made every effort to ensure I was kept fully occupied. I joined them at church or in taking tea with acquaintances staying in town for the season. Lizzie did her very best to lift my spirits. I will always be grateful to her.*

Mary recalled how special she had felt under Lizzies constant care. 'What a good and true friend she has proven to be to me.'

*My physical and mental strength improved. I began to feel capable of facing the realities of the changes affecting me. Thinking of my situation it was, in some respects good as I felt more positive about my life. And yet, in other ways I was still lost, as if I was floundering. In reality I had, over the last two years, lived a lie. My position in Mrs Maberley's house had been far better than any I could have expected. My current circumstances made me very much aware how far*

21

*beneath my current host's social standing I am. And I knew I must not forget that. I could not go back but neither could I go forward. I was a homeless person, totally confused and bewildered as to what was to become of me.*

*Lady Mountford must have realised my confused state. Perhaps thinking I was suffering a form of depression. She was very kind to worry about my health and state of mind. But Lizzie also worried. Unbeknown to me, she discussed my situation with her Mother, enquiring as to whether or not, there was something they could do to assist me. Fortunately, Her Ladyship, a most caring Mother who doted on her daughter, was prepared to help if she could.*

"I soon discovered what a considerate soul Lady Mountford was. She reassured Lizzie, she would give the matter some thought, even discussing it with His Lordship. I was grateful for their concern over me and my future," Mary said to herself.

*With a calmer mind, and being a resilient person, I decided not to allow any worries to take too strong a hold. I would face each day with a stout heart. However, as strong as I thought I was, it still came as a shock when returning from church to be summoned to His Lordships study. I had felt a little nervous, being sure I had done nothing wrong which required such a summons. Entering the study Lord Mountford must have noted my nervousness for he had quickly urged me to relax. Telling me not to be concerned as he merely wished to discuss my future with me.*

*Settling into a chair His Lordship had explained how Lady Mountford and Lizzie were concerned about my wellbeing. In particular about my future, wanting to see me happily settled.*

*I was not surprised by his comments as I knew, eventually, I would have to make a decision about my future. I had held my breath for a moment, waiting to hear the dismissal I thought was forthcoming. But it was not to be as His Lordship had gone on to surprise me by saying I was not to worry about the current situation. That he was there to offer me all possible assistance. And, that under instructions from his wife and daughter he had been investigating what options were available to a young woman in my position. I was surprised, quietly thanking him for his consideration. But he had brushed this aside going on to say he had found, hopefully, an agreeable solution.*

*Although I felt some relief, I had waited nervously to hear what the solution was. His Lordship being aware I could read and write had obviously felt me capable of teaching. And so, he had found a teaching position for me. As I sat thinking about his suggestion, the idea appealed to me. After all, if His Lordship had confidence in my abilities then there was no reason why I should doubt myself.*

*I had continued listening to the details. Discovering that the school was situated on a group of islands; part of the British Colonies near America. His Lordship had reassured me I would be safe. And, in order for me to take up the position he was willing to pay my passage. As well as providing me with a sum of money to cover my living expenses until I had earned my first wages. He further reassured me he would supply everything needed to help me set up the new school.*

*Silently I had contemplated all he had said. I knew I had to give the offer due consideration for I might not get another one so beneficial. The only difficulty, was it being a long way from England. Which meant my leaving those I knew?*

*Being astute, Lord Mountford must have noted my hesitation. Whether he suspected my fear at being put out onto the street, I know not, as he reassured me I did not have to take up the position if I chose not to. And that I was welcome to remain at Mountford House until you found a suitable position or place to reside." I admit I felt great relief at this comment and not wanting to appear ungrateful I thanked him and asked for time to consider his kind offer. He readily agreed and with nothing more to be said I stood up and left the study.*

Mary thought, 'The offer had left me astounded and yet

I was grateful for his generosity. All I could do was thank him profusely for his kindness. I think I knew I could not refuse, despite his reassurances that I could do so if I wished?'

*I chose to retire to my bedroom to think about the conversation. However, Lizzie had come looking for me and, finding me sat in the dark, had begun questioning me about what her father had wanted. Reluctantly I had explained. Doing my best to sound enthusiastic whilst carefully explaining what an ideal opportunity it was. While Lizzie had been pleased her father was assisting me the manner of it had shocked her.*

Perhaps she had realised it meant our not being able to be with each other anymore? I wasn't able to reassure her our friendship would continue, regardless of where either of us was. I tried my best to make her understand I had little choice in the matter for I am ill equipped to do much else. "I needed her to understand that as close as we were, I was only living in her house on sufferance of her parents. Neither she, nor I could have expected them to put up with me forever," Mary told herself. "Lizzies lack of comprehending the reality of my life is due to her being a Lord's daughter. She leads a blessed life with no worries or concerns to trouble her."

*In order to reassure Lizzie, and hopefully give her time to accept the situation, I agreed to sleep on the matter before making a final decision. Unfortunately, she left the room upset, and me feeling guilty at having distressed her. Dinner that evening was an uncomfortable affair as I believe Lizzie had spoken to her parents, telling them how unhappy she was. For the first time since arriving I was relieved when it was time to retire.*

*The following morning, I looked strained and tired but there was little I could do about it. His Lordship had left the house early and was to be away three days. His absence gave me more time to arrive at my decision. I was relieved. Lizzie and her Mother, were absent too, having left for town straight after breakfast. Lizzie was having a new evening gown as she was attending the end of season ball at the palace. Their absence allowed me time to think and consider what was best.*

*After breakfast I decided to visit my Aunt and Uncle. Being my closest relatives, they may be able to advise me. Later that morning I quietly left the house, making my way to the other side of town. It had been some time since I strolled so freely through the city, making me realise what a different person I had become. Arriving at my Uncle's house I was shocked to discover they no longer lived there, having moved some weeks previously. The neighbours, and those at the hostelry didn't know where my family had gone. I discovered there had been some trouble and my Uncle had been told to leave. And they were gone by the next day. But no-one knew where. For just a moment I felt a frisson of fear. It suddenly hit me I was all alone in the world with no-one to discuss things with. Likewise, it meant I had no-one to answer to either. With my only family gone, any decisions I made would now be mine, and mine alone. My mind was in a whirl as I tried to decide what to do?*

'It was a shock to find the family gone and myself alone. And yet, what assistance could they have given me? I'm not sure,' thought Mary.

*Returning to Mountford House I made my decision. I was going to accept what was being offered. But until I confirmed it with His Lordship, I would remain quiet on the subject as I didn't wish to upset my dear Lizzie. Strangely, that night I remember sleeping well.*

'That was the point at which I realised that I was now truly alone,' thought Mary. 'It was a feeling which cut me deeply and brought home to me that the only person I could now rely on was myself. I realised that from that moment on I was in charge of my life. I would have to make of it what I could.'

*Three days later Lord Mountford had returned home. I had immediately requested an audience with him where I happily accepted his generous offer. Looking back, I believe he was relieved as I am sure neither of Lizzie's parents really approved of our friendship. Our positions and status in life*

*are so widely different. A fact Lizzie appears blissfully
unaware of.*

*And so, two weeks later I was ready for my journey. Yes,
I was sad Lizzie was upset even though I did do my best to
explain fully to her my reasons for going. Hopefully, once she
gives it more thought she will realise it is the best solution
all-round. The last weeks were not the easiest. Lizzie grew
quieter and quieter the closer my departure day approached,
causing me not to speak of the future. I know we will not part
on bad terms for to do so would sadden me greatly.*

"It wasn't until yesterday Lizzie finally convinced her
father to allow her to come to the docks with me," laughed
Mary. "She did her very best to reassure him she would be
perfectly safe."

*His Lordship had objected strongly to Lizzie escorting
me to the docks. Telling her it was dangerous but she had
worked on him as only she can. Finally, he had capitulated,
agreeing so long as she didn't leave the carriage. Later that
evening Lizzie had sneaked into my bedroom, climbing into
bed beside me. I hadn't had the heart to refuse her when she
begged to stay. Although when I woke the following morning
she was gone. Maybe she just needed some reassurance of my
affection for her.*

*My packing was done and the footman had carried it
downstairs. I had not anticipated breakfast would be a light,
cheery affair. However, I was surprised to discover all the
family in attendance. Lady Mountford gave me a gift of
delicate lace handkerchiefs. His Lordship five pounds. When
I had expressed my concern at his generosity, he had given
me so much already, he dismissed the gesture, telling me to
put it away for a rainy day. I shall remain deeply grateful to
the family for all their kindness and care.*

*Finally, I took my leave of Lord and Lady Mountford,
having already made my adieus to the household staff. I shall
miss them all dearly having grown close to them as they have
in some way replaced my lost family. As we mounted the
carriage Lizzie and I settled on the seat and held hands. But,*

*as we pulled away from the house, I waved goodbye one last time to all those I had come to know and care about.*

Mary read through all she had written. Then at the bottom of the last page she wrote the following: *Tomorrow is the first day of the rest of my life. I wonder if I am being reckless in travelling so far, to take up a position, in a place I have no knowledge of. And yet, I know I have little choice in the matter, being an orphan. The unhappiest moment was having said goodbye to the only people I know. It makes me sad but the options available to me are limited.*

Satisfied Mary turned the page and started writing afresh: *My Journey Abroad - Having boarded the ship, I find my cabin comfortable. A nice young man called Adam is my cabin boy. The first evening I joined the Captain and the other passengers for dinner which proved to be a most affable affair. Although not a nervous creature by nature I was a little wary when it came to meeting new people. However, all those present made me feel welcome and I soon relaxed, joining in the conversation and laughter with ease. It bodes well for the start of my journey.*

# Five

A few days into the journey Mary spent some time with some of the remaining passengers, starting with Colonel and Mrs Johnstone. They were a lovely couple with no children being happy with their own company.

Mary would later write in her journal: *Today I met more of my potential island neighbours. I have learnt the Colonel is a retired Army officer who invested his money in property on the islands. The couple are returning home after spending time touring Europe, celebrating their 10th wedding anniversary. Mrs Johnstone has proven to be most friendly, insisting I call her Laura, which I am quite happy to do. The final passenger is a gentleman called Lord Falshaw. During the day he keeps very much to himself, although he does spend a good deal of time with the crew. Whilst his behaviour is most civil when addressed, he otherwise tends to ignore people. He also appears not to be averse to stripping to the waist to work alongside the crew. I find this unusual behaviour in a gentleman.*

When Mary questioned the Captain about this he apologised. "You must forgive His Lordship's behaviour. He is used to doing manual labour. Living on the island's workmen are scarce so His Lordship thinks nothing of joining in where work needs to be done on his estate. I trust you are not embarrassed by his behaviour."

"Not at all. It is just that I find it most unusual in a titled gentleman."

Strangely, it seemed no-one else found His Lordships behaviour unusual, greeting him with the respect his title deserved. Mary did wonder if he was perhaps a little eccentric.

The ship had been at sea about five weeks when it docked at a small harbour port to take on fresh supplies. The passengers were allowed to go ashore and the experience of placing her feet on terra firma had at first made Mary feel slightly dizzy. It took a few moments for her to gain her sense of balance.

She later wrote in her journal: *After we docked Jayne, Laura and I took a stroll along the wharf. I was amazed at the hustle and bustle of the place. Fortunately, we found a small establishment offering refreshments which gave us the opportunity to sit, take some food and a small glass of wine. On the veranda were some wicker chairs where we sat for some time, enjoying the afternoon sun. Although there was a slight breeze, the place was sheltered enough to make our stay comfortable. We enjoyed the day until Adam arrived, requesting we return to the ship which was making ready to get underway. The Captain wished to leave on the next tide. It was with great reluctance we took our leave of the establishment, slowly returning to the ship feeling exceedingly refreshed.*

Back on board ship the passengers found life quickly settling into a daily routine. They were fortunate with the weather, remaining good enough to allow them to exercise daily by taking turns around the deck. On these occasions Mary found the crew courteous, bobbing their hats or touching their foreheads in respect whenever the ladies passed. Mary also found her time spent in a variety of ways. Not just walking on deck but playing cards or having a game of Ludo with Jayne and Laura. However, once on her own she filled her time filling her journal or writing letters to Lizzie. Even though she couldn't send the letters until the ship docked, she decided it would help Lizzie settle if she wrote about the happenings on board ship. It also helped settle her own mind towards the journeys end.

Returning to her cabin after dinner one evening Mary took out her first letter to Lizzie. Sitting at the small table she read it through, checking she had included all she wanted to tell her dear friend.

*My Dearest Lizzie*

*My journey so far has been uneventful. I will admit to suffering regret and sadness after we sailed. However, having reassessed my position I realise I am fortunate and shall look upon this journey as a great adventure. The start of a new phase in my life. As I watch the movement of the sea it is beautiful and peaceful. It calms my mind, allowing me to sit in silent contemplation with an easy heart and a feeling of being at peace. The silence at these times is broken only by the soft mumblings of the crew going about their daily routine. Or by the sound of the water lapping against the sides of the ship as she glides majestically thro' the clear blue, green water. Why do they refer to a ship as 'she'? I am at a loss to understand and must ask the Captain as he will surely know.*

*My cabin is below decks, and is small and cosy. It contains a table, chair and chest of drawers for my belongings. There is a small window, or I should say porthole, through which the daily sun shines. However, once the sun goes down the cabin becomes dark. This is when my cabin boy Adam lights the lantern hanging over the table. At night the temperature drops considerably so Adam returns to light the brazier. A muted glow, envelopes the cabin making the place feel warm and cosy. Once the light expires, I am left with the glowing embers of the fire and the moonlit night shining through the porthole. There is a bed, or bunk as it is called, which I have found easy to sleep in. But I think I would sleep well regardless, having had so much fresh air during the day.*

*The Captain informs me our voyage will take about seven weeks as the ship will stop at a number of places along the way. Four weeks into our journey we stopped at a small port, being allowed to go ashore to stretch our legs, which proved to be most refreshing. I found the place basic but exceedingly busy and along the wharf we discovered a small inn offering good fare. It felt good to stand on solid ground once more. However, we only stayed long enough for the ship to take on fresh water, fruit and vegetables. The Doctor tells us it is most important the crew and us passengers get fresh food and water daily so as to prevent scurvy. I am not sure what he means but the crew certainly look fit and healthy. In a matter of hours, we were back on board and with the sails at full extent the ship made its way into the ocean. Since then I have found my time well occupied, so am content.*

*Looking back at our parting I am sorry we did not spend more time together before I boarded the ship. Know I miss you greatly but we can write to one another. I will send letters by the ships which call at the islands. I am positive we can keep in touch even though we are such a distance apart. Once we land, I have arranged to give this letter to the Captain to bring back to England for you. In the meantime, I shall write more of my journey so you are aware of my life and what is happening in it.*

*Night draws in so I will finish this letter and be away to my bed. The wind appears to be building and I fear the night will not be as calm as these last few days have been.*

*Think of me often as I think of you.*

*Your loving friend Mary*

Satisfied Mary folded and sealed the letter before putting it away in a drawer. She was aware the winds were indeed building, causing the ship to sway somewhat violently so decided it best to retire. She prayed the wind would blow itself out during the night. Unfortunately, as she lay down in her bunk, Mary was unaware she wouldn't be rising for a number of days to come.

The following morning when Mary woke, she did not feel at all well. In fact, she felt so sick she couldn't sit up without becoming dizzy. Again, she began wishing she had never left England. Hearing a knock, she struggled to rise from the bed. Managing to open the door she found Adam had brought her some fresh water. Seeing her pale face, he was immediately concerned, deciding to report her condition to the Captain. Once he left Mary crawled back into bed relief flooding over her as her head touched the pillow and the world stopped spinning. Not long afterwards Jayne came to enquire why Mary had missed breakfast. She was alarmed to find her in a state of distress, immediately sending for the ship's Doctor to bring a medicinal draft. Jayne offered to stay, but feeling so unwell, Mary declined the young woman's kind gesture. Wanting only to be left alone in her misery.

The draft helped settle Mary's stomach, allowing her to fall into a deep sleep. Later in the day Laura called to see how she fared, offering sympathy for her poor condition. It was some four days, once the sea had calmed, before Mary felt recovered enough to eat a few spoonsful of soup. And a week later before a much-revived Mary found she was able to rise without suffering any side effects. With her spirits much improved the Doctor allowed her to spend some time on deck sat in a chair wrapped in a blanket. Later, having returned to her cabin Mary penned another letter to Lizzie.

*Dearest Lizzie*

*It has been some time since I last wrote. As noted before, the night did indeed become unsettled. The ship swayed and rocked quite violently and the wind howled so loud it sounded like a dog in pain. My poor stomach became upset and I suffered with chronic malaise for many days. Finding I could not eat nor sit up. I believe the ship's Doctor was a little concerned by my distressed state. He has proven to be a most caring gentleman, calling every day to check if I am well.*

*Do not despair dearest for I am now fully recovered and am eating normally, being back to good health. I am hopeful of finding my sea legs once more. The wind has eased but remains strong enough to be refreshing and to fill the sails. Our progress is much improved and the Captain says we will sight land within a few days after which we will disembark and my new adventure will begin.*

*Lizzie dear I have been most remiss in not telling you more of my companions. Captain Morrison has proven to be a charming man. He informs me he has been married some years and has four children of varying ages. He runs the ship with a strong hand but for all his sternness the crew appear to love him dearly.*

*The Doctor on the other hand is a man of indeterminate years. I believe him to be a confirmed bachelor, very much set in his ways. Being a man of learning he is full of*

*information and knowledge about the world through which
we travel. Yesterday he was kind enough to point out the most
amusing of creatures swimming in the sea. They appeared to
be racing alongside the ship. The Doctor called them
Dolphins. They are the most adorable creatures I have ever
seen being grey in colour, fairly large in size, with long
pointed faces. We heard them making funny squeaking
noises, which the Doctor told us was their way of
communicating with each other. I found them delightful and
I am sure you would have thought them highly amusing.*

*The other passengers on board include Reverend
Morgain who travels with his sister Jayne. It is his intention,
so he informs us, to bring the faith to the islanders. He
appears staid and oppressive in attitude, whilst his sister on
the other hand, is gentle and personable. I think she may be
slightly afraid of her brother as she runs whenever he calls.*

*There is also Colonel and Mrs Johnstone (Laura) who
are returning to their home on one of the islands close to the
one I shall be living on. They have been most kind to me with
Laura calling every day to see how I fared whilst laid low
with the malaise. She hopes we will be good friends and
insists I visit them, once I am settled in my new island home.
I admit my dear the thought of having someone to talk to and
visit, relieves some of the apprehension I feel towards my
journeys end. I believe it will be comforting to have a friend
living close. Not that she will ever replace my dearest Lizzie
in my heart. With you being so far away from me I am sure
you will understand.*

*The final passenger I know little of. His name is Lord
Percy Falshaw. Although he appears a gentleman his actions
are peculiar. He has spent much of the voyage in the company
of the crew. I have to be honest and say I find him pleasing to
look at. Yesterday whilst walking on deck I came upon him.
He was stripped to the waist, working alongside the crew and
I believe I blushed when I spied him. His body is brown and
muscular. I swear his eyes glinted with amusement when he
saw me watching him. I was embarrassed, quickly walking*

*away without a backward glance. I am positive I heard him laughing as I departed.*

*Anyway, my darling friend I find my head is drooping and my eyes closing so I will complete my letter. Sleep well my dearest.*

*Think of me as I do you.*
*Your loving friend Mary*

Life on board continued with little incident. Both weather and sea remained calm. As the end of her journey came closer Mary found herself looking forward to being on dry land once more. Her recent malaise had left her slightly drained and looking a little pale. Jayne had been concerned for her but Laura announced a few days in the sun would soon change all that. 'The warmth will do me the world of good and I will soon be back to my old self in no time.'

Although the winds had eased, they had not dropped completely allowing the ship to make good progress. It was therefore a few days later the Captain dropped anchor inside a large bay. Mary's first sight of the island proved to be an exciting one. She had not been sure what to expect even though Laura had described what she could about the islands to her and Jayne.

With the ship at a stop inside the moon-shaped bay the Captain told them, "We drop anchor here as we cannot sail to the dockside for the port area is too shallow for larger ships such as ours. Tomorrow everyone will board the launch and go ashore."

Sitting in her cabin that evening Mary wrote her last letter to Lizzie. She would not be able to send any others for some time so wanted to reassure her friend she had arrived safely.

*My Darling Lizzie*

*We have arrived and the ship is standing in the harbour. We are to remain onboard tonight and disembark early in the morning. I am so excited Lizzie I believe I may not sleep this night. My bags are packed and ready to be taken to my new home.*

*The Captain has agreed to take my letters back to England with him. I believe he will honour his word, making sure you receive all three missives. Therefore, my Dear One if you are reading this then he is truly a man of his word.*

*Unfortunately, My Sweet Lizzie, this will be my last letter for some time. I know not when I will write again as I will have to rely on the ships which call at the islands. Please do not fret for me. In the meantime, I beg you please not to forget me. You are my sister-in-arms and I need to know you are well and are thinking of me. Knowing this will strengthen my resolve to enjoy my new life. When you write please tell me all your news.*

*Now I must close and try to sleep. Tomorrow is the first day of the rest of my life. Sleep well my dearest. I hope these letters find you in good health and high spirits.*

*Your loving friend Mary*

Satisfied, Mary retired for the night. Although she did not expect to sleep, being excited, it was not long after her head touched the pillow that she was fast asleep.

Early the following morning she requested an audience with the Captain. "May I beg your help Sir?"

The Captain looked at her questioningly. "Of course, Miss Watson. How may I be of assistance to you?"

Holding out the three letters she asked, "Is it possible you could take these letters back to England and arrange postage please."

Smiling the Captain replied, "I am delighted to be of service to you." Whereupon he placed the three letters in a small chest in which he kept his own papers.

Thanking him profusely for his assistance she left to join the other passengers waiting to disembark. Before joining them she took time to write in her journal: *Yesterday we finally arrived at our destination so this is my last entry while onboard. From the ship the island has a romantic yet wild look about it. I rose early full of excitement wanting to look on my new home. Yet, I am a little wary of what I will find when I arrive on land. My hope is that I am expected and will receive a warm welcome. I confess I will be glad to feel terra firma once more as I still find the movement of the ship a little unsettling. The Captain has shown such kindness towards me I will be sad to leave his company. I believe he worries about my being a young woman on her own and I am most grateful for his consideration.*

As she stood Mary was filled with feelings of excited anticipation. Looking across the water towards the island she saw a number of people standing on the shoreline. Allowing her eyes to travel slowly from the beach up the small hill she observed a large number of buildings of varying size; obviously a village. Beyond that all she saw were large trees and bushes.

Laura, noticed Mary's interest. "That's the forest. There is quite an assortment of fauna and flora with many beautiful and unusual flowers. However, I must warn you to be careful. Do not to enter the forest alone as there are some strange creatures living within."

At Mary's look of horror, Laura continued, "There is nothing to worry about as they never leave the forest so you are quite safe in the village." Mary relaxed but Laura's comments had left her feeling a little uneasy.

Half an hour later the passengers boarded the small launch. A thought crossed Mary's mind, 'this is the start of the next chapter in my life.'

# Six

Whilst Mary travelled to the islands, back in England Lizzie had been reflecting over the parting from her dear friend. After Mary had left the carriage Lizzie had felt sick to her heart. So much so she had nearly cried out for her friend not to go. Sadly, she accepted there was no other way, thinking, 'How fortunate I am that I have such good parents. And how terrible my dear friend is so bereft of a loving family.'

Having initially barred Lizzie from seeing her friend depart, Lizzie and her Father had finally managed to reach a compromise. His Lordship only agreeing if Lizzie remained within the carriage and did not put one foot on the dockside. This she faithfully promised to do. Although she nearly disobeyed, Lizzie knew if she had then Robinson, her driver, would have reported to His Lordship. After Mary had left the carriage Robinson was about to leave but Lizzie had objected, being glad they had waited, for Mary had returned to the ships side to wave a final goodbye. Once Lizzie had extended her arm through the window, waving warmly, Robinson had moved the carriage away.

Later that night Lizzie took up her pen to write in her diary: *Today I said goodbye to Mary. I do not know what I will do without her. Even though she reassures me she will be safe, I cannot help but fret for her. When will we meet again, I know not? We have vowed to write often. Poor Mama tried to cheer me up, for she knows I am sad at Mary's departure. My heart is breaking. I shall not sleep at all tonight.*

As it turned out, Lizzie slept quite well that night. And all the nights following Mary's departure. Although time seemed to hang over her, leaving Lizzie with little heart for anything else, as each day passed, she began to feel more like her old self.

It was during the month following Mary's departure

that Lizzie attended a ball at the palace. There she was introduced to Sir James Williamson, a delightful, good-looking young man. James found Lizzie to be a most charming creature, asking her father's permission to call on her. To which His Lordship readily agreed. Lizzie soon found solace from Mary's absence, in Sir James' company, often looking forward to his visits. And, before long he became a regular visitor to Mountford House where he heard much of Mary. Being a sensible young man Sir James quickly realised that Mary was an important friend to Lizzie, so he ensured to listen attentively.

A few short weeks into their relationship Sir James lifted Lizzie's spirits by bringing a gift. This action was not an act of artifice on his part but merely the caring actions of a young man who was fast falling in love with an adorable young woman. The gift was well received and he left that day with a spring in his step. After his departure Lizzie had the urge to tell Mary about Sir James and the delightful gift. She also wanted to tell Mary how much she was missed. Retiring to her room she sat at her writing slope. Lizzie wouldn't be able to send her letter until Mary wrote with an address. But it didn't matter as all she wanted to do now, was share her thoughts.

*My Dear, Sweet Mary*

*How much I miss you. It is many weeks since you departed, yet it seems a lifetime. I wander the house feeling lost and listless. Whenever I hear the doorbell, I jump up thinking it is you. Then sadly, I remember you are not here and I am disappointed. I confess my mother and father have been doing their best to console me.*

*Recently I attended a ball at the palace where I met a most delightful young man, Sir James Williamson. He has now called at the house a number of times being most understanding and attentive, often listening to me talking endlessly about you. I am sure he must be bored by my incessant chatter.*

*Today I received the sweetest of gifts from him.*

*Entering the room, he carried a large basket which intrigued me. Placing it on the floor, James removed the cover and the most delightful little creature popped her head out. It was a sweet, adorable kitten. She is white with a black patch over one eye. James has suggested I call her Mary, believing she may comfort me when I am missing you. I am delighted but hope you will not be distressed by his suggestion? Mary dear I find his caring so thoughtful. He has been most kind.*

*I know I cannot send this letter yet so will keep it until you write to me.*

*I hope and pray to hear from you soon.*

*Your loving friend Lizzie*

Daily life continued matter-of-factly for both ladies, it being many weeks since Mary's departure. The relationship between Lizzie and Sir James began to develop into something serious. Lizzie found herself looking forward to the young man's visits. Her father often inviting him to join the family for dinner. So far, he hadn't refused a single invitation, leaving Lizzie's Mother secretly wondering if he had any feelings for her daughter.

Eventually Sir James realised he was falling deeply in love with Lizzie. His constant attention made her realise she had no-one close enough to talk to with Mary gone. At these times she felt remorse for not having given her dear friend more thought. Especially as the only way she could confide in her friend was by writing to her. After one such bout she wrote another letter in which she asked the questions she wanted to ask, had Mary been sat next to her.

*My Dearest Mary*

*How time flies by. It over fourteen weeks since you departed. I hope you have arrived safely as I worry still about what awaits you. Tell me if the people are kind to you. Will they make you happy? Will you forget your dearest Lizzie?*

*Sir James has been such a solace to me but still, I miss you very much. His care of me, the way he speaks and behaves is most comforting. We spend a great deal of time together. He is not overbearing in any way, making me feel at ease. I wonder if he has feelings for me.*

*My dearest Mary what am I to do? I think I am falling in love with him. Should I follow my feelings? We have known each other but a short time and yet, it seems I have known him a lifetime. Am I too young?*

*How I miss you Mary for you are my confidante and I need your guidance so much.*

*Please write soon my dearest.*

*I am your sweetest, loving Lizzie.*


Lizzie was unaware that fortune would shine on her, for about two weeks later, she had an unexpected visitor. Entering the drawing room, the maid enquired if Miss Lizzie would receive a Captain Morrison who had some important news for her. Lizzie did not immediately recognise the name until she suddenly recalled that he was the Captain of the ship Mary had left England on. Having recognised him she quickly instructed the gentleman be shown into the room. Beginning to feel excited Lizzie stood waiting anxiously. A few moments later the door opened and a tall distinguished looking gentleman entered the room. Lizzie studied him silently for a moment.

Bowing the Captain introduced himself. "Captain Morrison at your service Miss Mountford. I am here, on behalf of Miss Watson, on a mission of extreme importance. I have been requested to deliver this small packet to you." Whereupon he presented the three letters Mary had tied together with a ribbon.

Surprised but delighted Lizzie took the package smiling. "Welcome. Please Sir, pray take a seat. Can I offer you some refreshment?"

Thanking her the Captain declined. "Unfortunately, I am on my way home to see my wife and children, so with all due respect Miss Mountford I would prefer not to delay too long as they are expecting my arrival."

Although a little disappointed Lizzie promptly

requested, "At least tell me how my dear friend Miss Watson was faring when you left her?"

Being of a kindly nature, the Captain was unable to resist the endearing quality of Lizzie, so he sat, politely asking, "What is it you wish to know Miss Mountford?"

At his response Lizzie's questions quickly began to flow. With great patience the Captain responded, doing his utmost to satisfy each of her enquiries. Hopefully he thought, to the point, where he could leave her settled about her dear friend's circumstances. By the end of an hour the Captain, feeling he had fulfilled his obligations, politely but quickly made his adieus and left.

As soon as the door closed, Lizzie, unable to contain herself fell on the packet with gusto. Removing the ribbon, she found three letters. Sitting on the chaise she began devouring the contents in excited anticipation. An hour later Lizzie had re-read all the letters, finding herself full of mixed emotions. From happiness to worry to happiness again, causing tears to flow.

At that moment Sir James entered the room, being immediately concerned by her distress. Moving quickly across the room he sat on the chaise and, without hesitation or forethought, took Lizzie in his arms, offering her comfort. When she finally managed to explain why she was crying a feeling of such warmth overpowered him and, before either realised what was happening, he kissed her. All of sudden Sir James became aware of his indiscretion. Quickly withdrawing from Lizzie's side, he apologised for his behaviour. For some strange reason, Lizzie couldn't explain why she was not concerned by his action. James, on the other hand, felt bereft at his ungentlemanly behaviour. Immediately rising from the chaise, he begged her forgiveness and left the room. Surprised by his sudden departure, as well as feeling confused, Lizzie burst into tears.

Calming herself Lizzie spied Mary's letters where they had fallen to the floor. Picking them up, she began reading them again, putting James' hasty departure from her mind.

Having understood what Mary had written, Lizzie took up her pen and wrote her reply.

*My Dearest, Darling Mary*

*At long last you have written. Oh, how my heart jumped for joy. I was so delighted to hear you had arrived safe and that at last I can send you my letters. Your journey appears to have been quite arduous and I was saddened when I read of your malaise. How sorry I am I was not there to look after you whilst you were ill.*

*At the precise moment I read of your illness Sir James arrived. Seeing my distress, he took me in his arms without any hesitation whatsoever to comfort and console me. Oh, my Darling Mary I had no control over what happened next. I offered no resistance when James' lips met mine. His kiss was warm, gentle and tender. Although I hardly felt it, the feelings it stirred within me were overwhelming. Mary, I pray, do not be anxious or disappointed by my actions but I allowed his lips to linger for at least a full minute. Of course, he apologised most profusely for taking advantage of my distressed state, but I feel no regret. I even told him not to be overly concerned about the matter. Am I a bad person Mary?*

*Oh! The doorbell has just rung. Perhaps James has returned. If so, I will finish this letter later and send it with the others I have already written. Hopefully you will have them at the earliest time. Then I will write again to let you know how things progress.*

*Know that I think of you often with love.*

*Your own true friend Lizzie.*

# Seven

Landing on shore the morning after the ship docked, Mary allowed her eyes to wander over the scene before her. The island looked charming. As she waited for her luggage to be unloaded, she was approached by a rotund woman, obviously one of the islanders.

Quickly Captain Morrison stepped forward, bowing to the lady. Turning to Mary he said, "Miss Watson, allow me to introduce you to Her Majesty, Queen Mumna."

Taken aback by the formal introduction Mary quickly gathered up her skirts, curtsying. "I am most delighted to meet you, Your Majesty."

Mumna smiled. "Welcome Miss school teacher. We will get on well I think, yes?"

Mary nodded in silent agreement thinking, 'I believe I am going to like this lady.'

Mary was surprised to discover the Queen spoke quite good English, having learnt it from the old missionary. It was the reference to this man which caused Reverend Morgain to quickly step forward and interrupt their conversation. Having noted the respect with which the Captain had addressed the lady Mary felt the Reverends behaviour somewhat impolite. He no doubt felt the interruption acceptable. His sister Jayne however, obviously aware that some form of protocol had been broken, quickly stepped forward.

"Our apologies for the interruption, Your Majesty, but my brother is so eager to settle and be about God's work, that he momentarily forgets his manners."

Mumna nodded but said nothing. Mary would later think about the interruption, wondering if perhaps he had offended the Queen. Maybe it was then that the Chief's wife took her dislike of the Reverend.

Jayne realised her brother should have waited to be

formally introduced. It seems even here on the islands, there is etiquette just as there is in England. But, being ignored and rebuffed by the Chief's wife did not settle well with the Reverend. It took much of Jayne's patience to calmly and quickly remove him from the immediate area. Fortunately, just then the old missionary came running down the hill, his arms waving wildly in the air. Arriving at the dockside the man immediately began apologising for his tardiness at being late.

Catching sight of the Queen, he stopped, and turned to Mumna. "Good-Morning Your Majesty, I trust you are well?" And he slowly bowed. "My sincere apologies for being late."

Acknowledging the man with a wave of her hand Mumna introduced him to Mary, explaining she was the new school teacher. Mary in turn, held out her hand which the missionary took in his. It felt limp, warm and sticky.

Hearing a cough behind him, the missionary turned towards Reverend Morgain, and holding out his hand he introduced himself. "Welcome."

At this point Mumna instructed some islanders to pick up Mary's baggage and carry it up to the village. Then, taking Mary's arm she turned, leading her away up the hill. As they walked away Mary heard Reverend Morgain complaining loudly to the old missionary about how rude the Queen was. "Well, I suppose one shouldn't expect any better from the natives?"

What the missionary replied she failed to hear. However, she later admitted to Laura how embarrassed she had felt by the man's outburst.

As they walked Mary stole a quick glance at Mumna's face, wondering if she had overheard the Reverend's comments. It appeared she hadn't for she continued walking, looking straight ahead with no expression on her face. Slowly the two ladies made their way, finally coming to a stop outside a small hut near the end of the village.

"We have built you a house to live in and a school room

next to it," Mumna explained.

Surprised Mary looked around in excited anticipation. She saw a large square structure with a roof of branches and palm leaves to one side of the hut. As they passed it, she stole a quick peek inside, noting some tree stumps, presumably for the children to sit on. Next to the schoolroom was the hut which was to be her new home. From the outside it appeared primitive but it still seemed welcoming. Mumna stopped, bent forward slightly and opened the door before leading Mary inside.

There was little natural light, taking Mary a moment to adjust her eyes to the interior after the brightness of the morning sun. As she became used to the dimness she looked around in anticipation, seeing a bed, table, chair and a dressing table. She was surprised by the size as the outside was misleading. Turning towards Mumna, Mary expressed her delight.

"The white folks on the islands have given something to make you a lovely home. You like, yes?"

Mary nodded 'yes' before looking around once more, this time noticing a smaller table in a corner upon which was sat a pretty bowl and jug, presumably for her ablutions.

Across the room in another corner was a small stove. Mumna pointed to it. "That is for you to cook on."

Looking further, Mary noted on the dresser and table were candle holders to provide all the light she would need. She was pleased with all she saw. Whilst Mary inspected the contents Mumna stood patiently waiting. Once she was sure Mary was satisfied Mumna, nodding her head, took hold of Mary's arm again and turning she started for the door. Being a large lady with a strong grip Mary had little choice but to follow.

Outside the sun was strong, causing Mary to squint after the darkness of the interior of the hut. She also started to perspire with the heat. She hoped she would be left alone soon as she needed to wash and change her dress. Mumna stopped to give instructions about her baggage, telling the men to place the cases in the hut and everything else in the schoolroom. Looking at all the boxes Mary realised how generous Lord Mountford had been, obviously ensuring she had all she needed for the school.

With instructions given, Mumna turned towards the village. Practically pulling Mary along the Queen strode towards a large hut in the centre of the village. As they passed some of the islanders, Mary noticed how everyone stopped working, turning to watch them pass. She wondered if they were curious about her. Approaching the large hut Mumna called something out in a foreign tongue. In response, a short, rotund man in a long-patterned skirt emerged from inside. Holding out his hand in welcome, he greeted Mary in the same foreign tongue.

"This my husband, Chief Tonga."

Placing her hand in his, Mary found he had a strong grip which somehow both reassured, as well as calmed her nerves.

"Good-morning Your Majesty," she responded, curtsying.

Acknowledging Mary, he encouraged her to enter the hut. Once inside she found a group of older men sat in a circle on the floor. These were the islands Elders who were, to her amazement, there to greet and meet her. She was astounded and delighted that these people, total strangers, could give her such a warm welcome. Once introductions were over Mumna took Mary back outside, indicating she sit on one of the mats which had mysteriously appeared on the floor. Settling down Mary watched as a number of young girls appeared, each carrying a tray laden with different types of food. Other young women carried a form of cup which Mary discovered held coconut milk. Sitting in the morning sun, eating strange foods was a new experience for her. It was only after they had finished that she was finally allowed to go to her new home.

Back in the hut Mary, at long last was able to wash and change her dress. Over the next few hours she sorted through her belongings and the school items His Lordship had thoughtfully provided. As she organised her new home Mary pondered over all that had happened to her during the last few hours. Life here might yet prove to be good. For the first time in a while Mary felt she might have made the right decision by agreeing to come here. The remainder of the day was spent making her little hut into a home.

Just as she was finishing sorting her clothes Mary heard a noise outside. Going to investigate she was surprised to find a young girl sitting by the door.

"What do you want?"

"Me Kuala. I belong Missie."

Mary was taken aback, unsure what to do next. About to send the girl away, Mumna appeared. "Girl okay for you?"

Not quite sure what she should say Mary hesitated. But in the few moments they stood looking at each other Mary realised to protest or refuse Kuala might not be very respectful. And so, reluctantly she agreed, that yes, Kuala was ok. Nodding her head Mumna smiled, then turning she left.

After Mumna had gone Mary went back inside the hut, beckoning Kuala to follow, where she was relieved to discover she spoke good English. Kuala explained, "I am your Criada." This, Mary understood to mean servant or maid in Spanish. She would later admit in her letter to Lizzie at being surprised for she had never expected to have a servant. At least not one of her own. Oh, there had been plenty of servants in Mrs Maberley's house, and of course, Lizzie had servants. In fact, Lizzie had her own maid to help her dress and do her hair. But Mary had never had anyone to wait on just her. Despite her reluctance to be waited upon Mary was unable to do anything but accept the situation. In some ways she was actually relieved, for it meant she would feel more secure, having someone else sleeping in the hut at night with her.

That night she made her first entry in her journal since landing on the island: *I have found my welcome to the island most peculiar. Having been met by the island's Queen. She is a formidable lady but one I feel I will get on well with. My reception was extremely warm. I was treated royally which*

47

*flabbergasted me somewhat. Mumna showed me to a hut which is now my new home. It is a delight and I have found myself settling in easily and quickly. Fortunately, most of the islanders appear to speak English. I am happy with my circumstances. I have seen naught of the other passengers on board ship since we landed, each of us going our separate ways.*

# Eight

The following morning Mary woke to the sound of banging pots. At first, she was confused as to where she was. Sitting up in bed she smelt the aroma of something cooking assail her nostrils. Looking towards the stove she saw Kuala making breakfast and the memories of the previous day flooded back to her. As her eyes travelled across the room they rested on the table where she noted a bowl and cup laid out ready. This was the first morning in her new home.

Deciding to get out of bed Mary put on her dressing-gown and sat at the table, just as Kuala brought the pan she had been stirring. Looking inside Mary was surprised to see it contained freshly made porridge which the young girl spooned into the bowl. Mary fell on the food with a hunger she hadn't realised she possessed. Kuala smiled, pleased to see her mistress's appetite.

After breakfast Mary washed before dressing in her lightest dress and going outside. Even this early in the morning one could feel the heat of the day. It would get warmer as the day progressed. No doubt as the sun got higher making it unbearable to wear anything heavier. Mary made her way to the school room. Not that one could really think of it as a room for there were no actual walls. Looking at it she noted a pole at each corner. Across the top were large palm leaves, which created a roof to keep the sun off the occupants during the day.

She had not been expecting to find anyone inside but as she entered, Mary discovered seven children waiting patiently, sitting on the tree stumps. She noted someone had placed the blackboard at one end of the room and on it were written the words, 'Welcome Teacher.' The message made her smile. Seeing her response, the children relaxed. They must have been on tenterhooks waiting to see what their new teacher was like. Walking to the front of the classroom Mary looked at each child in turn before announcing in a gentle voice, "Good-morning children. I am called Miss Watson" and turning, she wrote her name on the blackboard.

Being unsure what to do next Mary sat in the chair by the desk and faced the children. Gently she began asking each child to tell her their name and how old they were. The children took it in turns to reply after which she spent the remainder of the day learning as much about them as she possibly could. Their level of education and their families. That night Mary retired extremely relieved, believing the children had accepted her.

Within days Mary had a set routine. She would rise early and have breakfast with Kuala. Afterwards she would get ready, before going to the schoolroom. Setting the lessons for the day she made sure everything was ready for when the children arrived. Lessons ran until late morning when the sun became too hot for exertion. School would then close for about two hours. During this time the children would eat their lunch then lie down on mats in the shade to rest. By mid-afternoon, as the sun slowly waned, Mary would restart lessons and these would last for another hour and a half, with school closing for the day.

Once the youngsters left Mary was free to explore the island, which she did with Kuala. Sometimes they went to the beach as Kuala was teaching her to swim in the warm sea waters. Life on the island was proving to be so different to anything Mary had ever experienced before. And yet, in some ways she was finding it much like living in the village of her childhood. As the days passed Mary found her life becoming easier, leaving her feeling at peace with the world. She found the island a lovely place and the people were friendly towards her.

Mary wrote in her journal: *There are a number of islands making up the group. Over the last few weeks, I have learnt much about the other residents living here. Discovering they are either European or American. Most of the foreigners live either on the opposite side of this island or on one of the outer islands. The plantations grow coffee, cotton or sugar. Travel between the islands is achieved by boat. Mumna has put a small boat at my disposal* which *Kuala is showing me how to paddle. Although I find the heat somewhat oppressive, as time goes by, I am slowly becoming accustomed to it. Unfortunately, my English dresses are somewhat cumbersome. Mumna has suggested I cease wearing them but I am too embarrassed to tell her I have a lack of lightweight dresses. And yet she must be aware of my predicament for this morning she sent me some material. She has insisted Kuala and I sew some new dresses better suited to the heat and the island way of life. The Queen's generosity both surprises and delights me. I shall be eternally grateful for the lady's consideration of my situation. Yesterday she brought me some new footwear. When I looked at them, I found them similar to those worn by Kuala. It will take me a little time to get used to wearing them but I am sure it will make it easier for me.*

Mary soon discovered her new mode of dress and footwear allowed her more freedom of movement. She was soon feeling more relaxed and comfortable than she had since arriving. Before she realised it, many weeks had passed. So, it was a pleasant surprise when Kuala came running to tell her a big ship had dropped anchor in the harbour, and that the Captain was coming up the hill to see her.

Filled with anticipation Mary left the hut to watch Captain Morrison approaching. He appeared to be holding a small packet in his hand. As he arrived, she greeted him warmly. "Captain Morrison, what a pleasure to see you once more."

"And you Miss Watson. Tell me, how do you fare?" The man appeared pleased as well as relieved to see her smiling and looking happy. If he were honest, he had been concerned about leaving her on the island.

Smiling back Mary tried to control her excitement. "Please Sir won't you sit for a moment and take some refreshments?"

"I would be most honoured," and he sat down.

Having settled he conveyed Miss Mountford's regards and greetings. Going on to tell Mary about his visit to Lizzie's home where he had faithfully delivered the letters entrusted to his care. From the visit the Captain had concluded the friendship between the two young ladies was strong and that they were devoted to each other. He therefore endeavoured to sit with Mary for some time, taking care to satisfy all the details of his visit to the Mountford House.

Sometime later the Captain rose to leave. "My apologies but I must go and see the Chief. However, I will be most willing to carry any reply you may have for Miss Mountford should you so desire me to."

"You are a gentleman and are most kind. I will be grateful if you would do so."

Captain Morrison smiled, warmly promising to return prior to his ship sailing in two days' time to collect her letter. Handing her the packet, he left.

After the Captain had gone Mary sat back down, quickly opening the small packet. Inside she discovered three letters from her dear friend. With eager anticipation she began reading, the contents of which caused her a torrid ride of emotion. Having re-read the letters, Mary sat thinking. It dawned on her that, just as she had found solace in her school, the children and the islanders, dear Lizzie had found her peace with Sir James. She did not begrudge her friend her happiness but decided to sleep on what she had read before responding.

Closing the packet, she put it safely away before returning to her duties. During the day Mary often thought about Lizzie's letters, finding she was happy for her dear friend and also very glad to have heard from her at long last. That night she slept soundly.

The following morning Mary woke in a positive mood. Once school closed for the weekend she took out Lizzie's letters. Sitting in the sunlight she absorbed what Lizzie had written, after which she penned a reply. She had much to tell her.

*My Sweetest Lizzie*

*What a wonderful surprise to receive not one, but three letters from you. I cannot tell you how much I have missed you. What a joy to read of all you have done. In particular news of your friendship with Sir. James. From what you have said, he sounds to be a most personable young man. One who is obviously taken with the sweetness of my Darling Lizzie.*

*You say he kissed you. What joy you must have felt. But, of course, I am not disappointed if you have feelings for Sir James as I know in my heart, I will never lose our friendship. But my darling, please be sure of his feelings for you, before you commit yourself to him. I would hate him profusely if he were to hurt you in any way. You must write more as matters progress. You know your happiness is very important to me.*

*Now Dear One I will tell you my news. Life here is becoming more settled each day. I am developing a good routine. The school I run is small having just seven pupils. All are European or American. Apart for Jimbala who is the eldest son of the islands Chief. I was most surprised to find he speaks reasonably good English and I am delighted by his abilities in his studies. It seems the Chief and his family were all taught English by the old missionary Father Ignatius, who has now left the island. The Chief's wife, Mumna appears to have taken me under her wing and looks after me as if I were a daughter. I find this pleasing even though she has a somewhat daunting character.*

*The main island is large, being the biggest of the group and while the natives appear somewhat primitive, they are all very friendly towards me. I feel quite safe, but should I need assistance, I know it will be readily given. Everywhere I look there is bright colour. The sea is a mix of blue and green; the sky, a beautiful shade of blue, is clear most days. The forest is a landscape of different shades of green, interspersed with the bright reds, pinks and oranges of the flowers. All are peculiar in shape being nothing like those found in England.*

*The forest is most unusual. There are some strange creatures living within, many of whom are colourful, although a few are a little frightening. Otherwise the island appears to be a paradise.*

*Jimbala has been most kind. He has been educating me in some of the island ways. In return I give him extra lessons in reading and writing. He improves daily and I am pleased with him. I believe he will make a great Chief one day.*

*The Johnstone's left for their home on one of the outer islands the same day we landed. But not before Laura extracted a promise from me to visit them once I was settled. It is my intention to call on them later this week. The next time I write I will tell you about the visit.*

*My dearest Lizzie I must tell you about my new home and the life I now lead. You may be shocked to hear that I no longer wear the heavy woollen dresses I brought with me from England. They are too cumbersome and warm so I have resorted to wearing lighter clothes. At times the heat can be somewhat oppressive as it is summer time here, so I have sewn myself some new dresses. I also no longer wear my boots. I now have the same footwear as the native girls. The toes are open to the elements but they keep the soles of the feet safe when walking. I feel to have so much more freedom that it is quite heady and uplifting.*

*You will be pleased to know the islands Chief has provided me with a hut so I have a home of my own. I must tell you they look nothing like the houses in England as they are made from branches and leaves, yet surprisingly, offer all the protection needed. Inside I am well catered for having everything I need for a cosy, comfortable home. My furniture has been provided by some of the islands residents so I sleep on a proper bed, not the floor!*

*The schoolroom is unusual, being an open sided building. It has poles at the corners and a roof of big branches which affords us enough protection from the harsh midday sun. It is most fortunate that your Father provided me with everything I needed for my school. It certainly looks the part. Please thank him for his generosity and thoughtfulness.*

*The Chief and his wife Mumna are most supportive of me but I find they have little tolerance for Reverend Morgain. I am not surprised by this as he appears to show very little respect towards the pair. This is, I feel, unbecoming in a man of the cloth. Hopefully, if he learns to keep quiet and show more respect, he will find his reception friendlier. At the moment he seems to find it totally outside his power to hold his tongue, often he's overheard being derogatory about the islands and its people. I believe his position here was forced upon him and, as such, he bears a grudge. I trust he discovers, or at least remembers, some reverence before too long or I fear things will not improve and may get worse, which will affect his poor sister Jayne.*

*And there my dear Lizzie is where there is a difference as I find his sister Jayne a most pleasing person. When her brother is absent, she seems to smile more and the changes in her demeanour are most welcome. I know I should not be so forward, but I trust when her brother travels to the other islands, Jayne will stay behind. I have asked her to assist me in the school, which she does when she can absent herself from her brother. She teaches the youngsters the scriptures and makes the lessons so interesting the children appear mesmerised by her.*

*Lizzie dear I must tell you about Lord Falshaw. I have discovered he owns a large plantation on one of the outer islands and is a great friend of the Chief and his wife. Since we arrived, I have seen little of him, although, he did take time before leaving for his estate, to enquire if I had everything I needed for the school. At least this time Lizzie he was fully clothed!*

*Dearest you would have been proud by my demeanour as I spoke to him. I was calm, behaved in a most becoming frame of mind and chose to forget his mode of dress and actions whilst onboard ship. He seems more personable than I at first thought.*

*I am sure there is more to tell you, but I will close for*

*now as the night draws in. I must secure the hut before I retire. Captain Morrison is to call tomorrow to collect this letter and I want to ensure it is ready for him.*

*Take care my Darling Lizzie and know I miss you greatly.*

*With love from Your Mary*

Satisfied with her letter Mary sealed it, placing it to one side ready to be collected by the Captain the following day. As Mary thought about Lizzie, she realised how pleased she was her dear friend was not pining for her.

'At least my letter to Lizzie will reassure her I am well and settled,' she thought. 'If the relationship with Sir James progresses then not only will he be good for her but at least her parents will stop worrying about our friendship.'

Mary sighed saying out loud, "How quickly life can change but I bear no grudge if Lizzie follows her heart, for she is a timid creature who needs companionship and care. I hope Sir James is a good man and will treat my dear friend properly."

# Nine

Back in England Lizzie had finally come to terms with Mary's absence. Although her easiness was probably more due to the careful attentions of Sir James Williamson who now called at the house every other day. Being a man of means, Sir James owned a country estate of some one hundred acres, a large town house and had an income of some four thousand pounds per year. He also had two spinster sisters of indeterminate age, both of whom had stayed at home to take care of their late Father. Whilst they were civil to Lizzie when meeting in town, Lizzie did not always find them pleasant. So far, fortunately, she had only spent a limited amount of time in their company so was not overly concerned at their lack of friendliness.

Following Mary's departure Lizzie fell into a mild state of depression causing her to study her own lifestyle. While Mary had been living with her the two young women had done things which helped the poor. At the time Lizzie, who had automatically accepted she was privileged, had been enthusiastic in her endeavours to help. Maybe because Mary had persuaded her. Being of aristocratic birth it was accepted within their social circle that those better off aided, where they could, those who needed assistance. Of course, there were limits to what one would do. Even in this day and age there were still diseases such as cholera and consumption which might affect the health of a genteel person. So, it was that Mary and Lizzie had often spent their time sewing for the poor or making up baskets of food for distribution to the elderly, especially during the winter months.

During the months following Mary's departure Lizzie had, with Sir James help, reverted to enjoying her social life more. With her friend no longer guiding her, Lizzie's enthusiasm and resolve to aid those worse off than herself had slowly diminished. Her mind now occupied with other, more joyous employments.

Sir James invited Lizzie and her family to join him at his country estate, which they did, having recently returned from what turned out to be a most enjoyable stay. The Misses Williamson had, during their stay, been on their best behaviour. Perhaps they had been warned by their brother to be warm and friendly towards Lizzie and her family. Despite their coldness towards Lizzie, they loved their brother, and genuinely wanted him to be happy. Even if they didn't necessarily like his choice of future wife. And, it was obvious Sir James was indeed looking at Lizzie to be his wife.

The pair were now spending a great deal of time together, often being seen mixing in the same company at balls or soirées. Fully chaperoned of course. Lord Mountford was delighted at the friendship of the two young people. In fact, His Lordship was hoping that marriage was on the cards. In this he was not wrong, as a few days later his wish came true, making him a truly happy man.

Lizzie wrote in her diary: *Reading the latest letter from Mary, I was enthralled by the descriptions she used to describe her new island home. I think I am filled with a mixture of emotions. Relief that she is safe and settled but disappointed that she will not be returning to England in the foreseeable future.*

It was only as Lizzie sat reading Mary's last letter again that she realised how engrossed in her relationship with Sir James she had become. Giving little thought to Mary for some weeks. Having been so busy enjoying her own life it was only now she felt any guilt at her thoughtlessness.

'The problem is,' thought Lizzie, 'we are too far apart. Our only communication being through the letters we write, which take too long to arrive.'

It wasn't that Lizzie wanted to forget her dear friend it was just that she was young. And Sir James was attentive and caring. "Besides, he is here not thousands of miles away in a foreign place I know nothing about," she told herself. Feeling guilty, Lizzie became determined to think more of Mary by making sure that when she next wrote to her, she would have much to tell her friend or ask her.

As Lizzie sat pondering all these thoughts, she was surprised to hear Sir James unexpectedly arrive. He was requesting to be received. As such, all thoughts of her guilt towards Mary disappeared the moment he entered the room. Looking at him Lizzie realised how agitated the young man appeared. Rather than sitting he was prowling the room, causing her some concern.

She was worried by his behaviour. "Pray Sir, please sit? You seem disturbed. Do please give a reason for your state of mind. You will wear the carpet out should you not desist."

Sir James stopped moving. Looked at the carpet then at Lizzie before quickly sitting on the chaise next to her. Taking her hand in his he looked deep into her eyes, thinking what a beautiful pale grey colour they were.

Slowly Lizzie smiled at him. "Are you not well Sir?"

Her question seemed to give Sir James courage as he gently told her, "You are so beautiful. You do know how much regard I have for you? You do realise that don't you Lizzie?" Without waiting for her to answer he went on. "I wish to know if you could ever feel the same for me?"

There was a short silence, which for Sir James seemed to stretch into eternity. Then Lizzie's face lit up with a smile as she whispered, "Oh yes. I can. I do."

With such a positive response Sir James felt there was hope for his next question. Going down on one knee he solemnly declared his love before asking if she would consent to be his wife. When Lizzie breathlessly expressed her love for him, and that she would be honoured to be his wife, James was elated. Quickly taking her in his arms he proceeded to shower her face with kisses. Declaring between each one how much he loved and adored her. Lizzie sat totally bemused by his actions.

Shortly afterwards he left to see her Father, leaving Lizzie beside herself with worry. 'I cannot believe it,' she thought, 'James loves me. How wonderful that sounds – James loves me! I am so heady I could jump for joy.'

Looking at the clock on the mantelpiece Lizzie suddenly stood up, unable to sit still any longer being full of anguish at what her father was saying. She looked at the clock again. "He has been gone some twenty minutes," she told her kitten. "Please, dear God, let Father agree to James being my betrothed. I promise to be a better person if you do." Whereupon she began pacing the floor, feeling more agitated as each minute passed.

In the library James had an audience with Lord Mountford, where he had solemnly asked for Lizzie's hand in marriage. Not wanting to appear too enthusiastic His Lordship ensured he asked the appropriate questions regarding the young man's position in life. As well as his ability to provide for Lizzie. However, feeling slightly guilty at prolonging the inevitable, His Lordship finally gave his wholehearted consent, blessing the betrothal.

Half an hour later, leaving the library James walked as if on air. When he entered the drawing room, he found Lizzie pacing the floor. Looking at him she stopped, waiting expectantly for his reaction. And when he smiled to show consent had been given, she literally flew into his arms declaring, "I am the happiest person in the world."

A short while later Lord and Lady Mountford entered the drawing room, offering their heartfelt congratulations to the two young people. His Lordship ordered champagne to warmly toast the happy couple. Much later Lizzie's parents withdrew, allowing the couple some privacy. Whereupon the betrothed couple spent the next two hours discussing their feelings for each other, and what the future held for them; both amazed at how much they loved each other.

Finally, but reluctantly James declared, "I must go and break the happy news to my sisters. I promise to return tomorrow when I shall bring you, my sweet darling, wonderful Lizzie, an engagement ring."

Once he had left Lizzie retired to her room. She wanted

to write to Mary to tell her the wonderful news. There was much she wanted to share with her friend, including how happy she felt. Sitting at her desk the thoughts which had earlier bothered Lizzie about her absent friend were no longer in her mind. Probably due to the excitement of the afternoon. It was with a great feeling of joy that Lizzie picked up her pen and began writing.

*Sweetest, Dearest Mary*

*Oh, what joy I feel and what wonderful news I have to tell you. My dearest Mary I do hope you are sat down for I am sure you may faint once you read what I am about to write. Well, my dear, sweet friend, where do I begin? Imagine me sat in the drawing room reading your letter, feeling joy at the happiness of having recently heard from you. Sir James arrives anxious to see me. Upon entering the room, he seems very restless. For a few moments I am afraid but suddenly he openly declares his love for me and before I know it, he has asked me to marry him. Although I was taken aback, I am so excited. Mother and Father have agreed and are very pleased.*

*I wanted to tell you the great news that, my dearest Mary I write to you as a newly engaged person. I am so very excited but also sad for you will not be here to be my bridesmaid.*

*I must close my letter, for Mama is calling me. Tomorrow we are going to organise my engagement and wedding trousseaux with the seamstress. I believe Father wants me to wear my Grandmothers wedding dress but Mama will not hear of it. She insists I have a whole new wardrobe as befits a future lady of the manor. How excited I am. Oh I have already said that. But it is true I am excited by all that has happened. I find I am having to pinch myself to make sure I am not dreaming. I do wish you were here with me my dearest to share my joy. I know you will be happy for me.*

*Remember, I think of you often.*

*With warmest love*

*Your Lizzie*

Having finished her letter Lizzie sealed it before going downstairs where she gave it to the footman to take to the post. Then she went to find her Mother to discuss the plans for her future nuptials. Lady Mountford was, of course, highly delighted with the news. And so, Mother and Daughter spent the remaining part of the day engrossed in making plans for an engagement party and a future wedding. All thoughts of Mary disappearing from Lizzie's mind. In fact, any further thoughts of Mary were dismissed for the following days to come as Lizzie became totally embroiled in the pleasure of planning her future, and her many visits to the seamstress.

As for Lady Mountford, she enjoyed announcing to all her friends how her only daughter was now engaged to be married. His Lordship on the other hand, decided to hide away in his study. He knew that where his daughter's wedding was concerned, his wife would brook no interference. He also decided it was going to be a very expensive affair. But, as he told himself, he only had one daughter so there was no reason why his wife shouldn't be allowed her head.

# Ten

Mary had been on the island a number of weeks before she managed to complete the promised invitation of taking tea with the Johnstones'. She hadn't wanted to lose touch with Laura as she found her friendly. Besides Laura had been so caring to Mary whilst on board ship. It was, therefore, on Sunday morning after church, that Mary was seen heading towards the dockside. She was dressed in her new clothes, wore the sandals given her by Mumna, and was followed by Kuala carrying a basket of fresh fruit and some other small gifts. Both girls quickly clambered into the small boat waiting for them.

The journey itself was a short one which Mary found exhilarating. As they sailed over the calm waters Kuala pointed out the different types of fish swimming in the greenie, blue waters. Suddenly, off to one side, Mary spied the same large fish the ship's Doctor had shown her during her journey to the island. "Kuala, what do you call the big grey fish?"

Looking, Kuala answered in her native tongue, but Mary didn't understand, as so far, she hadn't learnt the young girl's language. As the boat glided along, the large fish kept time with it. They jumped in and out of the water, much to the delight of the two girls. Sometimes they appeared to be too close yet not near enough to cause a problem. Mary watched them closely, finding their antics amusing, being in awe of the large friendly giants.

As they arrived Mary saw her friend coming down the hill to greet them. Once the two young women had climbed onto the boardwalk, Laura greeted them warmly before leading the way to the house. Mary appreciated her warm welcome. Approaching the homestead Mary saw it was far larger than she had at first thought. Built on two levels, there was a wide veranda around the outside of both the lower and upper floors.

Reaching the house, a large brown dog left the veranda and slowly loped down to greet them. "Don't be afraid of Wolfie. I know he's large but he's a big softy really and won't harm you." And true enough, having sniffed Mary's hand, the dog decided she was friendly so he let her stroke him. Afterwards he returned to the veranda to settle down in the morning sun to snooze.

"Would you prefer to go indoors or sit outside?"

"Oh please, let's sit outside. It's nice and warm and the scenery is lovely," said Mary looking around.

Settling into the delightful wicker chairs, Mary found she was ready for a refreshing drink. A young maid set a tray down on the table. On it was set a jug of cool lemonade and what looked like a delicious creamy cake.

"I am fortunate to have an excellent cook who is a little gem. I know you will love the cake when you taste it."

The slight breeze blowing in from the sea, meant sitting outside was comfortable. After the refreshments were served the two ladies settled down to talk, each learning all they could about the other. Kuala had disappeared inside the house.

"You know Kuala comes from a big family?" Mary said she didn't so Laura went on to explain. "Well Kuala, and my maid Min are sisters. They are also cousins to the Chief's children." Mary was surprised by the news as neither Kuala nor Mumna had ever mentioned this to her.

The morning passed and the two ladies sat chatting and relaxing until Colonel Johnstone arrived. "How do you fare Miss Watson, well, I hope? Tell me, what do you think of the islands? Are you settled in?"

Mary smiled finding the Colonel a welcoming soul. "I am very well Colonel. I find myself liking island life and settling in easily. But please, do call me Mary. Miss Watson sounds so formal." Acknowledging her request with a smile, the Colonel made his excuses and left to change for lunch.

Laura stood up. "Come, I will show you inside the house. Then leave you to freshen up before lunch which, I think, we will take on the veranda." The light lunch proving to be a convivial affair, with the Colonel being most amusing.

Afterwards he invited Mary to tour their estate. She felt honoured by his invitation so he quickly whisked her away in a buggy. As they rolled along the Colonel told her about the planation. "We have a number of different crops growing on the estate, although it's mainly coffee and cotton." Time, and the delightful scenery, soon passed by.

At one point the Colonel stopped the buggy. "Come, I'll introduce you to some of the estate workers before we go back."

Returning to the house shortly afterwards they re-joined Laura on the veranda. "What a delightful tour I have had," Mary told her hostess.

The Colonel appeared pleased by her praise. Making his excuses he left the two ladies alone for the remainder of the afternoon, where the day passed in quiet companionship and a happy friendly atmosphere. Mary was sorry to see evening approaching, being reluctant to leave.

Laura, sensing her friend's desire not to go, asked, "Would you care to stay overnight Mary? If you wish you can join our other guests for dinner this evening." Mary looked up smiling, although she was hesitant to answer. "Don't worry about the boatmen, they will be quite happy to stay until tomorrow. It means they can spend the evening with their relatives here on the island."

Delighted by the idea of staying, Mary still had one concern. "The only thing is I am not really dressed for dinner."

"Oh, don't worry about that, you can borrow something of mine. We are of a similar build so I am sure I will have something to fit you." And satisfied she would not embarrass her hosts Mary happily agreed to stay.

Later that evening, refreshed and changed, Mary descended the stairs. Upon entering the drawing room, she was delighted to see Jayne sat on the chaise. Her friend had been absent from the island for two weeks due to escorting the Reverend on his visits to the various islands. Mary discovered they were staying at the homestead before returning to the main island. Apparently, the Reverend had an audience with the Chief and the Elders in two days' time which he could ill afford to miss.

As the two ladies sat talking the door opened, and looking up, Mary was slightly taken aback to see Lord Falshaw enter. Surprised to see her, he hesitated for a moment before approaching. "Good-evening Miss Watson. How are you? I trust you are settled in your new home?"

As he had walked across the room, Mary had taken the moment to study him, finding herself impressed by his bearing. He appeared to have made every effort to dress formally. And a thought flashed through her mind, 'at least he is fully clothed this time!' She had nearly laughed out loud but was, fortunately, saved any embarrassment as at that moment Laura entered the room, His Lordship turning away to greet her.

Turning back, he awaited a response to his enquiry. Mary was further prevented from answering as the gong rang out announcing dinner was served. Standing, Lord Falshaw presented his arm to her and, with only the slightest of hesitations, she placed her hand on it, realising it would be churlish to refuse such a gentlemanly gesture. Slowly the guests made their way into the dining room.

Dinner proved to be a delightful affair, with Mary taking care to compliment Laura on the quality and variety of food served. Throughout the meal, the conversation flowed as freely as the wine. Before long Mary felt a warm, happy glow spread through her, making her realise she felt as if she belonged amongst these people. Looking around the table she was amazed at how easily all the guests had settled comfortably together. They seemed to have little regard for their different levels of social status. Something which unfortunately, Mary was most conscience of. However, the atmosphere went a long way to helping her relax, making the evening enjoyable.

After dinner the gentlemen retired outside to smoke cigars and take brandy, while the ladies went into the drawing room to drink coffee. This was a new drink for Mary. One she found strange, yet fairly pleasant once sugar cane was added to sweeten it. Later, the gentlemen joined them, and the evening was spent in either quiet conversation or listening to Laura or Jayne play the piano. As the hall clock struck eleven the ladies retired for the night. Bidding goodnight to everyone Mary left the room. She felt satisfied with way the day, and the evening, had gone.

Once in her room, Mary was surprised to find Kuala waiting to help her prepare for bed. She had not expected the young girl to stay up so late, expecting her to have retired some time earlier. People on the islands got up early to take advantage of the cooler morning weather. This meant they retired early.

"Have you enjoyed your day Kuala?"

"Oh, yes Miss. It was a very good day. I spent it with my sister." Mary smiled, glad her young charge had been well looked after. She realised she was developing a soft spot for the girl.

After Kuala had left, Mary lay down in the big, soft bed. Sinking into the deep comfort of the feather mattress. Lying in the dark she thought about the day. Of how Lord Falshaw had engaged her in conversation throughout the evening. She thought him a most enigmatic person, leaving her feeling slightly confused by his attentions. It was on this thought that Mary fell into a deep, undisturbed sleep.

The following morning Mary was woken by Kuala entering the bedroom. She was carrying a tray of tea for her. When asked the hour, she was told, "Not too late. Miss Laura gave me strict instructions not to disturb Miss too early, but to let you sleep."

Mary smiled at the seriousness with which Kuala had made the announcement. "Thank you. I feel a special person

67

at being allowed to stay in bed." Whilst she drank her tea, Mary lay back against the pillows enjoying being spoiled.

Later, once dressed, she went downstairs. Entering the dining room, she found Laura sitting at the table enjoying her morning coffee.

"I hope you slept well? Please, come and join me?"

Smiling Mary took a seat. Together the two ladies enjoyed a delightful breakfast of fresh fruit, ham, eggs and toast, all washed down with hot tea. After breakfast it was, sadly, time to leave. She had missed the Colonel as he had left earlier with Lord Falshaw on business. Thanking Laura warmly for her hospitality, Mary and Kuala boarded the boat to sail back to the main island. Mary was highly satisfied with the visit.

Back in her island home Mary wrote in her journal: *What a delightful weekend. Laura's home is lovely being filled with beautiful objects which, I must admit, made me feel a small pang of jealousy. They have travelled so far and seen so many wonders. My amazement at her ceramics collection must have shown on my face for Laura asked what I thought of each piece. Not that I think she wished to extol the pieces but merely to educate me on their origin. The Colonel appears to be a fine upstanding gentleman. I found his company on the tour of the estate most comforting and knowledgeable. I was also pleased to meet Jayne again, although I feel she is looking a little tired. Perhaps when she returns to the main island, we can spend more time together. As for Lord Falshaw, he too has surprised me somewhat. For a moment I could not believe he was the same aloof man who was my co-passenger on board ship. After spending time in his company, I have to be honest and say I find him most companionable and attentive in every way. Yet he causes some confusion in me?*

Mary soon settled into the daily routine of school, needlework and teaching Mumna to write. It was a week later when a large ship docked in the harbour, causing great excitement in everyone. Knowing she wouldn't be able to keep the children concentrating on lessons, Mary took them down to the shore. They would enjoy watching the small boat put out from the ship. As Mary followed its progress, she secretly hoped the Captain would have a letter for her, and in this she was not to be disappointed.

As soon as the Captain spied Mary, he strode towards her. Letter in hand he quickly passed it over. "Pray forgive me for not staying to talk Miss Watson but, if convenient, I will call upon you later. I must go see the Chief at once."

Mary smiled warmly. "Of course, Captain. I thank you for the letter. I will expect you for refreshments once your business is concluded." And turning away, she gathered up the children and marched them back up the hill to the schoolroom, setting them the task of writing a short story about the ship.

Later, after school had closed for the day, Mary hurriedly returned to her hut to sit and read her friend's letter. Kuala entered just as Mary had finished reading it for the second time. The young girl was alarmed to see tears in her mistress's eyes. "Tell me Missy what is wrong? Who upset you? I fight them."

Looking up in surprise, Kuala's reaction made Mary laugh. "It is nothing. All is well. I am crying with happiness for I have received the most joyous of news from England." Kuala looked at Mary strangely. Mary's admission was, to her, most confusing. If, as Kuala thought, the news was good, then why was Miss upset? It took Mary some time to explain the reason, and although Kuala seemed satisfied, she remained a little puzzled.

Delighted with the letter Mary mulled over its contents. Sitting thinking about Lizzie made her want to say so much to her dear friend. However, she had plenty of time to write a response before the ship left. She wanted to reassure Lizzie how delighted she was with the happy news. That night Mary retired feeling pleased with the world.

The following morning, she rose early. After breakfast she prepared the school room for the day's lessons. Only returning to the hut to write a response to Lizzies letter.

*My Dearest, Darling Lizzie*

*What great happiness your letter has brought me. I cannot believe you are to be married. How I wish I was there with you. But even though I am not, know you are in my heart. What feelings of joy I have for you? But my dear Lizzie, you have failed miserably to tell me more of your future husband. I need to know him. Pray tell me, how tall is he? What are his looks? Is he fair or dark? Tell me of his stance and his demeanour? Oh! And how deep are his affections for you? I must be sure he is the right person for you in every way. Lizzie dearest, please ignore my ramblings. Of course, he is right for you or you would not love him. Nor would your Father have agreed to your marriage. Therefore, I am settled I will love him as a brother. The same as I love you my sister.*

*I am quite excited to hear more of your forthcoming wedding. You must write and tell all. About your trousseau! What colour and style will it be? What flowers will you carry on your Wedding Day? Also, tell me where you are to be wed? Where you will reside once you become Lady Williamson? How nice that name sounds. There is so much I wish to know. I shall think of you on your special day. Remember, I wait in eager anticipation for your next letter.*

*And now my dearest here is my news. I went to visit the Johnstones homestead. Their island home is quite large and the house most grand. The Colonel designed and arranged the building himself. Laura and the Colonel were most warm in their welcome. Maybe Laura has missed some feminine company these many years and so the arrival of Jayne and myself has brought some new life to her. The other guests during my visit were Jayne, her brother and Lord Falshaw. You can imagine my surprise, when His Lordship arrived, for he looked quite elegant in his formal attire. Such a bearing has he; he is almost regal. Throughout dinner he took great care to engage me in conversation which I found surprising. His manners were impeccable and he was most courteous towards me throughout the evening, even enquiring after my*

70

welfare.

After dinner we ladies drank coffee. It is the drink most people take here but a new experience for me. It is readily available as the beans are grown here on the plantations. The room I was given had such charming décor and the bed was so comfortable I slept deeply. Overall, my visit was an extremely enjoyable affair.

Life on the island is peaceful and I am settled into a good routine. Everyone rises early including myself. Each morning I take a short walk along the edge of the sea which is the most delicate blue, green colour. So clear is the water you can sometimes see the small creatures swimming on the seabed. I have been given the use of a small boat. And, you will be shocked to hear, I have been learning to swim in the sea. The water is quite salty but I find the experience most refreshing and invigorating. People here eat a great deal of fish which is caught fresh every day. I find I am beginning to enjoy the taste but dislike the cleaning process involved in preparing them. This is one reason why I am glad to have my maid!

Oh yes, my Darling Lizzie, I have a maid. Well, at least I call her my maid. Her name is Kuala. She is teaching me the island way of life. So far, she has taught me to cook and light a fire. Also, how to plait ropes from the fronds which hang from the trees at the edge of the forest. This means I have been able to provide skipping ropes and climbing ropes for the children. Life is most enjoyable. I am well and feeling more contented as each day passes.

Ships visit regularly but are not always encouraged to stay long as sometimes there is trouble between the crews and the islanders. This is also probably why we see more of Lord Falshaw than usual at these times. I believe he brings his men to the main island to police the area and keep order. His men are polite to us ladies, making sure we are not disturbed by any unwanted attentions. I do declare I feel quite safe when they are around.

I know it is early my dear but I have enclosed a small

*gift for you for the forthcoming festive season. It has been made by one of the local islanders. You may find it most unusual but hopefully useful? Please try not to open it until Christmas morning. Remember, I shall be thinking of you on Christmas Day.*

*School is due to start so I shall close my letter. We start and finish early these days. Plus, the Captain will be calling to see how I am and to collect this letter. I am so happy you received him when he called as he has been most kind to me. I start to look upon him as a father figure. When you write please remember to tell me all you can.*

*Think of me always.*
*Your loving friend Mary*

Sealing the letter Mary placed it to one side to await the arrival of the Captain. She would share with him the joyous news of Lizzie's betrothal for she knew he would be interested.

Much later after the Captain's departure Mary wrote in her journal: *I have received the most joyous of news. My sweet, Darling Lizzie is to be married. I can only imagine the feelings of great happiness she must be experiencing at this time. How happy I am for her. Unlike me she needs to be cherished and loved for she is such a delicate creature. I will admit, if only in this journal where I write my most intimate thoughts, that for a fleeting moment, I experienced pangs of jealousy at her good fortune. I have scolded myself for being a shrew. I love Lizzie dearly and want to see her truly happy. She is my sister-in-arms. I would never wish her harm. May God bless and keep her.*

# *Eleven*

Back in England, Lizzie was enjoying the attention being showered upon her, in her new status as an engaged person. Since the official announcement in The Times, Lizzie, James and her family had received a number of invitations. Their acquaintances were delighted by the betrothal and, in some cases, envious as James was an eligible bachelor. Being too much in love she would hear no wrong of him from anyone, not even his sisters. Surprisingly, those two ladies, had behaved most pleasantly towards her. The only time Lizzie felt any discord with her situation was when giving thought to her absent friend. Lady Mountford, perceptive of her daughter's sensibilities and feelings over the loss of Mary, has done her best to keep Lizzie fully occupied.

The buying of the engagement and wedding trousseaus excited both mother and daughter. They had spent a great deal of time checking and choosing different dress materials, laces and flowers, to adorn the new outfits. As much as Her Ladyship was set in her ways as an aristocrat, she was also modern minded. Insisting her only daughter must have the most up-to-date style of wedding dress. Knowing and caring deeply for both his wife and daughter, Lord Mountford raised no objections.

During the weeks leading up to the wedding, which was to take place in the local church, Lizzie found herself quite busy. Inspecting everything she was highly satisfied. After much discussion with James, her mother and Father, it was decided the two Williamson sisters, along with Lizzie's cousin, Penelope were to be bridesmaids. This pleased James. Lizzie felt, for one day, she could be magnanimous regarding his sisters. Not that she would have been otherwise. Such was her nature she could not be unpleasant to anyone.

It is during one of their shopping trips that Lizzie

purchased a pretty stole. When questioned why she declared it was a gift for Mary. Her plan was to send it to her dear friend the next time she wrote to her. Her Mother said nothing, although she quietly hoped married life would limit the time Lizzie spent brooding over the absent girl. What Lady Mountford couldn't do as yet, was prevent the letters which passed between the two young women. However, she believed in time these would eventually cease. Therefore, when a few days later Lizzie received another letter from Mary, Her Ladyship kept her peace on the subject.

Receiving the letter brought home to Lizzie how remiss she had been. And how, in the excitement of her wedding preparations, she hadn't spared a thought for her dear friend. With this in mind she raced to her room to sit and read without being disturbed.

Much later, Lady Mountford entering the room, enquires, "And how is Mary?"

The question surprises Lizzie. "She is very well Mama and appears to be settled in her new life."

The warm glow on Lizzie's face shows Lady Mountford her daughter is still very much attached to her young friend. Her Ladyship realises she must tread carefully on the subject. It isn't that she dislikes Mary but, being of noble blood, she is very much aware of the difference of standing between the two girls. However, she is perceptive enough to understand the turmoil her daughter suffered at the loss of her friend. She hopes in time, James will displace Mary in Lizzie's thoughts and affections. The focus might have changed but it is obvious Mary is still very much in her daughter's thoughts. Despite Lady Mountford praying time would change all that, little does she know that the missives between the two young women would continue whenever they were apart. Nor would they cease until the day one of them passed away!

When pressed, Lizzie willingly tells her Mother what Mary has written. Hearing her daughter's young friend is settled in her new life, Lady Mountford feels some relief.

Descending the stairs, she chooses to pass news of Mary onto her husband. He too will feel easier knowing the girl has accepted her future life. It will also perhaps, ease his mind at the guilt he occasionally feels in being the one to instigate Mary's removal from Lizzie's vicinity.

After her Mother left Lizzie read Mary's letter again before taking up her pen, to write her response.

*Dear Sweet Mary*

*I so enjoyed your last letter. You appear to be settled and I am pleased you are happy. Please do not be cross but Mother entered my room and I shared some of what you had written with her. She sends her best regards and says she will pass on your well wishes to Father. I speak of you often to James and he has been most complimentary. He expressed the opinion how brave you are to be all alone in a strange place. And how he regrets not having met you.*

*One evening at dinner James mentioned you sounded quite settled in your life. But what a shame you had to go so far away to achieve this. Fathers responded, 'that you had little choice considering your situation.' I found this a little disturbing for I know how much Father has assisted you. Mama though, was most kind in her remarks and, to my surprise, reminded Father not every girl is as fortunate as his dear Lizzie in having such caring, loving parents. James and I looked at each other surprised for it seemed Mama was reprimanding him! I find it a sad world when people, as sweet as you my dearest Mary, are left in such dire straits.*

*Now, to answer your questions about James. He is taller than I and is fair in colouring, having the most beautiful pale brown eyes. His waist and hips are sleek, and he sits a horse well. When he speaks his voice is soft and gentle but he has such an infectious laugh. I know you would find him as attractive as I do. His manner is gentle and caring and I know he loves me deeply. So yes, my dear Mary, you can love him as a brother. I am sure he would welcome your affections so.*

*With regards my trousseau. Father says Mama is trying to bankrupt him. How we both laughed for he jests of course.*

But even I am surprised at the cost of my wardrobe. My wedding dress is a beautiful, creamy silk and lace concoction. It looks a little like a fluffy cream cake. The seamstress has worked hard to make it perfect. There are six petticoats beneath and the bodice has been embroidered to match the veil which is ten feet in length with little flowers sewn all over.

Mama also bought me ten new dresses in pink, lemon and pale blue with shoes to match. I am so very fortunate. James has promised me a cape of fur and a horse of my own as my wedding gifts from him. I have chosen a set of silver buttons engraved with his family crest as his gift from me.

We are to live at his family estate in the country part of the year, and in his town house the rest of the year. This way I will be able to see Mama and Father quite often. Father says he will never be rid of me but Mama says he is secretly very happy with the arrangement.

The nights are now drawing in and it is cooler each day. Soon it will be Christmas and my Darling Mary will have been gone for many months. Tell me my Sweet One how will you celebrate Christmas? Do the islanders understand the meaning of our Lord's birth and the celebrations we keep?

I am sending you a gift with this letter but you too must promise not to open it before Christmas morning. I am sure you will love it and will think of me often when you look upon it. I have put your gift to me away until we return from church on Christmas morning. I am so excited to know what it is you have sent me as it feels quite heavy but I will resist opening it until the day.

The flower you sent arrived safely. It is most unusual and I have kept it with your letter so I may look on it again and again knowing it will remind me of you.

Please take care, my Darling Mary. When next I write it will be as Lady Williamson from the address I have given at the end of this letter.

With all my love
Your very dear friend Lizzie.

With her letter finished and sealed Lizzie returned to the drawing room, surprised to find her father waiting to speak to her. Entering the room, he bade her sit and tell him what news there was from Mary. Although surprised by his request, she was in fact quite pleased, for this was the first time he had shown any interest in how her dear friend was doing. Settling on the chaise she told him all Mary had written.

Well, not all as there are some personal confidences a young girl should never share with her parents; particularly her father!

# Twelve

Mary, like Lizzie, gave little thought to her friend, apart from when day-to-day life allowed her to do so. Recently, Kuala had asked if she could join the school. Mumna had agreed but only after finishing her jobs in the hut. As Mary made little mess, nor needed much doing for her, this proved to be easy for Kuala to agree to. Making requests to Mumna had now become second nature to Mary. She realised, that though her husband was Chief, it was really Mumna who ruled the islands, and did so with a rod of iron.

School life progressed well. Jayne, who had returned to the main island not long after Mary's visit to Laura's home, came three times a week to teach the scriptures. She also relieved Mary from teaching some of the younger children, helping them with their reading. Mary in turn concentrated on teaching writing and arithmetic to the older children. The system worked well. Over the last few months Mary had learnt much more about the people living on the islands. She was fortunate to receive a number of invitations to tea from the children's families. Her island life was becoming much more settled. Most days England and her lost family were rarely in her thoughts, although sometimes she and Jayne would talk about the past, and the future. As time passed, she began to believe it had been her destiny to come to the islands. The only time she ever felt homesick was when reading Lizzie's letters.

Sitting at the table one evening she wrote in her journal: *Christmas fast approaches and I cannot believe how time has flown by. It is many months since I first arrived on the island. How quickly I have come to feel at home here. This year it will be a different type of festive season to any I have experienced before. There will be no snow to cope with, nor will it be as cold. I find it strange to think of celebrating our*

*Lord's birthday in the hot sunshine and yet he was born in a hot climate. After talking to Laura about her travels I have discovered how Christmas is celebrated in many different ways in lots of countries. How little I know of the world.*

*Since her return to the island, I have found myself drawing closer to Jayne. I feel so comfortable in her company. She has such a caring, warm nature that one can do no other but like her. The difference in demeanour between her and The Reverend amazes me. He appears so cold-hearted for a man of God. I am still at a loss to understand him.*

With Christmas a few weeks away, Mary began looking forward to organising the celebrations they were to have at the school. She decided the children would perform a Nativity play and give a Carol concert. She was also eager to see how the event would be celebrated by the islanders. With Jayne's help, Mary started showing the children how to make Christmas decorations. The youngsters were looking forward to seeing the school hung with the results of their labours. And, with Lord Falshaw's assistance, Mary obtained any items needed to fasten the decorations and dried foliage the islanders collected for her. Thinking of Lord Falshaw, Mary also realised they had seen much more of him in recent months. Without realising it she had begun looking forward to their meetings. It was after one such meeting that Kuala told her Mumna wished to speak to her about Miss Morgain. Surprised by the request, Mary left to see the Queen, wondering what was wrong.

Arriving at the big hut she asked, "What is wrong Your Majesty?"

"It is the Reverend. He bad man. He shows no respect to Chief. Even after Chief give him meeting. I not pleased at the way he speaks to Chief."

Mary, surprised by the outburst, took a moment to think before answering. "Yes, I agree it isn't good. It does seem to be a problem." Not knowing what else to say or suggest she waited for Mumna to speak again.

"What do you suggest Chief do about him?"

Taken aback Mary was slightly disturbed. What could she say as it really wasn't her place to advise? "Err... I think perhaps I am not the most suitable person to ask such a question. Err... Might I suggest Your Majesty speaks to Lord Falshaw. He is, I am sure, much better qualified to help you with such an important matter!"

Mumna smiled. "You' clever lady. I think is good suggestion. I will speak to His Lordship." Breathing a sigh of relief Mary, happy to have been of service, returned to the schoolroom.

It should not therefore, have been a surprise when, a few days later, she discovered Lord Falshaw waiting at the entrance to the school room. Gaining her attention, he asked for a private audience. Agreeing to his request the pair left, much to Jayne's surprise. As they headed towards the shoreline Lord Falshaw spoke. "I have just spent some time with the Chief and Mumna. It seems they are both disturbed by Reverend Morgain."

He stopped speaking, waiting for Mary to digest his comments.

"So, I understand. Mumna mentioned to me they were unhappy with him."

At her response he continued. "Yes, I believe you suggested Mumna speak to me about the situation. But pray tell me, what are your own thoughts on the matter? What do you think should be done? As Jayne's friend I wondered how we could sort the problem out without hurting her."

Mary looked up in surprise. This was the last thing she had expected to hear but knew she must respond. "It is such a shame the Reverend has not been able to communicate more agreeably with the Chief or his wife. Perhaps if he were to listen to someone like yourself, who could explain the matter to him...? Maybe show him the error of his ways?"

His Lordship thought about her response. "Mumna thinks it would be better if the Reverend left the island."

Alarmed by his comment, she turned towards His

Lordship, a questioning look, upon her face. "But what about Jayne if he leaves?"

"Mumna has asked me if I would consider allowing the Reverend to stay at my estate. The hope being that his demeanour will change. However, I believe Miss Morgain should not suffer the same fate as her brother. Could I therefore ask a great favour of you?"

"If it is to help Jayne, then please ask?"

"What I wish to know Miss Watson is... would you consider allowing Miss Morgain to live with you while her brother is absent? That way she will not be left alone."

"But of course, she may live with me. I think it a most suitable solution."

Breathing a sigh of relief Lord Falshaw smiled at her. "Thank you. I am grateful for your generosity. I will inform the Chief the matter is resolved."

Reluctantly it seemed, on both their parts, they returned to the school-house whereupon His Lordship took his leave. The conversation left Mary much to think about. Deciding to close the school early, much to the delight of the children, she was left with a questioning glance from Jayne. After the children had left, she told Jayne she had a headache and needed to lie down. Returning to the hut without saying anything further, she left poor Jayne a little confused. Settling inside Mary thought, 'Poor Jayne. I feel so bad for lying to her but it is not my place to tell her of the changes being made. I feel guilty but I will be there for her when the time comes, as I am sure she will be distressed by her brother's banishment.'

Two days later Reverend Morgain left the main island to journey alone to Lord Falshaw's estate. At the same time Jayne moved her belongings into Mary's island home. Jayne was at first concerned and distressed by the removal of her brother. But, as the days passed and Christmas drew nearer, she seemed to relax. Before long she was enjoying her new-found freedom.

The decorations for the schoolroom were almost

finished. Once complete the two young women decided they would hang them up on the Thursday afternoon, after school closed for the day. This meant when the children arrived the following day, they would find the place looking highly festive. Mary and Jayne were excited, eagerly wanting to see the children's reaction to the finished results. They also decided to give the children a small party with some nice treats for them. Jayne suggested baking a cake but as neither Jayne nor Mary knew how, it wasn't possible. Then Jayne suggested asking Laura if her cook would bake one. Laura readily agreed, declaring she would also come and help with the party.

On the Thursday after the school was closed, both young women began decorating the schoolroom inside and out. Later, the pair wrapped a small gift for each child, placing them in a sack ready for the following day. By the time they retired that night both ladies were tired but happy.

Early the next morning Laura arrived with the cake and buns for the party. Just before the start of school the three ladies stood outside waiting for the youngsters to arrive. As the children walked through the village the ladies were filled with excited anticipation. They were not disappointed for as soon as the children saw the schoolroom their faces lit up.

Much later Mary wrote in her journal: *Taking lessons this morning I knew would not be easy, it being the last day before the holidays. Jayne and I planned a fun day. We organised games for the children until lunch time. Laura and Kuala helped us get the party table ready with lots of nice food. The children enjoyed everything, including the sweet treats Laura had brought with her. After lunch the parents and the other residents arrived for the concert. The Chief and Queen Mumna were guests of honour. After the Nativity play the children sang Christmas Carols with everyone joining in. Before going home, we gave each child a small gift which delighted them. Later, after wishing everyone a Very Merry Christmas school was officially closed. Watching the children walk away smiling and chatting filled me with such happiness. With school closed Jayne and I are to stay at Laura's for a few days, returning in time to celebrate my first Christmas in my new home.*

When, a few days later Mary and Jayne returned home from Laura's, they discovered a ship docked in the harbour. Mary was pleasantly surprised to discover Captain Morrison waiting, holding a small parcel for her. Inviting him in for refreshments they spent the next hour in friendly conversation until reluctantly he bade her farewell. "I am afraid I must leave now for I have to see the Chief. However, I am sure I will see you over the next few days as we are staying on the island for the festive celebrations."

"But you will not be home for Christmas, Captain. Will your wife not be disappointed and upset by your absence at this time of year?"

The Captain shrugged his shoulders resignedly. "Unfortunately, as Captain of my own vessel I occasionally have to stay away at these times. It does not happen every year. I am fortunate my wife understands. But we will have a good celebration once I am back home." And standing he bade her good-day.

The following day, despite Jayne's mixed feelings, Reverend Morgain returned to the island, albeit under a cloud. He was given permission by the Chief to take the Christmas morning service, and to visit his sister. On Christmas morning Mary arrived at the small church and was pleased to find it full. It seemed all the islanders, residents and the crew from the ship were in attendance. The service went well and afterwards Jayne and her brother left to spend the remainder of the day together. Thinking of the Reverends demeanour, Mary was unsure what sort of day her friend would have, for it appeared he had still not learnt any humility. On the contrary, he seemed more put out by his situation.

As she was leaving Lord Falshaw approached. "Miss Watson, I wondered if you would care to join me for lunch on board my yacht."

Surprised, Mary wondered whether to refuse him but she didn't really want to be on her own for the rest of the day. "Thank you Lord Falshaw. I would be delighted to join you." And taking his proffered arm, she allowed him to lead her to his large yacht which was tied up at the dockside.

As they boarded Mary was pleased to see the Colonel and Laura sitting in some wicker chairs on the boat's deck. She felt slightly relieved having been a little wary of being on her own with His Lordship. With a gentle breeze blowing and the warm sun shining down Mary soon relaxed. Lunch proved to be a delightful affair with Lord Falshaw doing everything possible to ensure she felt at ease. Later, he walked her back to her home.

"I wondered if you would do me the honour of allowing me to escort you to the celebrations later on." Although she protested, he need not trouble himself, he insisted. "It will be no trouble at all." And so, she acquiesced to his request.

Later, when His Lordship returned to collect her, he found Mary had changed, re-done her hair and around her shoulders she wore the beautiful stole sent by Lizzie. A gift Mary was highly delighted with. Gently taking hold of her arm he led her towards the village centre where they sat down on the mats next to the Johnstones. Once settled young island girls began bringing food and drink for everyone. Looking around Mary was disappointed to see Jayne absent, realising there was little she could do about it. The rest of the evening saw the islanders singing and dancing, with the celebrations going on long into the night.

As dark descended the Colonel insisted the two ladies should retire. Standing, he escorted Mary and his wife back to Lord Falshaw's yacht where the pair spent the night. Back onboard, Laura and Mary settled down in their bunks. As they chattered, they listened to the intoxicating music pounding through the night. Fortunately, tiredness overtook them and eventually both drifted off into a deep sleep. Neither woke until the following morning. And it was to an island suffering from being too 'chippy' (hung over) from drinking too much of the local brew.

Returning home after breakfast Mary met Captain Morrison. He was attempting to round up his crew as he wanted to sail on the next high tide. As he passed, he informed Mary he would call prior to sailing, to collect any correspondence she might have for him. Once inside the hut Mary sat and began writing a reply to Lizzie.

*My Dearest Lizzie*

*Thank you so much for the wonderful gift you sent. I admit it took all my will power not to open the package before Christmas morning. The paper and decorations on the parcel were so pretty I have given them to Kuala as she admired them so much. I do believe she has been showing them to the other young girls. They appear to be envious for it is something they do not have here.*

*Life has gone on much the same. Although, I must tell you of poor Jayne's brother, The Reverend Morgain. May God forgive me my thoughts, but he has been so arrogant when speaking to the Chief that he has upset him. Now the Chief will have nothing to do with him and has banished him from the main island. The Reverend has been sent to Lord Falshaw's estate. Poor Jayne remains here with me. I am grateful to Lord Falshaw for the happy solution and admit he has risen in my estimations. Yet, when I try to thank him, he seems a little brusque, saying no thanks are necessary. It being the best solution all-round. He believes Jayne should take over as spiritual advisor to the islanders. Especially as her temperament is much more suited to the role than her brothers. I am more than happy to agree to his suggestion.*

*Jayne it appears has found a new lease of life. She moved into my hut to live with me during her brothers' absence and we found ourselves quite comfortable together. Our days are well spent and I have seen her become more relaxed. She smiles more and walks with a lighter step. Almost as if a weight has been lifted from her shoulders. God surely works in mysterious ways.*

*Christmas morning, we celebrated with a service in our*

*little church; conducted by The Reverend whom the Chief allowed back for the occasion. Poor Jayne spent most of Christmas Day in the church house with him where, I am sure, she had to listen to his litany of complaints. No doubt aimed against the Chief, the islanders and anyone else whom he believes has slighted him. They were not even allowed to join in the village celebrations. I was unhappy for her. But she said it was a small price to pay as her brother is to return to the other island in the morning. I am sure he is most put out by this, but the Chief is quite insistent.*

*After the church service I took lunch on Lord Falshaw's yacht. I was at first a little hesitant about accepting his invitation. But there was no need for me to worry as the Colonel and Laura joined us. The meal was delightful and the whole morning proved to be most relaxing. In the afternoon there followed a big celebration in the middle of the village. The islanders made lots of music with dancing. This went on all day and well into the night. Laura and I spent the night on Lord Falshaw's yacht as the Colonel wished to ensure we were safe. Laura said it was because the islanders sometimes lost control when drinking the local brew. It is called Juju and is, I understand, quite intoxicating.*

*I find the island way of living most enticing and my life here is enjoyable. I am delighted with my new-found freedom. I must remember to be careful or I may become a little native in my actions and appearance. Ha Ha! I am only teasing you my dear for even here etiquette and good manners are still observed.*

*You will my Dear One, have been married for some weeks now. Please write to tell me all about your special day. I hope you are happy in your new life? Does James's family treat you well? I know your life will be different from now on but please do not forget me.*

*Write to me soon Lizzie and remind me of all I am or should be.*

*Your dearest friend Mary*

Satisfied with her writing Mary sealed the letter and taking up her journal she wrote: *Christmas this year has been a strange one. Yet, I have found it most enjoyable. My heart went out to Jayne for having to spend the day alone with her brother. His Lordship provided us with roast chicken for dinner which makes a change from fish. The celebrations held later that day were exciting. The islander's music seems most intoxicating. Sounding wild and carefree. I was sorry not to be able to stay and watch the dancing but the Colonel was most insistent Laura and I left. Sometimes I wonder what it would be like to have been born a man. They appear to have so much more freedom than we woman. My night aboard the yacht was comfortable. Laura and I get on well together. So much so, I found myself confiding in her the story of my life. The telling of it reminded me of my parents and for the first time in a long while I found myself missing them. But there is no reason for regret. My life is what it is and I accept it readily.*

# *Thirteen*

As her wedding day approached Lizzie began feeling nervous at what lay ahead. Having talked to some of her lady friends they had told her stories of what happened on the wedding night. As such she was beginning to worry. The fact that most of what these silly girls said was hearsay and not based on actual experiences didn't alter her thoughts. The closer the day approached the more concerned she became. It was then she wished Mary was still with her.

Lady Mountford, although a formidable character, was also quite a perceptive woman. She soon realised something was bothering her daughter for she appeared to become paler and more listless. As each day passed Lizzie was losing her initial excitement at the idea of marrying James. One morning Her Ladyship took Lizzie to one side. "I think something is worrying you my child, please, tell me what is it?"

After some hesitation Lizzie burst out, "I am afraid of getting married."

Her Mother was surprised. "Why? Why do you feel this way?"

It took a while before Lizzie could speak. "The girls tell me strange things happen when you get married. Things in bed that are, err…… perhaps not normal."

At her daughter's outburst Lady Mountford has to turn her face away to control her smile. It isn't that Her Ladyship finds the matter funny, only that she is relieved the problem isn't a major one. Sitting Lizzie down she carefully explains all she needs to know. Reassuring her there is nothing to worry about. By the end of the conversation Lizzie, although embarrassed, feels calmer. Not wishing to leave her mother worrying about her she tells her she feels better, even though secretly she remains uneasy.

With her wedding day closing in Lizzie becomes so

busy that any thoughts of her wedding night flies from her mind. The house is cleaned from top to bottom. And the kitchen becomes a hive of activity as the cook and kitchen maids prepare the wedding feast. Everything is going to plan. Her own maid is instructed to ensure all Lizzie's clothes are cleaned and pressed, and that her wedding trousseau is ready. The celebration meal is organised and the invitations are sent out.

However, things do not go to plan, as a few days prior to the wedding Sir James calls with some unhappy news. Not wanting to tell Lizzie on his own he hopes Lord and Lady Mountford will be present. Possibly because he believes they will be better able to calm her than he can. Especially as he knows she will be upset by what she hears. Entering the house, he instructs the maid to inform Lord Mountford of his arrival, requesting he join the family. Entering the drawing room, he finds Lizzie and Lady Mountford sitting reading. Although surprised by his sudden appearance Lizzie thinks nothing of it and the three of them sit chatting about the forthcoming wedding until His Lordship enters the room. Taking a seat near the fire Lord Mountford waits to hear what it is James has to say. Looking at the young man's face he realises it isn't good news.

Taking a deep breath James begins. "I have something important to tell you. It isn't good news."

Upon hearing this Lizzie becomes concerned and agitated. Lady Mountford, perceiving something is amiss tells her, "Pray be quiet child. Calm yourself until we know what is the matter."

Once she is settled James goes on. "It seems war has broken out in one of the colonies. The Minister of War has summoned gentlemen to gather groups of fighters for entry into Her Majesty's Army." He pauses to allow the news to sink in. "This means I will have to leave to attend the Ministry a few days after the wedding ceremony."

At this piece of news Lizzie gasps. "But you can't. It's not right."

"I know my dear," says James gently. "There is little I can do but conform to orders. I am afraid, it means our honeymoon will have to be postponed until I return."

Lizzie, shocked by the news, is distressed at the thought of James' fighting and bursts into tears. Whilst her Mother attempts to calm her, Lord Mountford takes James into the library to obtain more details. Thus, allowing his wife, enough time to sooth his daughter. Fifteen minutes later James returns to the drawing room to find Lizzie is calmer. With his return Her Ladyship leaves the two young people alone while she goes to speak to her husband, hoping they won't have to postpone the wedding.

By the time James leaves, later in the day, he has managed to reassure Lizzie it is not as bad as she thinks. "The war won't last long. Before you know it, I will be back with you once more." Reluctantly, Lizzie agrees for she realises there is no alternative but to accept the situation.

Writing in her diary later that evening she puts down her thoughts: *What a miserable day it has been. I should be the happiest person in the world. Yet, I find myself sad as my Darling James will have to leave for foreign shores not long after we wed. Could life be any more unfair to me, I think not. My heart trembles at the risk he takes, even though he tries to reassure me he will be safe. What is worse, is that I have been so happy I have given little thought to my dear Mary. Today's sad news has reminded me how much I miss her not being here. How can I abide such sorrow when I have no-one close to share my fears with? It is unbearable and intolerable. Damn the military.*

Over the following days James spent what time he could with Lizzie, doing his best to reassure himself she had accepted his impending departure. Wishing to take her mind away from the war he encouraged her to make any changes she wished, to their new home. However, as Lizzie felt the town house was perfect it needed nothing doing. The household staff were always welcoming. Treating her with such deference it made her feel at ease. Had Lizzie but known it they were in fact relieved by her manner. To them, her gentle, caring nature was a sharp contrast to the Williamson sisters who were the opposite of Lizzie. Uncaring and inconsiderate as mistresses. Lizzie would be taking her own maid Lucy with her when she married. Lucy was pleased to be going as she had looked after Lizzie for over four years and adored her mistress. As the wedding day drew closer there was much excitement and activity in both households. After all, the changes would affect many.

On the morning of her wedding, Lizzie, though still troubled by news of the war, nervously allowed Lucy to prepare her for the most important day of her life. Once bathed and dressed in her undergarments, Lucy prepared Lizzies hair. She then fastened fresh flowers into the long curls hanging down her back. With great care and ceremony, the maid helped Lizzie into her wedding dress. Looking in the mirror Lucy noted how pale Lizzie looked so she lightly powdered her mistress's face, before rouging her cheeks and lips. Afterwards, she carefully placed the jewellery Lady Mountford had given Lizzie as a wedding gift, around her neck. To finish, Lucy added the final item. A long wedding veil.

As Lizzie looked at herself in the mirror, the maid stepped back to admire the finished result, gasping with delight. "You look beautiful Miss Lizzie." The compliment made her mistress blush profusely.

Lady Mountford, wanting to see her daughter, knocked lightly on the bedroom door and entered the room. As Lizzie walked slowly towards her Mother she trembled ever so slightly, waiting with bated breath. Taking a short intake of breath her Mother said, "You look beautiful. What a wonderful bride you make." At her Mother's words Lizzie breathed a sigh of relief. Bending down Her Ladyship kissed her daughter's pale cheek lightly before gently taking her arm to escort her from the room.

Standing at the top of the stairs Lizzie looked down, seeing her Father waiting. As she descended the stairs Lord

Mountford was taken aback, swallowing hard to hold in his emotions. He had never seen his daughter look more beautiful. As she reached the last step, he moved forward to take hold of her hand, whereupon he bent forward and kissed her gently on the cheek.

Lizzie later wrote in her journal: *Taking my arm, Father escorted me towards the front door. As we passed the maids, I heard them whispering, "You look beautiful, Miss Elizabeth. Good-luck." I remember smiling at them. Leaving the house, we climbed into the carriage and set off for the church. The journey wasn't a long one but all the way Father held my hand tightly. I believe he was trying to instil confidence in me. Offering me his reassurances, which I was happy to receive. My stomach felt as if it was full of butterflies, flitting around excitedly.*

As the carriage approached the church, Lizzie saw the Williamson sisters and her Cousin Penelope waiting. As her maids of honour, they would lead her down the aisle. Stepping from the carriage, Lizzie watched her Mother enter the church. Then taking her arm, Lord Mountford led his only daughter into the dimness of the church. Walking up the aisle, the church organ played and the choir sang. Lizzie noted the church pews were crowded with many people she knew. Then looking towards the altar, she saw James waiting for her.

'There is my future husband. He looks so handsome and grand in his red uniform,' she thought just as James turned. Seeing her he smiled warmly in reassurance.

With the service over the newly married Sir and Lady James Williamson left the church through an archway of drawn swords, created by two lines of men from James' garrison. Lizzie laughed gaily, feeling relieved that a major part of the day was over. Reaching the church gates James led her to the waiting carriage which was decorated with flowers and ribbons. Climbing inside they both threw coins towards the poor people waving at them. Then, settling down close together on the seat they held hands all the way back to the house.

During the drive James bent forward, taking every opportunity to kiss Lizzie. "You are the most beautiful of wives. I love you Lady Williamson."

Shyly Lizzie whispered back, "And I love you too Sir Williamson." How they both laughed.

During the family's absence the servants had laid out the wedding banquet. As the happy couple alighted from the carriage there was, much to Lizzie's delight, a loud burst of applause and cheers from the household staff. Not long afterwards the wedding guests arrived and the celebrations were underway. There was much cheer and goodwill for the happy couple. Some hours later Lizzie left the party to remove her wedding dress and to change into her travelling outfit. She and James were spending a few days at their country estate before returning to town. Lizzie would reside at her family home, rather than the town house, as James didn't want her to be alone while he was away.

Before she left her bedroom, Lizzie completed her diary: *What a glorious day it has been. I am at last Lady Williamson. My only sadness, is that my dear Mary was not here to share in this special day of mine. I am now changed and ready to leave. My husband and I, (how wonderful that sounds). My husband and I, are to leave soon for the country estate. I am determined not to think of James going away to war until we return to town. How sad it makes me but I will be brave for him.*

The day was a long one but eventually the happy couple arrived at the Williamson estate. It was late in the evening and Lizzie was feeling quite tired. Once settled in the drawing room, James insisted she sit on the chaise, her feet up on a footstool, drinking hot chocolate to help her recover from the journey. As she sat, Lizzie looked around the room, remembering how delighted she had been the first time she saw it. Hanging over the fireplace was a large portrait of James' father, the late Sir Williamson. Lizzie wondered what sort of man he had been when alive.

Turning to ask her husband she caught him looking at her. "And why are you watching me like that?"

Taking a moment, he smiled. "I am amazed at how beautiful my wife is and how happy she makes me."

Lizzie blushed at his compliment. Seeing this, James leant forward, to gently kiss her. It was a warm kiss. His lips lingering over hers for some time, before a knock at the door made them reluctantly part. As James called, "Enter" the door opened to reveal the butler and two footmen carrying trays of food. Bowing the butler announced, "Supper my Lord. Is there anything else, Sir?"

"No, thank you," replied James and the servants left. After which the happy couple sat in companionable silence eating their supper of cooked meats, bread and salad.

Finally, it became obvious Lizzie was trying to hide her yawns. Removing the tray James stood up and gently pulled her into his arms. Kissing her, he slowly led Lizzie from the room and up the stairs to the bedroom. Climbing the stairs Lizzie felt unsure what to do or expect.

As she entered the bedroom, she discovered a young woman waiting. "This is Alice. She will be your maid while we are staying on the estate."

Lizzie smiled. "Hello Alice."

Curtsying the maid said, "Welcome, my Lady." Satisfied, James left the room, leaving Alice to help Lizzie prepare for bed. Once she was ready, the maid curtsied and headed for the door. "Goodnight Madam."

Lizzie wondered what to do next. Deciding to get into bed she climbed under the covers, finding herself sinking into a large feather mattress. Ten minutes later there was a gentle knock at the door. As it opened James entered wearing a dressing-gown. He had obviously gone into another room to change into his night attire so as not to embarrass her, this being their first night together. As he walked towards the bed Lizzie shivered slightly. Even though her Mother had explained the duties of a wife, she was still nervous at what was to come. But she need not have concerned herself for her husband would prove to be the most considerate of men.

James, perceptive enough to realise Lizzie was probably wary of what was going to happen, sat on the bed next to her. "Do you have everything you need my darling?"

She replied in a small voice. "Yes, I think so."

James smiled warmly at her before removing his dressing-gown, revealing a white night gown. Carefully climbing into the big bed, he lay down close to her. Lizzie felt her heart beat faster. She was concerned James would hear how loud it sounded. She was also shaking slightly, wondering if he might think her afraid of him. But she need not have worried as, leaning forward, James gently started kissing her. Carefully he increased the pressure of his mouth against hers, gently encouraging her back against the pillows. Withdrawing his lips, for a moment he looked deep into her eyes before smiling. She smiled back in response.

Turning he blew out the candle, then lay down next to her. With ease James took his wife into his arms, and began showering her with gentle kisses. Within a short period of time Lizzie was lost in the moment. James was stirring feelings to which she responded. As their kisses deepened, he slowly began to caress her body. Soon she was experiencing sensations of pure delight. And so, Lizzie discovered the true reality of what her wedding night should be.

One of joyous happiness and heightened elation. Later, she fell into a deep sleep, feeling happy and contented, a small smile spread across her face.

The following morning when Lizzie woke, she found herself alone. Lying still, she took the opportunity to relive the previous night, thinking how foolish she had been to worry. James had been so gentle and caring. Now she understood what being a married woman meant. Picking up her husband's pillow, Lizzie stroked it gently as she smiled to herself, feeling full of his love.

Sometime later there was a knock at the door.

"Enter."

Alice entered the room, carrying a large jug of warm

water. "Good-morning, Madam," Alice curtsied.

"What time is it Alice?"

"Ten o'clock Madam. The master gave strict instructions that you were to be left to sleep until ready to rise," she said as she poured warm water into the wash bowl.

Hearing this Lizzie smiled. "Well I'm ready now," and she promptly jumped out of bed feeling as if she was on top of the world. When her toilette was complete, Lizzie descended the stairs in search of her husband.

After a few blissful days in the country, Sir and Lady Williamson returned to town, going straight to the Mountford Manor House. Eagerly waiting to greet them were Lizzie's parents. As they entered the house Lady Mountford took her daughter in her arms, before leading her up to her old room to change out of her travelling clothes. Her Ladyship was pleased to see her daughter looking happy. James stayed a few hours but finally he rose to leave. "I must go to the town house to take leave of my sisters." The two ladies had stayed in town whilst the newlyweds were in the country, thus allowing them some privacy. "I will return later my darling to say goodbye before I leave to join my regiment."

The parting which later took place, was not an easy one for either Lizzie or James. And, it took all of his strength of will to walk away from his sweet adorable wife without a backward glance. Lizzie was bereft and upon seeing her daughter so distressed, Lady Mountford took her upstairs, instructing her to lie down until she was more composed.

Lizzie wrote in her diary: *I am bereft. My darling husband has left for places unknown. This is the saddest of days for me, especially following the glorious time we spent on our short honeymoon. My fears of my wedding night were unfounded. Even though there was some pain James did his utmost to be considerate and caring of my sensibilities. Now I am a true woman, and I find nothing more fulfilling than the caresses and love-making of my dear sweet husband. What a foolish girl I was to cause such a fuss. I vow I will be strong whilst James is away but please dear God, I ask you bring him back home safe to me.*

Over the next few days Lizzie wandered around the house listlessly, feeling totally lost. However, as the days passed, she began to feel more like her old self. But once her friends learnt she was back in residence the house was soon filled with the noise and laughter of young people enjoying themselves. It was while Lizzie was feeling low that she wrote a letter to Mary.

*Darling Sweet Mary*

*When I first read your letter, my heart skipped a beat. I wanted to tell you my dearest to please be aware of your actions. I would not wish to lose you to such primeval instincts. When I read your admissions, I became most concerned. Perhaps you can speak to Jayne for guidance as she seems to be a most sober person in thoughts and actions. Please, please do not distress me like this again.*

*And now to my news. Well my Dear One. My wedding day went exceedingly well. There were lots of people in attendance, too many to name here. Needless to say, you probably remember them all. My dress was wonderful and James looked exceedingly gallant in his red uniform. Yes Mary, I did say uniform. You see dearest it seems war has broken out somewhere in the colonies and poor James has been commandeered to lead a troop of infantry from his estate. I hoped it would be close to you as then you could meet him. But I am glad it is not for it would mean I would be worried about your safety as well as his. I admit I was most distressed when told the news for it came but a few days before our marriage. I thought it would cast a dark cloud over our day, but it did not. The only thing lacking was my Mary, who wasn't here to comfort me. However, Mama tried her best to soothe and calm me.*

*James' two sisters, along with my Cousin Penelope were my bridesmaids. They were dressed in red taffeta, which seemed most becoming as their outfits showed off my wedding dress beautifully. And they matched the uniforms of the Guard of Honour provided by James's regiment. My bouquet was a delight. I have pressed a small corsage as a keepsake for you, which I have enclosed. After the ceremony we returned to the house for a great banquet, with wine and port to drink. It was late when James and I left for a short honeymoon at the country estate. Our planned trip to Europe has been postponed until he returns home. When that will be, I know not.*

*Oh, Mary, nothing prepares you for your marriage bed. I have to admit to being most concerned about it some days before and throughout the journey to the estate. But I should not have fretted for James was the most courteous and caring of husbands. My wedding night passed in such a wonderful world of emotion. I cannot begin to describe it to you. Now I am a true woman and find the thought of being taken to bed by my husband quite exciting.*

*My Sweet Mary you must ensure that when you find a husband, he must love you dearly. And be as considerate and as caring as my dear James is to me. Not, perhaps, that you may achieve this where you are. Can you not return to England? I will ask James if you can live with us as my companion. Then I would have you with me all the time and I could help find you a suitable husband. Oh, how I miss you not being here.*

*We returned to town a few days ago and soon afterwards James departed for foreign lands unknown to me. Parting from him was so distressing I cried for a full two hours after he left the house. Father tried his best to calm and cheer me but to no avail. In the end Mama sent for the doctor to give me a sleeping draft. And so, I am once again alone. My friend is gone and now my dear husband. I am left with only my cat for company.*

*I need your comfort Dear One so I will close this letter. I wish the angels could fly this to you but I know it will be many weeks before I hear from you.*

*Think of me my sweet dear friend*
*All my love Lizzie*

# Fourteen

Christmas passed and life on the islands settled back into its daily routine. School re-opened in the New Year with the children returning full of stories about their presents and celebrations. The friendship between Jayne and Mary deepened as they supported each other, talking on all manner of subjects. Their friendship pleased and delighted them both and they were happy with their current living arrangements. Mary was especially delighted for Jayne was now more of a sister to her.

During the following weeks a number of ships visited the island. As such, the two young women managed to obtain an assortment of goods allowing them to have hobbies other than needlework. Such as painting and reading. These new occupations increased their opportunities in meeting the other lady residents. Their social circle was quickly growing. As the ladies now met at least once a week it was apparent that island life was becoming much more pleasant for all concerned.

At one of their regular visits to Laura's house, Jayne and Mary met a Mrs. Oldfield. The two young women found the lady to be very personable as she made their weekly meetings amusing and enjoyable. During one of their get-togethers Mary learnt a great deal about Dorothy and her husband and how they came to be island residents. She also learnt more about America as well. Mary realised how open the American people were. Yet not in a way that one took any offence from, for Dorothy's demeanour was so pleasing.

As the ladies sat chatting at one of their weekly meetings Laura announced. "Do you know I think it is time we had a ball!"

Everyone agreed what a wonderful idea that was, wanting to know what they could do to help. Life on the islands was slower than on the mainland, meaning entertainment was limited. Most of the ladies missed those social events, such as dances, balls and soirées. After much discussion a date was set, with Laura agreeing to act as organiser. The idea of a ball caused quite a stir, so when Dorothy suggested it would be a good excuse for new dresses as well, everyone agreed. Thereafter, their time was spent making a list of items needed for a successful event.

It was as the ladies sat sewing one day that Mary happened to mention news of the war. And how it had affected her dear friend. At that moment Colonel Johnstone, returned to the house. Overhearing the conversation, he shook his head, a dismayed expression on his face.

"Yes, the news of the war is very sad indeed. It will affect many people. One can only hope it does not go on for too long." Mary was surprised, wondering how he was aware of the news? But felt unable to ask. Nor did she get the chance as her attention was diverted back to the job in hand.

A few days later Lord Falshaw called to speak privately to Miss Morgain. He had come to give her some bad news regarding her brother. After he left, Jayne appeared distraught, being unable to communicate until she had calmed herself. Making her excuses she left for a short walk by the sea shore. But when she returned Mary saw her friend was still distressed. Fetching some water, she made Jayne sit, waiting silently until she was ready to speak. What Mary heard made her cry out in alarm.

Jayne was physically shaking as she told Mary what had happened.

"According to Lord Falshaw there has been a meeting of the Elders. They have decided my brother is to leave the island at the earliest time possible." Taking a deep breath, she went on. "It seems he has... forgotten... his calling, for he has.... molested... one of the young island women? I... I cannot believe it. But... his Lordship assures me it is true."

Mary, was astounded by the news. "It cannot be so. Surely such a thing is beyond him. He is a man of God."

Jayne took a moment before responding. "I know... but it is true. I am so very... very... angry with him. And ashamed of his actions."

Mary didn't know what to say. "I am sure you are but what is to happen now?"

"Well," said Jayne taking a deep breath. "He has been brought back to the church house. I may visit him if I wish. I will go as I am determined to have it out with him. What am I to tell our parents? They will not be pleased...! Neither will the Bishop be... He is such a fool." And the tears flowed down her face. The minutes passed but eventually calming herself Jayne looked at Mary. "I want you to know I may visit him but, I... will... not... welcome him back? Does he not realise the damage he has done?"

Mary thought how considerate His Lordship had been, to call in person and explain everything to Jayne. Thinking about the situation she was worried for her friend. What if she were to lose Jayne because of her brothers' actions. It seemed so unfair.

Once Jayne had calmed down, she went off to visit her brother. It was late in the evening before she returned to the hut. Mary thought her friend looked drained and exhausted. And seeing her arrive back in a state she made Jayne get ready for bed, all the while listening to what she had to say. After her friend had fallen into an exhausted sleep Mary sat thinking once more about the bad news. 'Poor Jayne,' she thought.

The next morning, not wanting to disturb Jayne, Mary quietly left the hut. Knowing how exhausted her friend had been from the meeting with her brother, Mary left her to sleep on. At lunchtime, while the children rested, she returned to see how she fared. Entering the hut, Mary discovered Jayne sat at the table. Looking up she gave Mary a wan smile, looking as if she was ready to cry. Yet there was something else in her eyes – determination.

Shaking her head Jayne told Mary, "I just don't understand what came over him.... I cannot find it in my heart to forgive him." Mary had to agree with her. But Jayne did not want to dwell any longer on the situation. "I think the day will be better served if I put my time to good use, rather than my sitting here, mulling over my stupid brother's actions." And, with her decision made she stood up and ran her hands over her hair. "I am going to the schoolroom to work with the children." Whereupon, her head held high, she left the hut. Silently Mary applauded her friends resolve, deciding to give her all necessary support.

Needing time to ease her own mind Mary took out the letter she had started writing the previous evening. A ship had anchored in the harbour two days previously, meaning the Captain would call soon to collect any correspondence she might have. Wanting to ensure she included all her news Mary re-read her letter.

*My Dearest Sweetest Lizzie*

*What tribulations you seem to have experienced these past few weeks. I am so sorry I was not there to aid or comfort you. It has left me feeling most remiss. If I am honest, I must confess when I read your letter I was devoured with a deep feeling of homesickness and loss. One I cannot describe. Every day since receiving your letter, Jayne and I have prayed for James' safe return.*

*Following the Christmas celebrations things have settled down on the islands and we are returned to our daily routines. Jayne and I meet regularly with the other ladies of the islands. We have also met a new friend, a Mrs Dorothy Oldfield. I find her a most agreeable person. She and her husband have lived here for some years, only returning to the island recently after visiting her family home in New York. Apparently, the Oldfield's met in her hometown where their love blossomed. They were married before leaving for the islands. According to Dorothy, it took her some time to convince her Father that Reginald was the man for her but they love each other deeply. I cannot see how he could not have known this for they obviously dote on each other.*

*Their plantation is owned by Dorothy's father, who has*

appointed her husband to act as his manager. Like most of the plantations, they grow a mixture of crops, including coffee beans, bananas and cotton, which the islanders help collect at harvest time. You would be most amused by Dorothy for such is her accent and she is quite outspoken in manner. But one cannot take offence. I have to say how very much I like her, finding her manner refreshing and uplifting. I am sure you would think so too were you to meet her.

It has been decided we are to have a small ball and so all us ladies are busy sewing new gowns. The colour of mine, according to Dorothy, makes my skin glow. To be honest I am not sure you would recognise me, my Darling Lizzie, as I am quite brown, having lost much of my English Rose complexion. As the sun can easily burn ones' complexion Jayne and I always carry parasols when out walking but still, we are colouring nicely.

Over here the war seems so remote, our being such a distance away. Strangely though, it seems Colonel Johnstone is already aware of the situation. I am at a loss to understand how he can be so well informed. We hope and pray it ceases soon and James returns to the bosom of his loving family.

The other news I have to impart is in regards to Reverend Morgain. He has returned to the main island in deep disgrace as it appears, he has been too friendly with one of Lord Falshaw's native girls, whom we discover is the daughter of the Chief. Unfortunately, she is with child. Lord Falshaw is very angry, as is the Chief. Jayne has berated her brother for his lack of duty and apparent abandonment of his faith. And so, after a meeting of the Elders it has been decided The Reverend is to leave the islands on the next ship. He is quite put out by this and has been attempting to make Jayne go with him. You will feel as proud of her as I do, for she has found new strength, telling him she will not go. I can only hope her stamina and determination lasts and she does not falter. But who can say, blood is thicker than water? We will wait and see.

The ship which arrived recently is due to sail soon so I

*will finish my letter. Know my thoughts are with you at this difficult time.*

*I close with all my love.*
*Your devoted friend Mary*

Happy with her letter Mary sealed the envelope, putting it to one side ready for collection.

Taking out her journal she wrote: *It has been a sad time these last few days. I cannot believe the news of The Reverend. Having been brought up a God-fearing Christian I find it strange I have no feelings of forgiveness towards Jayne's brother. Neither Jayne nor I are able to comprehend what came over him. Jayne says he is evil for taking advantage of the young woman. He must be aware of the consequences of his actions. He has wrought great sadness on Jayne, as well as disgrace upon himself. How she suffers because of him. My heart goes out to her as the news has affected her badly. My one hope is that she is allowed to stay when The Reverend leaves. I feel the sooner he goes the better.*

# Fifteen

Back in England Lizzie was feeling as lost and lonely as poor Jayne, albeit for different reasons. With only her cat for company she became more and more melancholy as time passed. Each day she waited in anticipation for news of James. Whenever the doorbell rang, she would eagerly run to the hallway in search of a letter. Only to return, shoulders drooping, as disappointment enveloped her after discovering there was none. Try as they might Lizzie's friends could not cheer her, even though they did their best. For a short period of time she would rally and become cheerful. Only to return to feeling despondent once alone when all her fears and worries over James returned.

Each night she would write in her diary: *I miss James. I love James. I miss my dear husband. Please God keep him safe.*

A few weeks later something unexpected happened to change her mood. That morning Lizzie woke feeling sick to the stomach. Rising from her bed she found herself overcome with a sudden rush of nausea. When she hadn't come down for breakfast by the time her father left for town her Mother had sent the maid upstairs to discover what was wrong. Quickly returning, Lady Mountford was informed Miss Lizzie was confined to her bed.

Going upstairs she discovered Lizzie vomiting into the wash basin. She looked exceedingly pale. "I don't feel well Mama. I don't understand it as I cannot remember eating anything to upset me. I feel too ill to come downstairs."

Looking at Lizzie a sudden twinkle flickered in Her Ladyships eye. "I believe I may know the reason why you are not well."

"You do?" said a miserable sounding Lizzie.

"Yes. I believe you are going to have a baby."

The news so astounded Lizzie, for this was the last thing she expected to hear, that she burst into tears, wailing, "Oh no, no. It cannot be true. What am I to do?"

Doing her best to calm her daughter Lady Mountford insisted Lizzie stay in bed. "Now, now my dear calm down. I shall arrange for the doctor to visit. In the meantime, I will send up a draft to settle your stomach."

Laying down in bed Lizzie found she felt a little better. Her Mother pulled the bed covers up and sat stroking her brow, making soft cooing noises, as if to a young child. Fortunately, it had the desired effect for in a short time her daughters' eyes closed and she was soon fast asleep.

Later in the day the doctor called to examine her, happily confirming Lady Mountford's diagnosis. Lizzie was indeed expecting her first child. Declaring her a fit, healthy young woman the Doctor said, "I will call again in a few days' time to check everything is going satisfactorily."

After the doctor, left Lizzie, having taken some medication, began to feel much better eventually finding herself able to eat some soup. Leaving her daughter to rest Lady Mountford went downstairs. Discovering her husband had returned from town she happily gave him the wonderful news. To say His Lordship was pleased was an understatement. In fact, he was highly delighted. A son for Lizzie and James. But, more importantly, it meant a Grandson and heir for him, and his wife.

Later, feeling much better, Lizzie dressed and went downstairs. Hearing his daughter coming His Lordship went to meet her. Taking her in his arms he told her how happy he was. Then becoming all fatherly he promptly insisted she must sit down. Taking her arm, he led her into the drawing room where he placed her on the chaise, telling her to put her feet up on the footstool.

"Now my dear Lizzie, you must take great care of yourself, and my Grandson," and he smiled endearingly at her. Lizzie, smiling in return, found his concern both amusing and caring.

From that day, life for Lizzie became different. She suffered morning sickness for a number of days but, with the help of her mother's drafts, these soon ceased. Slowly she found herself becoming used to the idea of being a mother, feeling much happier about her condition. Her only worry was that they still hadn't heard from James. Still, now there was some wonderful news to tell him.

Once recovered from the morning sickness Lizzie began feeling quite well. Her intention was not to mention the news of the forthcoming baby. Wanting to keep it a secret from everyone until after James had been told. However, he still hadn't been in touch with her. Besides, her parents were excited by the prospective addition to the family so wanted people to know. Her friends were delighted with the news, so Lizzie found herself receiving many gifts for the baby, which pleased her.

Although the days passed slowly Lizzie and her mother were kept occupied making plans for the new arrival. They decided which room would be converted into a nursery with the two ladies taking great pleasure in shopping for it. Even though baby clothes tended to be the same style, whether a boy or girl, Lizzie still enjoyed choosing all the other items. The only thing still worrying her was lack of a communication from her beloved James.

Often, Lizzie sat on the parlour window seat, watching for the postman coming along the street. As he approached, she would hold her breath, waiting to see if he mounted the steps to the house to deliver any letters. When he passed by Lizzie was deflated, feeling distressed for some time afterwards. When this happened, her mother would scold her. "You should not become so distressed. If you do not take care of yourself then you will upset the baby."

Concerned for her child, Lizzie made every effort to pull herself from the doldrums, trying to appear more spirited. Sometimes she fooled her mother but at other times she knew she was unable to do so. Then she would make her excuses and retire to her room to be alone. After one such day Lizzie was sat at the desk in her room when her eyes fell upon the pile of letters from Mary. Thinking of the forthcoming baby she decided to write and tell her friend the news. She knew Mary would be surprised. Taking out the last letter from her dear friend she re-read it, finding her spirits lifted. Then taking up her pen she began writing.

*Dear Sweet, Sweet Mary*

*How much your letters lift my spirits. You seem to be having so many adventures on your island. Here, however, all is dismal for I still await news of my beloved James. I hope and pray he is safe and well.*

*At the moment I suffer from a malaise of my own. The reason why you may never guess, so I will tell you. My Dear One I am with child and am some three and a half months' expectant. Mother and Father are highly delighted. I have, however, suffered with morning sickness over the last few weeks. It was so bad I was unable to rise afore noon. How I wish you had been here to comfort me with your sweet talk and soothing manner. Unfortunately, I still await a communiqué from James so I can give him the wonderful news. The absence of any contact concerns me but I try not to dwell on it too much.*

*You say the Oldfield's are American, how interesting. I mentioned this to Mr Smithson, the church curator, asking if he knew of the place and he does. He is much travelled so was interested to hear your friend comes from New York, a place he visited some years ago. He was quite effusive when talking of the city. I am sure he has many happy memories from his time spent there. You sound to have developed such good friends. I am most envious of them having my Mary's time and attention. Oh, Darling Mary, Mama has just entered the room so I will leave this letter for the moment……*


Entering Lizzie's bedroom Lady Mountford held out a letter to her. Seeing the handwriting Lizzie rose from the chair. Literally grabbing it, she tore it open in her excitement to read what her husband had written. Her Mother waited patiently while her daughter absorbed every word. Looking up, Lizzie gave her Mother a big smile, telling her James was well. However, there was little else, other than him saying he was abroad somewhere. That he had arrived safely, and he loved and adored his darling wife. Initially it was enough to lift Lizzie's spirits. And although she felt satisfied at having finally received a letter, she was still left feeling frustrated by the lack of content.

Seeing her daughter, a little more settled and at ease, Lady Mountford left her alone. Having read the letter at least twice more Lizzie returned to complete her missive to Mary.

*I have returned to writing my letter and am pleased to say I am in greater spirits for, at long last, there has been news from James. He has managed to write me a short note letting me know he has arrived, is safe and well and that he loves me dearly. He says he cannot tell me where he is situated until such matters are settled, which should be soon. I suppose I must be satisfied and thankful with what little news I have of him. My one hope is he will be returned to me before my time is due.*

*Other than that, my life continues, albeit in a quiet way. The kitten is quite grown now and is still a joy to me, responding whenever I call her name. 'Mary.' Funny how she knows who she is. I spend most of my time working on my needlework for I am making clothes for the baby. I have decided if it is a boy, I will call him James after his father. But, if a girl she will be called Mary, after my closest friend.*

*I am sorry this letter is so short but I have done little with my time other than worry about James. Plus, suffering with morning sickness has not helped. Next time, I am sure I will be able to write more.*

*Take care of yourself my dearest.*
*Your loving friend Lizzie*

At long last Lizzie had heard from James. She was happier, becoming a changed person, and was seen smiling more often. Later that evening she took out her diary: *At long last what good news I can write in my diary. James has written, sends his love and tells me he is safe. I am full of joy and happiness. Yet I know so little of where he is. He writes he is well and I thank God for listening to my prayers. Mother says I should be thankful for what little I have received, no matter how small the amount. And I am. But all I want now is for him to come home safely to me.*

# Sixteen

The New Year on the island had begun with a number of events. The first being the departure of Reverend Morgain. Throughout the days up to his leaving, poor Jayne suffered unwarranted verbal abuse from her brother whenever she saw him. It appeared he was blaming everyone but himself for the sorry state he found himself in. Finally, Jayne could take no more and, for the first time in her life she told him exactly what she thought of his disgusting behaviour. The man turned white at her tirade.

Thinking about Jayne, Mary knew that what made her snap was her brother's condescending manner. Starting with his attitude towards Lord Falshaw, then the other plantation owners and finally the Chief and his wife. Jayne was so incensed that it left her feeling disgusted at his total disregard for his predicament. The fact he didn't care about the young girl he'd made pregnant, plus his derogatory manner was just too much for her to bear. Especially considering how friendly the islanders had been towards her. Jayne was definitely not amused by his rantings. Unable to bear his company any longer she had returned to Mary's home where she knew she would be made most welcome.

The day the Reverend left the island Jayne did not say goodbye, being too angry still to be in the same room or even look him in the face. She told Mary, "I know I will slap him for showing no regard to anyone."

Lord Falshaw and Colonel Johnstone were at the dockside to ensure the Reverend left the island. His Lordship had spoken to the Captain the previous day, explaining why the man was being expelled. The Captain, being a good Christian man, felt some pity for the Reverend. However, he also appreciated, that as he traded with the plantation owners, he must reluctantly accept the commission given him.

Once the ship had sailed Lord Falshaw, accompanied by his Estate Manager Thomas Craven, called to see Mary. "May I ask how Miss Morgain is holding up."

"Quite well thank you, under the circumstances. I am obliged to you for asking Lord Falshaw." She then went on to reassure him, "All will be well with her in a few days, once everything returns to normal." Satisfied with her reply His Lordship bade good-day and left to visit the Chief.

Thomas, however, remained, having started a conversation with Jayne. He was offering her assistance in collecting some much-needed foliage for a school lesson. Mary smiled as shortly afterwards she watched them walk away in companionable silence. It was some time later before Jayne returned to the hut.

Looking up, Mary noted a warm glow on her friend's face. "And how was Mr Craven?"

Jayne became animated as she described what a pleasant man he was, and how much she liked him. It appeared to Mary, for so short a period of acquaintance, her friend knew a great deal about Thomas. She also noted the use of his Christian name. Mary smiled to herself before returning to her reading.

A few days later, as school was closing Thomas Craven arrived. "I wanted to ensure you ladies were in good health and spirits?" Both acknowledged they were.

Smelling romance in the air Mary discreetly withdrew, leaving the pair alone. As she strolled away, she turned to look back, catching sight of Thomas holding Jayne's hand. Mary was happy for her friend. She knew Jaynes life, where romance was concerned, had not been good, as her brother had often disrupted any potential liaisons before they could develop. 'At least he isn't around to spoil this one,' thought Mary.

As she approached the village centre, Mary was surprised to meet Lord Falshaw.

"Are you well Miss Watson? And, Miss Morgain too?"

"Why thank you. Yes, we are both well, Sir. I have

absented myself as Jayne has a visitor. Mr Craven."

His Lordship smiled. "I am not surprised. I felt some time ago that Thomas and Jayne were attracted to each other. There were often shy little conversations between them whenever the Reverend wasn't around." He then surprised her by asking, "I wondered if you would care to go for a short walk down by the water's edge?" Mary willingly accepted his invitation.

As they strolled along, both were relaxed, the conversation between them convivial. Eventually, making their way back to the hut, they found Jayne and Thomas sat outside. Before leaving His Lordship formally took Mary's hand and kissed it. "Good-evening Miss Watson. Miss Morgain."

Thomas, taking his leave of Jayne followed suit and the two ladies watched the two gentlemen walk away down to the water's edge, each lost in their own thoughts. Visits from Thomas or Lord Falshaw, sometimes both at the same time, soon became a regular occurrence.

Over the next few weeks the romance between Jayne and Thomas blossomed, until finally they announced their betrothal. Everyone was delighted with the news, gathering around the happy couple to offer their heartfelt congratulations. The wedding was planned for a few weeks' later, not long before the Johnstones left the island. It seemed the Colonel had given much thought to the war situation, deciding to return to his old regiment in England. The news had come as a shock to everyone. None more so than Laura, who did her best to hide the disappointment she felt at having to leave the island so soon after returning. As their departure was imminent the Colonel, with Lord Falshaw's agreement, had offered Thomas the role of plantation manager. He would take up the post after the wedding. This meant Thomas and Jayne would move into the Johnstone homestead after their marriage. And so, Jayne and Thomas's wedding plans were put in place. The first item on the agenda being the creation of Jayne's wedding trousseau.

Later in the week, as the pair sat outside their little home Jayne broached the subject of who would give her away. Mary gave it some thought. "Perhaps the Colonel or Lord Falshaw could perform the task. Perhaps Thomas could ask one of them to oblige?"

Jayne decided that was a good idea and so, the next day she broached the subject with Thomas. As he left, Thomas promised to ask His Lordship when he returned to the plantation. Although he had already asked him to stand up as his Best Man, he was willing to choose someone else to please Jayne.

Jayne also confided in Mary. "As you know I have no family here, only yourself, whom I look upon as a sister. I wondered if you would consider being my Wedding Maid. Please say you will Mary?"

Mary smiled. "But of course. I would be delighted to be."

Surprisingly, when Mumna heard of the forthcoming nuptials she insisted on acting as Jayne's mother. The idea both amused and concerned Jayne. If truth be known Jayne was secretly a little afraid of the Queen. However, the two girls, laughed at the absurdity of the situation although they both realised what an honour it was.

"I think I will accept Mumna's offer for she has been good to me regardless of my brother's indiscretion." Mary agreed, knowing Jayne's decision would please Mumna.

Writing in her diary later she put: *The idea of Mumna acting as Jayne's Mother seems quite comical. Yet, I cannot fault the Queen's consideration of Jayne after all that has happened. I am pleased my friend is settled since her brother's departure. At last she has found a new sense of freedom.*

Shortly afterwards the hurricane season hit the islands, but soon passed over. The summer season would soon follow as the winds wouldn't last long. And, with the change of seasons new life would come to the islands. Due to the windy weather no ships had docked in the harbour for some weeks.

It was therefore with great excitement, the islanders were seen racing down to the sea shore one day, to watch a small boat rowing across the water. The excitement at the ship's arrival was infectious. Even Mary and Jayne left what they were doing and followed everyone down to the seashore. As the boat pulled alongside the landing stage, Mary searched out Captain Morrison. She was hoping he would have brought a letter from Lizzie. She was not disappointed, for once the Captain landed, he sought her out, quickly handing over a small packet. Thanking him profusely Mary took the letter, and returned to the hut to read her missive in peace.

When Jayne returned to the hut, she found Mary sat in silent contemplation, tears on her face. "My dear Mary, pray tell me what is wrong? I hope it isn't bad news."

Mary smiled. "No dear Jayne. It is the best of news. Please sit and I will read what Lizzie has written." As she finished Mary felt she might have been a little unkind in telling her of Lizzie's baby and of her being separated from her husband.

But she need not have worried for her friend was warm in her feelings. "What wonderful news. How happy I am for Lizzie. You do know I feel as if she is my friend too since you share her letters with me. I feel I have got to know her well."

Mary was pleased by Jayne's response, deciding a small glass of sherry to celebrate was warranted. Raising their glasses, they toasted the future baby. As they sat sipping their drinks they talked of their lives. Discussing the changes each of them had experienced over the last few years. Mary had never felt as comfortable in anyone else's company, other than Lizzies, as she did in Jayne's. That night both ladies retired happy and contented.

The following morning Mary woke feeling full of vigour. Reading Lizzie's letter again she decided to write to express both hers, and Jayne's delight, at the glad tidings. As she sat Jayne returned from her walk, telling Mary the Captain would call later to collect her correspondence.

"Please give my best wishes to Lizzie, won't you?" Jayne said before leaving her friend to write in peace and quiet.

*Dear Sweet Lizzie*

*What wonderful news you send. My heart is filled with such joy for you and James. Do not despair My Sweet. I am sure James will return before the birth. Jayne and I will pray every day, he remains safe and well until he is back with you once more.*

*Oh, Lizzie dear what changes have been wrought us this last year. Who would have believed I would travel many miles to a new life and you would now be waiting to bring a new life into this world? You must take great care of yourself and the baby. I am so sorry I cannot be by your side but I know you are well supported by your parents. Please let me know how it goes with you.*

*Since I last wrote there have been changes here. The Colonel and Laura will leave the islands within the next few weeks to return to England. They plan to travel via New York. Dorothy is writing a letter of introduction to her family for them. I shall miss them but mostly Laura as she has become such a dear friend to me. It is my dearest wish Lizzie, that you look to receiving them when they arrive in England. I have told Laura all about you as she often asks how you are when I have received your letters. I will write a note of introduction for her to present to you. I think the Colonel has intentions of returning to the Army. I believe he feels the loss of his command and wishes to attend the war in some capacity. However, I am sure Laura does not care for his decision but she accepts it with all the steadfastness she can muster. Please look after her Dear One.*

*Jayne has been full of joy since her brother left and, dare I say, light of feet. Although she suffered some moments of anguish after his departure, her life seems more fulfilled for she now has a romantic acquaintance. So, you see dearest Lizzie, romance blossoms even here. The gentleman is called Thomas Craven. He is Lord Falshaw's Estate Manager, soon*

116

to take charge of the Colonels estate while they are away. He is tall, fair of colouring and hails from Scotland. He is such a charming man one cannot but like him. I am so happy for her. Jayne certainly deserves someone special as I have discovered, what a hard life she has endured these past few years. Their love has developed over time. They made the announcement of their engagement at the Spring Fair.

As for The Reverend he parted with much grumbling. My hope is he does not return. But should he, not until after Jayne and Thomas are wed. I imagine he would object most strongly to the union even perhaps trying to prevent it. He seemed to enjoy having his sister at his beck and call, often treating her like a servant. We are not sure if Lord Falshaw or Colonel Johnstone will give the bride away. However, the Chief's wife is to act as Jayne's mother. We find this most amusing. Jayne has also done me the honour of asking me to be her Wedding Maid. I am of course, delighted.

As for myself I am kept busy with my school and needlework, an example of which I enclose with this letter. This is for the new baby. It is nothing too fancy for I am not yet the best of seamstresses. Although I am much improved since we last sewed together. Tell your daughter (I believe it will be a girl) about her Auntie Mary, who has sewn this little gift with much love. However, if a boy, tell him the same for I will love him just as much.

My further news about babies is that the Chief's daughter grows close to her birth date. She seems too young to have a child but the islanders are well practiced in the way of births and deaths. They treat these events quite naturally with no worries at all.

These past few months have been interesting for Jayne and I have received many visits from Lord Falshaw. His continued presence has been surprising and his reasons for calling varied. One day he called to enquire if we needed any items for the school room as he was arranging an order of goods to be sent from England. Another day he called with a basket of fresh fruit, declaring it was excess to his needs. He

117

*believed Jayne and I would enjoy the delicious contents, which we did. Jayne believes he has an eye for me but I think she imagines things. He is just being a gentleman by showing me the same consideration he does the others on the islands.*

*I will close now as the Captain will be calling soon. Take great care of yourself my dearest Lizzie.*

*Think of me as I do you.*

*Your loving friend Mary*

# Seventeen

Lizzie woke one morning with a feeling something was not quite right. For some reason she could not shake off the premonition that something was dreadfully wrong. Carefully she made her way downstairs to find her Mother. As she entered the drawing room her mother looked up, sensing her daughter was not in good spirits. "Are you ailing my dear?"

"I feel out of sorts but I don't know why. I have a feeling of unrest."

Taking Lizzie in her arms Lady Mountford did her best to reassure her daughter. "It sometimes happens when a woman is expecting."

Listening to her Mother Lizzie nodded. "You are probably right." Yet still, she found it difficult to settle, spending the rest of the day feeling ill at ease.

After lunch Lizzie returned to the drawing room to read, feeling only slightly better. Sometime later the doorbell rang and not long after the maid entered with a despatch for her. Accepting it Lizzie tore open the envelope. As she read it, she turned pale, let out a cry, then fainted to the floor. The maid started screaming and shouting for Her Ladyship, who came running with all haste. Seeing her daughter lying on the floor her Ladyship demanded her husband attend at once. Throughout the maid stood sobbing and wailing until Her Ladyship was forced to slap the young girl's face to bring her to her senses.

Running into the room Lord Mountford stopped. "What the hell is all the cat-a-wailing about?" But, as soon as he saw Lizzie on the floor, he shouted for the butler to come and assist him. Together they carefully lifted Lizzie onto the chaise. "What happened here."

In between sobs the maid told him. "I brought a letter to Miss Elizabeth. She was reading it when she cried out.

Then she fainted dead away."

Picking up the letter from the floor Lord Mountford read it. As he did, he was filled with dismay. It was a missive from the Ministry of War, notifying his daughter that Sir James was wounded, and was being brought home.

With help from the butler Lord Mountford carried Lizzie to her room. Leaving his wife and her maid to settle her in bed, he returned downstairs and despatched the footman to fetch the doctor. The crying maid he sent to the kitchen, sternly telling her to stop her silly blithering and go wash her face. The young maid left the room, feeling quite sorry for herself.

Approximately fifteen minutes later the footman returned with the Doctor. Having examined Lizzie, he gave her a sleeping draft to help settle her nerves. Once she was comfortable the Doctor and Lady Mountford left the room. Downstairs His Lordship and the Doctor discussed the terrible news, learning what could be done to prepare the house for Sir James' return. The Doctor then left, promising to return once Sir James was in residence. Later, Lady Mountford returned to Lizzie's room. Luckily, the Doctor's draft meant Lizzie remained asleep until the following morning.

The next day when she opened her eyes Lizzie wondered, just for a moment, where she was. Then it hit her. James was wounded and he was coming home. Ringing the bell for her maid she got out of bed and started to dress. A knock at the door made Lizzie look up. It was her Mother.

"How do you feel this morning Elizabeth?"

Lizzie burst into tears. Taking her daughter by the arm her Mother led her to the bed, making her sit down. Whereupon she began comforting her. "Now, stop the tears. You mustn't worry, everything will be ok."

"Do you," *'sniff'* "think so," *'sniff'* "Mama?"

"Of course," she told Lizzie, secretly hoping she was correct.

Once Lizzie was calmer Lady Mountford told her.

"That's better. Now you are going to have to be strong. There will be much to do. First, we have to prepare a room for when James returns. Then we have to make sure we have everything necessary for an invalid."

"I never thought about that," whispered Lizzie. "Of course, I will help."

"I know you will," said her Mother gently. "In the meantime, we will have to find a nurse."

"Oh no! I will nurse James myself," Lizzie cried out.

"You will not, Elizabeth," her Mother said sternly. "That's silly. You are in no condition to be sitting up every night to take care of a poorly man." Reluctantly Lizzie agreed with her Mother, even though she didn't want to. Feeling better now she had a goal in mind, Lizzie stood up ready to face the world.

The days prior to James arrival were drawn out. Lizzie often found herself checking and re-checking the room prepared for him. It was on a day when Lizzie was feeling particularly vulnerable that James' sisters paid a visit, much to her annoyance. She showed them the sick room which had been prepared. Being perfect the sisters could not complain even though wanted to. Although they made it obvious, they did not agree with Sir James being nursed at Mountford House. However, there was little they could do considering Lizzie was their brothers' wife. The two ladies were so lacking in warmth Lizzie was relieved when they finally left.

As the days passed Lizzie grew bigger. Knowing her time was due, she fretted that James had not yet arrived home. Her Mother did her best to keep her daughter's spirits up, getting her involved in completing the room for James, the baby and interviewing for a nurse. But without much success for Lizzie remained listless. As her birthing time drew near it was agreed Christmas at the house would be a quiet affair, which might also have added to Lizzie's low feelings.

Not long after the Williamson sisters visit, the vicar unexpectedly arrived. To Lizzie his attitude seemed slightly condescending. Yet for some reason she couldn't explain, she actually got some solace from his visit. However, she was relieved once he took his leave. Not long after the vicar left the maid entered with a small package for her. At first, she was afraid to read it, in case it was about James but looking at the handwriting she recognised it was from Mary. Falling on the letter with gusto, she hoped for some cheering news. And, for a short time, it did help. When Lady Mountford entered the room, for the first time in two weeks she saw her daughter smiling. However, as Lizzie was looking tired, Her Ladyship suggested she go lie down and rest. Smiling, Lizzie rose from the chaise, kissed her mother on the cheek and left the room.

Upstairs in her room she lay on her bed re-reading Mary's letter, feeling better than she had for some time. Opening the package sent with the letter Lizzie was delighted to find a lovely baby blanket inside. '*Oh, my dearest Mary, what a lovely friend you are,*' she thought, holding up the blanket and seeing the beautiful little flowers her friend had embroidered on it. She thought of the time it must have taken Mary to sew them, and smiled as she remembered how Mary used to find it difficult to sew. Holding the blanket close to her heart Lizzie felt happier than she had for some time. Finally, she decided to write to Mary and thank her. After all she might not get another chance once James arrived home as her time would be spent with him.

*Dear Sweet Mary*

*What a joy to receive your letter. You cannot realise how much I needed to hear from you. It arrived at a time when I needed cheering up. What I am about to tell you will be a shock. It is such sad news. A courier arrived some two weeks ago to inform me my beloved darling James has been wounded and is being brought home. When I read the news, I fainted from fright and shock. The poor maid screamed so loud Father thought I was dead. Mama had to slap her face to quieten her. They put me to bed and sent for the doctor who declared me well if somewhat distressed. I do not know how long it will take them to bring him home so I wait with bated breath.*

The baby fares well and my time draws near to when I will retire to my birthing bed. Everything has been arranged, including the midwife and wet nurse, who are to be in attendance. I must admit I am dreading the forthcoming event. Mama tells me not be silly as childbirth is quite natural. I am most vexed with her. Does she not realise I am facing this alone, without my James or my Mary to comfort me?

Last week, James' sisters called. I cannot understand how anyone as caring and as gentle as my James can be related to such people. My dear Mary, I have tried so hard to think kindly of them but they are so lacking in warmth it fair behoves me to be civil to them. No wonder they remain spinsters, for what man would wish to wake up to faces as sour as theirs. Oh, I must be really bad and should perhaps pray to God to forgive my wicked thoughts.

The weather remains fine. I do not go far these days, only taking short walks in the park across the way. You would laugh at me as I am becoming quite maternal, as I begin to like the idea of being a mother more and more each day. In between I try hard to keep my spirits lifted. Mama and I have prepared a room for the baby. I will be relieved once the birth is over, for I am becoming so large of stomach I cannot lay with any degree of comfort. The baby's bedroom is a delight with a cot, table and rocking chair. There is also a small bed should I need to lie down. The wet nurse will have the room next door so she is on hand at night. Thank you for the lovely blanket, it is beautiful. I shall lay it on the baby's bed. The embroidered flowers match the colour of the baby's room. My dear Mary, my heart goes out to the Chief's daughter as I surely understand how she must be feeling. We have also prepared a room for James. Mama has appointed a nurse to care for him as I am not able to in my current condition.

I am glad to hear Jayne has found love. Mr Craven sounds to be a most personable young man. I am delighted for her. Please give her my best regards and tell her I am *praying for her. Yes, it is true Mary, praying is all I seem to do these days. The vicar called to bless me and to let me know he is available should I require his services. For some reason I find the man insufferable. Oh, yet again I am behaving badly. It must be my condition causing such wicked thoughts in me. Do you think God will forgive me?*

*As regards accepting a visit from your friend Laura? Of course, I will make her most welcome. She will be able to tell me all about my Mary and what her life is like. In the meantime, my days continue, however dull, but I manage. At least I no longer suffer with the malaise which possessed me through those early weeks.*

*I will close now as I am writing this when I should be lying down. Mama will be most annoyed by my not resting.*

*Please take care and write soon.*

*You're loving friend Lizzie*

Having sealed her letter Lizzie instructed her maid to take it downstairs for the post. Then feeling a little tired she lay down, promptly falling asleep to dream of beautiful wild flowers, sunshine and her dear friend far, far away.

# Eighteen

When Mary woke, she realised that at long last the weather was improving. Spring being upon them meant Summer was not far behind. The winds blowing across the islands had been quite terrifying. So severe, that at one point the noise had been frightening to listen to. During this time, Kuala and Jayne had done their best to calm Mary's mind.

With the storms finally blowing themselves out, everyone on the island assessed the damage. Jayne and Mary were happy at how well the hut and schoolroom had survived the bad weather, being pleasantly surprised to find limited damage. Mumna came to inspect the hut and school, taking it upon herself to arrange the necessary repairs, much to Marys relief. School had remained closed during the hurricane mainly because the children were unable to travel. During the bad weather the two young women were confined to their home, spending time preparing new lessons and learning more about each other. Mary discovered Jayne was the only girl in her family, being the youngest of four. Overall, their confinement hadn't been bad. They enjoyed each other's company and were kept fully occupied, taking the opportunity to complete Jayne's wedding trousseau. Kuala had gone to stay with her family.

The only time the two ladies left the hut was during a lull in the storm. Mumna had sent someone to fetch them as her daughter was in labour. Mary later admitted to Jayne how she had found the whole experience most distressing. "As I watched the young girl giving birth I was reminded of my dear Lizzie. She too will soon be suffering in the same way. My heart goes out to both her and the Chief's daughter."

After ten hours of labour the girl gave birth to a baby boy. Everyone was relieved. While she may have come through the birthing process safely, to Mary it seemed no-one was overly happy with the new arrival. Jayne told her, "I believe that normally they would have celebrated the birth but under the circumstances what can we expect." Thinking about it, Mary had agreed. You could see the child was predominantly European, with little of his Mother's features or colouring. She felt such pity for them both.

After returning to the hut Mary thought Jayne appeared a little sad. This was confirmed when she admitted, "I was thinking about my brother and his absence from my forthcoming nuptials. Also, if I am truthful, I was also thinking about the baby. He is my nephew. I just don't know what to do about him."

Mary did her best to reassure Jayne. "Try not to be too concerned dear one, for your brother is obviously not worried about you, or the baby. If he were, he would have sent a communication about his destination. As regards the baby. You are right, he is your relative. Unfortunately, you will have to wait to see how things develop before approaching Mumna with your viewpoint."

Jayne gave much thought to Mary's comments, finding herself reluctantly agreeing. It was fortunate Thomas arrived at that time and diverted her attention.

With the weather vastly improved, life settled back into a normal routine. Thomas called often, as did Lord Falshaw. Their visits creating much merriment with the two occupants of the little hut. On one such a day, while Jayne was out walking with Thomas, Mumna came to visit Mary. With her was a young girl who appeared younger than Kuala. Raising her eyebrow questioningly Mary waited for the Queen to speak.

"I think, with Miss Jayne leaving at the end of the week, you will need someone new to stay here. So, I bring Kuala's younger sister Chula to live with you." Mary was embarrassed. It had taken her some time to get used to having Kuala, so having two young girls in attendance seemed most frivolous. However, she realised refusing Mumna's generous offer would be both churlish and disrespectful. After a moment's thought Mary reluctantly but gracefully thanked the Queen.

Upon her return Jayne was surprised to hear the news of the new addition to the household. Mumna's insistence caused the two young women to laugh at the absurdity of it all. However, they both agreed it was kind of Mumna to think of Mary's wellbeing.

That evening Mary wrote in her journal: *I am most concerned for Jayne, wishing her only the best. I cannot see how her brother can return after such a bad deed. I know having to watch the Chief's daughter give birth caused Jayne great sadness. I believe she worries for the child. After all he and she are related but what can she do? I know not. I hope she does not ponder long on the matter. Perhaps Thomas can help her cope with the past few days' trauma.*

*Now I find myself with another young girl as a servant, which is strange. Despite myself, I cannot treat either Kuala or her sister as maids. They are more like younger sisters than servants. It is all so amusing. I must write and tell Lizzie as she will find it funny, I am sure.*

The following day Jayne and Mary, hearing a commotion outside, realised something was happening. Going to investigate they watched the islanders running down to the dockside. A ship had been spotted dropping anchor in the harbour. They eagerly followed. Mary was hoping for a letter from Lizzie and ten minutes later, after the small boat docked the Captain passed one to her. Thanking him warmly, Mary returned to the hut where she sat outside to read it.

When Jayne returned, she found Mary still sat outside. It was obvious she had been crying, causing Jayne some alarm. When questioned, being unable to say anything, Mary passed the letter to her friend to read. Taking it Jayne sat and began reading. All of a sudden, she let out a sharp gasp, shocked by the contents. Finally, standing she went towards Mary, placing her arms around her friend to offer comfort. "Poor, poor Lizzie. We must pray for Sir James' safe return. And for his quick recovery to good health. We must also pray for Lizzie's wellbeing."

Unable to speak, Mary silently agreed and bowing their heads the two ladies prayed. Much later, after Jayne had left with Thomas, Mary sat in silent reflection. She was deeply worried about Lizzie, wishing with all her heart she was with her. Deciding to write to Lizzie she hoped she might be able to offer her dear friend some small comfort.

*My Darling Lizzie*

*How low you sounded in your last letter and what sad news you sent me. I hope and pray by the time this letter reaches you that James is once again in the bosom of his family, and is safe and sound. Know our thoughts and prayers are with you at this most difficult and worrying of times. How I wish I were by your side to comfort you. Please keep your spirits lifted for both the baby and yourself.*

*My news is about the Chief's daughter who has given birth to a baby boy. Both Mother and son are doing well. Lord Falshaw's physician called to see if he could assist but the island women sent him packing. You would have laughed at the look of disgust he threw at them as he left. He was heard muttering something about 'meddling women.' We did not hear all he said which may have been a good thing.*

*Jayne and I were present at the birth. While it was quite frightening to hear and see, the sight of a baby being born it was the most amazing thing. We are a truly remarkable species when we can produce life so easily. I am sure you will make a wonderful, loving, caring mother.*

*On a happier note, Jayne and Thomas will be married next Sunday in our small village church. A ship arrived today and the ships' Chaplain has agreed to perform the ceremony. We have all been busy making new dresses for the occasion. Jayne's wedding dress is beautiful. She has borrowed a dress from Dorothy, who has allowed us to adjust it to fit Jayne for she is slighter in figure. It is cream in colour and I swear Jayne looks exceedingly beautiful in it. I am sure Thomas will be so proud of her, falling more in love when he sees her enter the church.*

*We are hopeful Jayne's brother will not return for the service. I believe Jayne is relieved as she believes he would probably try to prevent their union. Not that I think Jayne would allow that to happen being too much in love.*

*It has now been agreed Colonel Johnstone will give Jayne away as Lord Falshaw is to stand up for Thomas. After the marriage they will move into the Johnstones homestead. As previously mentioned, the Colonel and Laura leave shortly afterwards to travel back to England. Jayne's departure from my little home, does not mean I will be left alone. Apart from Kuala I will have a new companion as Queen Mumna has given me another young woman to look after me. Her name is Chula and she is Kuala's younger sister. I shall feel so grand having two people to look after me.*

*The hurricane season has passed and summer is nearly upon us. We saw little of Thomas or Lord Falshaw as the winds prevented travel between the islands. However, His Lordship called unexpectedly yesterday to inquire after our wellbeing and to bring us fresh supplies. I am grateful for his continued support and concern over our safety. Dearest Lizzie, the more I see of him the more I am attracted towards him. He is not the eccentric or arrogant person I first thought him to be.*

*Soon it will be time to pick the crops. Once ready all the islanders will leave to assist the plantation workers in the harvesting. When they do, I will go too so I can help the ladies with the refreshments for the workers. It means I will not be left alone and will return once the work is finished. A few of His Lordship's militia will stay to guard the main island, the Chief and the Elders. Queen Mumna, however, may take the opportunity to visit her children who live on the other islands.*

*There is a great community spirit here which, I believe you would enjoy. Everyone, including the islanders are extremely friendly. we celebrate all types of events. Besides the usual births, deaths and marriages the islanders also celebrate the end of bad weather, the return of good weather and a good harvest. The list is extensive but overall, they*

129

*enjoy their lives to the fullest. I am sure you would enjoy living on the island as much as I do.*

*I will close now. It will soon be time to eat and I can smell nice things coming from the kitchen as Kuala and Chula prepare a meal for us all.*

*Take care my Darling Lizzie. Let me know how you fare when you are able. Know our prayers are with you, James and the baby.*

*Your loving dearest friend Mary*

# Nineteen

Bringing Sir James home took longer than anticipated. Each day's delay caused Lizzie to worry more and more. As she was getting closer to her lying-in time, she wanted her husband home before the baby's birth. Moving around was difficult as she was large in girth, especially for someone slight of build like her. Going up and down the stairs easily tired her.

Three days later Lizzie took to her birthing bed, soon finding herself in the full throws of labour. The midwife arrived early, demanding all the necessary items for assisting Lizzie through the birthing process. Once ready the midwife chased Lady Mountford and the maid from the room. Then taking Lizzie's hand, she did her best to calm her. After the midwife's assistant arrived, the pair set about preparing the expectant mother for the birth. Sitting down they let Mother Nature take its course.

If she were honest, Lady Mountford was relieved to be removed from the room. Descending the stairs, she was in time to see her husband leave the house. A squeamish man, he was loath to stay and listen to the noises of childbirth. Particularly when it was his own little girl going through the process. He therefore intended spending the day at his club. Her Ladyship felt a little betrayed by his absence but, as childbirth was a woman's job, she could not blame him for absenting himself. Going into the drawing room Lady Mountford would occupy her time whilst she awaited the arrival of their first grandchild.

For Lizzie the day dragged on and on. She was tired and began to think she was dying. The pain grew worse and worse. The frustrating part for Lizzie, was that the two women attending her appeared so matter of fact about it all. So much so, she wanted to scream at them that they were being insensitive to her feelings. Slowly the pains increased. Lizzie couldn't hold out. And with all her might she began to push as hard as she could, letting out an almighty loud scream. The final stages lasted some ten minutes or so. During which time Lizzie wished she had never been born, never met James, never got married or done anything else she could think of. With one final push and a terrifying scream Lady Elizabeth Victoria Williamson gave birth to a son.

Shortly afterwards Lady Mountford, entering the bedroom, was introduced to her first grandchild. She was the happiest of Grandmothers. Returning downstairs, the butler was informed Miss Lizzie had given birth to a baby boy and the footman was to be sent to fetch His Lordship from his club. Expressing his delight at the news he left to do her bidding. And also, to share the happy new with the rest of the household staff.

Half an hour later, Lord Mountford returned in high spirits. Rushing into the house, he went straight upstairs to meet his new Grandson. Entering the room, he saw Lizzie lying in bed, ready to receive visitors. Stopping he looked and smiled, thinking she had never looked more beautiful. Satisfied Lizzie was well; His Lordships attention was immediately drawn to his new Grandson. Approaching the bed, he saw the little 'mite' lying, sound asleep next to his mother, bundled in a pretty blanket. Lady Mountford, looked up at her husband and smiled. For just a moment their eyes met. Perhaps both were remembering the day Lizzie had been born. And now, here was a new life. Their first grandchild. How proud they both looked.

After her parents had left the nurse came in to settle Lizzie. Taking the baby from her she settled him in the crib. "You should try and sleep Madam. We need you fresh for when the little mite needs feeding." Although Lizzie didn't want to let go of her son, she realised how tired she was. Snuggling down under the covers she watched her new son sleeping. 'How beautiful he is,' she thought and closing her eyes, she drifted off into a deep sleep.

The following morning Lizzie woke feeling as if she had been through a grinding mill, for she ached from head to toe. Suddenly a tiny scream shattered the silent air, causing her to sit up abruptly. Concerned with the baby's cries she was about to shout out when the nurse entered the room.

"Good-morning Madam. Don't you worry about him, he's just letting us know he's awake and he's hungry. You have to feed him."

"How?" It was obvious from Lizzie's response she didn't know what to do.

"I'll show you," said the nurse and carefully she showed Lizzie how to place the baby to the breast, and start him sucking at the nipple. Lizzie found the experience embarrassing. But as the baby began suckling, the sensation was unusual yet pleasing. Having suckled for some time the nurse explained. "Now you need to burp him before putting him to the other breast. Place him on your shoulder and pat his back. Not too hard" At the end of feeding time Lizzie felt pleased, realising she had succeeded in satisfying her baby's needs.

A few days later, feeling recovered enough to leave her bed, Lizzie was helped downstairs. She was placed on the chaise in the drawing room with a blanket securely placed around her legs and the baby settled in a small basket cot close by.

Over the next few days Lizzie regained her strength. By the end of the week following she was able to move about the house easily. The nanny helped her and the baby settled into a daily routine. Lizzie believed being a mother was quite easy. Of course, in her naivety, what she didn't realise was just how much work was actually involved in caring for a young child. It wasn't that she was ignorant, but someone like her in a privileged position usually had servants or a nanny to do the hard work. Regardless, Lizzie felt like all new mothers do, proud of her new son.

She later wrote in her diary: *I am a happy Mother. Giving birth was quite exhausting and at times painful. But as I look upon my son's adorable face, I think it has all been worthwhile. I do wish Mary was here to share my happiness. I am sure she will love my son as much as I do. My only prayer now is for my darling James to be brought home as soon as possible.*

Two days later Lizzie's prayers were answered when her husband Sir James finally arrived home. On seeing him Lizzie became concerned for he did not look at all well. Making sure he was settled in the bedroom made ready for him, the doctor was sent for, Lizzie not leaving his side until he arrived. Being shooed from the room, the doctor checked Sir James's wounds while Lizzie went to feed her son. Once finished she returned, only to find she could not gain entry. She was pacing up and down the corridor outside the sick room when Lady Mountford came across her. Realising how worried she was, her Ladyship gently took her daughters arm, forcing her to go down the stairs. "We will wait in the drawing room until the Doctor has completed his examination."

It was a long wait but half an hour later the doctor entered the room. Lizzie standing demanded to know if she could go to her husband. The Doctor willingly agreed as he wished to speak to Lord and Lady Mountford, before discussing their son-in-law's condition with his young wife. Taking a deep breath, he began his report. It quickly became apparent that Sir James was seriously ill. Apparently, the journey had taken a great toll on his already poor state of health. Lord Mountford questioned the doctor. "Can you give us any idea how bad his state of health is Doctor?"

Reluctantly the Doctor admitted, "If I am honest, then I must confess I hold out little hope that he will recover from his wounds."

The news sent shock waves through Lizzie's parents as they became concerned for their daughter and her new son. When asked how long their son-in-law had to live the Doctor wouldn't be precise. Reluctantly saying, "I do not think Sir James will last beyond the end of the month. Maybe two or three weeks at the most." Nothing was said, both were being deeply shocked by the doctor's words. After he had left Lord and Lady Mountford sat in silence, each lost in their own thoughts as to the effect the news would have on Lizzie.

Finally, Lord Mountford looked at his wife. "I think Lizzie will have to be told the bad news. And of course, James' sisters will also have to be notified. I will send a note to the ladies now." And leaving his wife to ponder the matter further His Lordship left the room. Whilst writing to the sisters he also wrote to his solicitor as things should be in order before the inevitable happened. Having completed his letters His Lordship sat pondering how they were going to break the sad news to their beloved daughter. It was a task he was not looking forward to. But it had to be done.

Evening was drawing in when the sound of the gong rang for dinner, bringing His Lordship to his senses. He realised he had been sat in the library for over two hours. Going upstairs to change, he joined his wife for dinner. It was a quiet affair as Lizzie had ordered a tray be sent to James room, being loathe to leave him. Apart from taking time out to feed the baby and sleep, Lizzie intended remaining at her husband's bedside. After dinner, Lord and Lady Mountford accepted they could not put the dreaded moment off any longer. And so, sending for Lizzie they prepared to give her the worst news she would ever hear.

Quietly entering the sick room, the maid coughed slightly, causing Lizzie to look up from the book she was reading. "Sorry Miss Elizabeth but your parents request you join them in the drawing room at once."

Surprised by the request, but unable to disobey the demand, Lizzie laid her book down on the table. Standing she bent to kiss her husband before reluctantly leaving the room. As she left, she instructed the nurse. "You must fetch me the moment Sir James awakes."

"Yes Ma-am," said the nurse.

Downstairs Lizzie entered the drawing room with some trepidation. She was surprised to find both her parents waiting for her. Sitting in the chair, a sudden, most awful feeling possessed her. A premonition that something was not right. Her fears were not unfounded. Taking her hand, Lizzie listened as her father gave her the news. It caused her to gasp and cry out with shock. Throughout the explanation she cried uncontrollably. It took her Ladyship some time to calm her daughter. Once she was, Her Ladyship took Lizzie to her room and made her retire, despite her objections that she wanted, nay needed, to stay with James.

The doctor was sent for and he gave Lizzie a sleeping draft before going to check Sir James. Within ten minutes Lizzie was fast asleep. As the doctor left the house, he promised to return in the morning to check on both patients.

Waking in the early hours of the following morning Lizzie picked up her diary to write: *I am in despair. My poor, poor darling James has not got long for this world. What am I to do? How will my son know his father if he no longer lives? Life is so unfair. My heart is broken and I am devastated. Oh, Mary, why are you not here when I need you the most?*

Over the next few days Lizzie lived in a haze. Wandering around the house listlessly, she spent her time between looking after her son and watching over James. When her husband had a few moments of lucid wakefulness, she took the opportunity to introduce James to the baby. Even in his pain and suffering he showed delight in his son. Managing to communicate what the baby's name should be. He was to be called, James Marshall Williamson the Third.

Unfortunately, Sir James' health quickly deteriorated with everyone becoming aware that he didn't have long to live. His sisters called daily, often sitting in silence on one side of the bed, usually ignoring Lizzie or treating her with disdain when alone with her. Lizzie, troubled by their attitude, felt as if they were blaming her for their brother's predicament. Each day, after they had left, Lizzie sighed in relief.

On the day Sir James Williamson passed away everyone who mattered was by his bedside. Lizzie, her parents and his sisters. Even the baby, who somehow sensed something was wrong with his father for he made little noise while in the sick room. As James took his last breath Lizzie sat and sobbed. She had left him only once during the day to feed the baby. Even then she knew her husband would never wake again.

# Twenty

Following her husband's death, Lizzie was left totally devastated, not knowing what to do. The house was quiet with the servants going about their daily tasks sadly. The only disturbance was the occasional sound of the baby crying. It was only the needs of her son which kept Lizzie sane.

Three days later after the lying in period, Sir James Williamson the Second was returned to his estate home. There to be interred in the family vault set within the grounds of the local church. Lizzie managed to control herself throughout the torment of seeing her beloved James' coffin being placed in the family crypt. The little family church was full of people. Not just friends and acquaintances but those living on the estate who had a great love and regard for the 'young Sir James.' They were very sad to have lost their master, for he had been a kind and caring benefactor. Their hope was the new master, when he grew up, would be like his father.

After the service most people returned to the house where the butler and staff had organised refreshments for the mourners. Lizzie ate little, leaving the room only once to feed her son. Other than that, she stayed close to her mother as the various mourners came to offer their condolences. Later, once everyone had left, the Mountford's returned to town, whereupon Her Ladyship sent Lizzie to bed. For the next few weeks Lizzie did little, devoting most of her time to looking after her son. Of Mary she gave no thought, being too immersed in her grief.

One evening, unable to sleep, Lizzie wrote in her diary: *What am I to do for I am all alone. My dearest husband is no more. How I miss him. I cannot remember how I managed to keep control during the funeral service. Wanting to scream out his name and beg I be allowed to be buried with him. I know he will be cold and lonely without me. It is only my son who keeps me sane. Stopping me from sinking into the depths of despair. He is all I have left. I am distraught.*

Over time, Lizzie regained her strength and composure. Finding she was able to do more, including accept those visitors who came to commiserate with her or to meet her new son. During these visits Lady Mountford stayed by her daughter's side, offering moral support, as well as ensuring Lizzie didn't overtire herself. However, as Lizzie's health and state of mind improved Her Ladyship decided the time was right to leave her daughter on her own. She chose to do it one Thursday afternoon, going with her husband to visit some acquaintances. They were to be gone a matter of three hours so left with the confidence that Lizzie would be okay. Unfortunately, it was during their absence that the Williamson sisters decided to pay Lizzie a visit, whom they hadn't seen since the day of the funeral.

As the two sisters were shown into the drawing room Lizzie steeled herself to receive them, whilst secretly wishing her Mother was with her. Having been brought up a well-mannered young lady, Lizzie knew she must do her best so politely asked the two ladies to sit, offering them refreshments, which they curtly refused. Their response made Lizzie hope the two ladies didn't intend staying too long. The elder sister Edith, made polite small talk, with Lizzie doing her best to answer in a similar vein. Then after ten minutes Edith suddenly turned the conversation to the baby. "And how is our nephew? We want to see him."

Such was her attitude that Lizzie felt annoyed. "I am afraid the baby is sleeping and cannot be disturbed."

"Is he not in good health?"

Surprised by the comment it took Lizzie a moment to gather her thoughts. "On the contrary. Baby James is quite well and is growing fast. He is a picture of health." For a moment, it appeared to Lizzie the ladies were slightly put out by her comment. And the thought came to her that they were perhaps disappointed he was doing so well. The idea caused her to shudder slightly.

Nothing further was said about baby James. It became obvious to the ladies they were not going to be allowed to see him. So as the flow of conversation dried up the two ladies remained sitting in total silence. Finally, Lizzie could stand it no more. Rising to her feet she politely asked, "Is there anything further you wish to say?"

Becoming aware they had perhaps outstayed their welcome the two ladies rose. Just as they were about to depart Edith stopped and turned to face Lizzie. "As you are now in full time residence at your parent's house, we presume you will not be using the town house or returning to the estate."

Lizzie was shocked by her statement. So much so that she nearly exploded with anger at her affront. Taking a moment to gather her thoughts she finally responded. "I do not believe you should presume anything at this moment in time. Remember, any property of my husband's, now belongs to myself and my son." Pausing, she took a deep breath. "I have not as yet made any decision as to where I and my son will reside. The matter is not open for discussion while I am still in mourning. I shall be meeting with the family solicitor shortly, only then will I consider what my arrangements will be. Once that happens then, and only then, will I make any decisions regarding the properties. AND,'" she stressed the word, "as a matter of courtesy, you will be informed in due time as to what those decisions are. Until then, there is nothing further to discuss." It was on that note the two ladies were left with no other option but to depart. What they failed to realise, as they left was just how angry and upset Lizzie was by their affront.

For some time after the lady's departure Lizzie paced the drawing room floor. She was shaking with anger. Which was how her parents found her! When pressed for the reason she told them about her visitors, repeating the gist of the conversation having taken place. Her Mother was angry, stating that unless she was present the two women would not be allowed entry to the house again.

Her Father however, congratulated Lizzie on her behaviour and control, telling her how proud he was in the way she had handled the situation. "In the meantime, I think I will arrange for the family Solicitor to call tomorrow to resolve the situation. We need to get James' affairs resolved as soon as possible." Whereupon he left the room to send a note to his Solicitor, Mr Smythe-Green, requesting he attend at his earliest the following day. Lizzie would have been surprised to discover her father smiling to himself. He thought his daughter must be feeling better. But how proud he felt that she was growing into a confident young woman.

Much later, after Lizzie had calmed down, she went to write to Mary, intending to tell her all. Sitting in her room she sat at her writing slope, feeling guilty at not having given one thought to her friend. But she knew once Mary knew the circumstances, she would forgive her tardiness. It was now she needed her the most but she was thousands of miles away.

*My Dearest Mary*

*I know you will think I have been remiss in not having written for so long but once you read why, you will understand and hopefully forgive me. I have both good news and bad news to send you. Firstly, the good news. I am born of a beautiful baby son. His name is Sir James Marshall Williamson the Third and he is the 10th Lord of Williamson Manor. He is adorable and I love him very much.*

*From this piece of information, you will have gathered the bad news? My beloved James is with me no more. He passed away some four weeks ago. My heart is definitely broken and I am drowning with deep sorrow at my loss. I will tell all once I wipe my tears.*

*Poor James was brought home and put to bed. His wounds were so bad, that during the journey he contracted an infection. Such was his weakened state he was unable to fight it. After he was settled, I visited him. It hurt me deeply to see the joy within his pained eyes as he looked upon his son. He was so proud of his child. But dear James did not survive long and within a matter of three weeks my beloved husband was with me no more.*

*My dear, dear Mary what am I to do. I am totally shattered by the events of this past month. For some time after his demise I wished only to lie abed and wallow in my misery. My only consolation has been our dear son and so I am being brave and strong for him. James Junior is a delightful child. You would love him dearly. He has his father's colouring and demeanour being gentle in his nature. It is he who keeps me sane, causing my spirits to rise.*

*Now I must tell you of a recent visit by Baby James Aunts, the Williamson sisters. The meeting was most unpleasant and I have told Mama I do not wish to see them again. She has instructed the servants they are not to be admitted if I am home alone. I do believe they have no regard for Baby James or me. I am so angry and devoid of any respect for their lack of emotion towards their nephew. Plus, I am sorely tempted in my moments of ire to dispossess them.*

*Do not be shocked my dear Mary. They are not penniless having incomes of their own. But they have taken advantage of their brothers' absence in residing at the estate. I should ask them to leave but I am too genteel and kind to do such a thing. Besides, whether I care for them or not they are still James' sisters and therefore Baby James' Aunts. I know my beloved husband would want me to try and be friends or, at the very least, courteous towards them. We are therefore meeting with father's Solicitor soon to hopefully resolve the situation. I will tell you more when next I write.*

*For the time being I shall reside here at Mountford House with Baby James until I am strong enough to make decisions regarding our future residence. I believe Father is pleased with my decision and, of course, Mama is delighted. Both dote on Baby James and are enjoying being Grandparents.*

*In the meantime, I must tell you I have told Baby James all about you. Telling him what you look like. How gentle and caring you are. And that you love him dearly. He is lain in his cot wrapped in the blanket you sent him, so he is surrounded with your love.*

*Oh, Mary I am too young to be a widow. I know I mustn't dwell on this too much but at the moment I can do no other but think of my poor lost love. I never realised how cruel life could be.*

*I must rest now for the day has been a long one and I need to keep my strength up. If only for my son's sake.*

*Send me your words of comfort for I desperately need them.*

*Your heartbroken Lizzie*

# Twenty-one

Everything which had been happening to Lizzie in England was unbeknown to Mary, which left her worrying as to why she not heard from her dear friend for some time. "I am at a loss to understand why Lizzie hasn't written," she told Jayne. "There have been at least two ships arrive since I last wrote. Yet neither Captains had any correspondence for me."

Jayne, could only sympathise with her friend. "There must be a good reason. Remember, poor Sir James was wounded. He may have needed more nursing than they first thought. And surely Lizzie will have given birth by now." Mary agreed but still, she was disappointed whilst remaining deeply concerned. She didn't like to think badly of Lizzie but sometimes she wondered if married life and her new child were perhaps diverting her friend's thoughts.

Fortunately for Mary, her own time was well spent, being kept busy and pre-occupied with little time to worry. Preparations for Jayne and Thomas's wedding were complete. And on the following Sunday morning, everyone gathered in the little church to witness the joyous nuptials. The bride looked lovely in the altered wedding dress. Mary looked delightful too, with her dress complimenting the bridal outfit. The church was picturesque due to the island women having collected an abundance of fresh flowers to dress it and to make the bouquets.

Walking up the aisle behind Jayne and Colonel Johnstone, Mary thought what a beautiful bride her young friend made. Looking towards the altar, Mary saw a great deal of pride shining in Thomas's eyes, causing a lump in her throat. The service was taken by the ships Chaplain and, as the couple made their vows, Mary watched how tenderly they stared at each other. She later admitted to Dorothy, at having a moments' feeling of envy at Jayne's good fortune in having

144

found someone as caring and loving as Thomas. A party followed and once this was finished it was time for the groom and bride to retire for the night aboard Lord Falshaw's yacht. Mary retired that night feeling tired but happy.

Before turning out her light she took out her diary and wrote: *What a wonderful day it has been. Jayne and Thomas are married. After the service the whole congregation gathered in the centre of the village where the island women laid out a fabulous feast. We sat on the mats scattered on the ground and there was music and singing from some of the ships' crew. The day was filled with lots of laughter and happiness. I felt no sadness at not having heard from Lizzie. As the evening drew to a close the bride and groom were escorted to the dockside where they spent the night on Lord Falshaw's yacht. Tomorrow they leave for the Johnstones' estate. I am so happy for them but I will miss Jayne not living here with me.*

Once in bed Mary found herself thinking about being held in His Lordships arms, dancing. It had felt wonderful. However, before she could examine the feelings he aroused in her further, she fell into a deep, exhausted sleep; not stirring until late the following morning.

Having just finished breakfast Mary heard a knock. Going outside she found Lord Falshaw waiting to speak to her. "Did you sleep well?

"Yes, thank you Lord Falshaw. I slept exceedingly well."

"I wondered if you would care to take a stroll by the sea shore?"

Although slightly surprised by his request, Mary agreed. She was finding him an easy person to talk to, enjoying their times together. Taking his proffered arm, she allowed him to lead her down the hill.

At first, they walked in companionable silence until Lord Falshaw enquired, "How did you enjoy the celebrations?"

"I enjoyed them very much. Jayne made a beautiful

bride. I have to say how much I enjoyed the Colonels speech. And yours of course; both were most amusing." And she laughed lightly at the memory.

"Why thank you Ma-am," said His Lordship touching his forelock in mock salute. Suddenly stopping, he turned to face her. "Tell me, is there any reason why you cannot address me by my given name? It's Percy."

Mary thought for a moment. "But it would not be proper for me to do so. You must remember I am only a simple school mistress while you are a titled gentleman."

At her response he started laughing. "Don't be so silly. You have been living on the islands for some time now, so surely such formalities are no longer necessary."

The request and his response certainly surprised Mary and she could think of nothing further to say, except, "I am sorry but I do not think I can oblige you. If I am honest, I believe I would find it difficult, for it is not in my nature to be so forward."

His Lordship laughed again before taking hold of her hand. "I do understand but, in all seriousness, could you not try to find it in your heart to think about my request?" And he looked deep into her eyes. "I would be most honoured if you would. Especially as I am finding it quite difficult to keep addressing you as Miss Watson, when I just want to call you Mary."

After a short pause she carefully said, "Very well. I will give it some thought but, I am not promising." His Lordship nodded his head in acknowledgement after which they returned to a companionable silence. Mary was thinking how delightful she found his laughter.

Returning to the hut they were surprised to discover the ship's Captain waiting for her. Expressing his good wishes, he enquired, "I wondered if you had heard anything from your dear friend in England as unfortunately, I have no letter for you."

Shaking her head, Mary was glad of the interruption. She still felt slightly uneasy at her conversation with His

Lordship, although she was sorry it had ceased. Offering her apologies, she thanked His Lordship for the walk before asking the Captain to wait whilst she fetched the letter she had written earlier. Before sealing it, she re-read the contents, ensuring everything she wished to say was included.

*My Dearest Lizzie*

*I am at a loss to understand why I have not heard from you? Although, when I think about it, I realise you may have been busy with your new son. And of course, the return of your beloved husband whom I trust is returned safely and is now recovering in the bosom of his beloved's family.*

*Here is some good news to cheer you up. Jayne and Thomas are married. Their Wedding Day was a splendid affair with everyone on the islands attending. The Colonel did a grand job as surrogate 'Father of the Bride.' He kept telling everyone how beautiful his 'daughter' looked, and how proud he was at having been allowed to give her away.*

*Lord Falshaw, as Best Man, gave a splendid speech. He was most amusing, causing everyone to laugh. Especially when teasing Thomas about him once getting stuck up a tree. Even Mumna strutted around in her chosen role as 'Mother-of-the-Bride.' It seemed quite funny. Jayne looked beautiful and truly happy. Everyone had a wonderful time. There was lots of music and dancing. I danced with Lord Falshaw a number of times. An experience I admit to finding most enjoyable.*

*Slowly I am settled at having both Kuala and Chula living with me. The three of us get on well together, although I do miss dear Jayne's company in the evenings. The two young girls have been teaching me to speak their native language and I am pleased to find I have an aptitude for it.*

*Life here on the islands offers me much contentment and I find I miss England less and less. But I do worry about you my dearest Lizzie for I need to know you are happy in your married life.*

*My apologies this letter is so short. If you no longer have time to write due to your family commitments, then*

*please tell me. While I would suffer some distress, I will*
*understand. I only hope and pray all is well but will close*
*now. The Captain has called as his ship is due to sail shortly.*

*Please write as soon as you are able my dearest.*
*Your loving friend Mary*


Having given the Captain her letter, Mary sat outside thinking about the events of the last few days. Suddenly she heard her name being called. Looking up she saw the Johnstones approaching. It was approximately an hour before the ship was due to sail so they were calling to take their leave of her. Mary knew Laura was still upset at having to leave the island so soon after returning. She also realised her friend was doing her best not to show her husband the depth of her feelings. She loved him deeply and did not wish to cause him any upset.

Coming closer, Laura held out her hand towards Mary. Sat inside it was a small token of her esteem. It was a figurine of a young girl in a pretty dress. One of those Mary had admired whilst visiting Laura's home. Mary was deeply grateful at her friend's thoughtfulness. She gave Laura a gift in return. A shawl, embroidered with flowers the colour of those growing on the island. The idea being that whenever Laura wore it, she would think of her island home. Hopefully giving her good memories.

Once their goodbyes were made the Johnstones left to board the ship. They were accompanied to the water's edge by all the islanders who stood on the dockside waving farewell. Watching the small boat take the couple out to the big ship the islanders began singing. A native goodbye song which Kuala told her was their way of saying goodbye, safe journey but remember to return home. Mary thought it delightful. Once on board the couple waved to everyone until the ship had left the harbour. Suddenly Mary was overcome with sadness. Jayne was lost to another island and now Laura was away to another country. Her country.

That evening Mary wrote in her diary: *What am I to do?*

*I am deeply aware of the honour His Lordship bestows on me to be so familiar in the manner by which I may address him. But still, I do not feel it is correct or proper for me to do so, even with his kind permission. He does not seem to accept the difference in our social positions, which still exists even here on the islands. And yet I have to admit to liking the idea of calling him Percy. It seems normal to do so. When I am in his presence I feel as if I have known him all my life. I am so confused by the feelings I have towards him. I am also sad not to have heard anything from my dear Lizzie and am worried something is not right. I can only pray God takes care of her and that she writes soon.*

Mary did not see His Lordship again until about a week later. As she was tidying up, having just finished school for the day, a loud cough made her turn and she found Percy standing, watching her. Bowing he smiled. "Good-day Mary. How are you?"

"I am very well, thank you."

"How are you managing without Jayne's help."

"Very well, thank you. Kuala and Chula are both ably assisting me."

Smiling, he asked, "I wondered if you had given any more thought to my request to call me by my given name."

At his question Mary blushed slightly. "I am still not sure it would be proper to do so."

Laughing he told her, "Well, I trust you will try your best to accommodate me," and he smiled to show he understood her reticence in the matter. Without realising it Mary found herself smiling back.

Going towards her, Percy took hold of her hand and kissing it, teased, "Do you realise that I think you look quite delightful when you blush." Mary quickly turned away in an effort to hide her embarrassment, picking up the books she had been tidying earlier.

His Lordship moved to the entrance. "I shall, with your permission return after I have visited the Chief. I am hoping

149

you might oblige me with some refreshments?"

Turning back to see him leave she called out, "But of course. I will be delighted to offer you some refreshments."

As soon as His Lordship was out of sight Mary raced inside the hut, calling for Kuala and telling her to prepare a tea tray for when Lord Falshaw returned. "We will take it outside," she said as she brushed her hair. Kuala smiled in a way Mary found disturbing. It seemed the young girl was reading more into the visit than perhaps she should.

However, half an hour later His Lordship returned. With the sun slowly descending they sat drinking their tea and making small chit-chat which went a long way to settling Marys nerves. With tea finished His Lordship stood. "I'm sorry but I must take my leave. Thank you for the tea. I trust you have a good evening." As she watched him leave, Mary thought his step somewhat jaunty!

After that, His Lordship calling to take tea soon became a regular occurrence. Each week when visiting the Chief, he took the opportunity to spend some time with Mary. His constant attentions found her relaxing, and looked forward to the time spent in his company. Yet despite his continued insistence, she was still unable to address him by his first name. It was one night after such a visit when Mary lay in bed thinking about His Lordship. Being honest with herself Mary knew she enjoyed sitting, talking and drinking tea with him. "Percy," she whispered to herself. Then she tried the name again. "Percy." 'I like the sound of that,' she thought. 'Maybe I could get used to addressing him so?' However, by the following morning Mary's worries about any feelings Lord Falshaw might be stirring in her disappeared when Jayne called.

Delighted by the visit Mary thought how happy and contented her friend looked. And, yet there was something else, a kind of mystery. Having been sat drinking tea for a while Mary realised there was an air of excitement about her friend. As if, she had a secret she was having trouble keeping to herself. Finally, Jayne blurted out, "I have something to tell you... There's going to be an addition to our household."

Mary was trying to work out what Jayne meant, then it dawned on her. Looking at her she knew why she looked so lovely. A smile spread across her face Mary. "You're pregnant?"

Confirming her suspicions left Mary overjoyed. As they sat talking Mary was further surprised when Jayne asked, "Thomas and I wondered, when the baby arrives, if you would consent to being Godmother."

Mary gasped then grinned. "What an honour you show me. I will be delighted." And the girls spent their time chatting about the forthcoming addition.

Shortly afterwards Thomas arrived. When Mary congratulated him, he blushed, grinning like a Cheshire cat. He was obviously delighted about the baby and happy Mary was to join the Chief and Lord Falshaw as Godparents. They left Mary glowing with delight for them.

# Twenty-two

Seven weeks later a ship dropped anchor in the harbour and Mary was delighted to discover the Captain had, at last, brought a letter from Lizzie. Receipt of which brought her much relief regarding her dear friend Lizzie. Being about to sit and read the letter Mary found herself disturbed by the arrival of Tara, one of the Chief's daughters, who told her, she was needed urgently by Mumna. Feeling slightly frustrated at the interruption, Mary put the letter in the pocket of her dress before racing after the young girl. Arriving at Mumna's hut she discovered a number of the island women waiting outside. As she approached, Mumna came outside beckoning her to enter. As she did, she was surprised to discover the Chief's daughter sat on the floor, her young child lying beside her. The ship's doctor was examining him.

Going towards them Mary asked, "What is amiss?"

The Doctor explained the baby was ill, having breathing problems. Sitting down next to the young mother Mary offered what support she could. As the young woman looked at her, there was a worried expression on her face. Taking her hand Mary gripped it tightly offering whatever support she could through her grip. But, to no avail. The child was too ill. Two days later he passed away and the islanders went into mourning.

Mary later told Jayne. "I know he is your nephew but, whilst the young mother is sad at her loss, I somehow feel she is also relieved."

Jayne nodded her head. "I agree and understand. The circumstances of her pregnancy were not the best. I cannot be upset by her attitude, though I am sad at the loss of such a young life. It is all in God's hands." No more was said on the subject.

Later, thinking about Jayne's comments Mary realised

how strong a person her friend was. Having become so since her brothers' departure, and having married Thomas. She was also pleased with Mumna when she agreed to Jayne's request to bury the child in the church cemetery. As such, a small funeral was held a few days later. The only people present being Jayne, Thomas, Lord Falshaw and Mary. Not that it mattered for at least the child had been given a Christian burial which pleased Jayne.

It wasn't therefore until some days later that Mary remembered the forgotten letter in her pocket. Sitting she began reading. As she turned the page's tears slowly fell down her face. The news was sad. Causing her great pain at her dear friend's loss. However, mixed with the sadness was the joyous news of Lizzie having given birth to a baby son! Being deeply concerned for her dear friend Mary decided to write a response immediately, asking Kuala to bring her writing implements out to her.

Lost in thought Mary found herself filled with anger at the cruelties of life. Suddenly the peace was shattered as the islanders raced past heading for the shoreline. Looking up she saw a ship had dropped anchor in the harbour. Taking her writing implements inside Mary washed her face. About to follow the islanders, she spied Dorothy walking towards her. Waiting for her, the two of them set of towards the dockside together.

Once at the shoreline Mary was delighted to see Captain Morrison. Watching from the side line she noticed a number of new people landing onshore. Spying Mary, the Captain came over. "Good-day Miss Watson. How are you?"

"I am well Captain Morrison. How are you and your family?"

Smiling in return he replied, "In good health, Miss Watson. We are all in good health. Thank you for asking. Miss Watson, I wondered if you would allow me to introduce you to some passengers who have just arrived on the islands."

"But of course, Captain, I would be delighted to meet them."

153

Mary spent some time becoming acquainted with the new residents. As the group stood getting to know each other Mary realised her school numbers had suddenly grown. The two couples had four children between them and she was delighted to hear they all spoke good English. Having welcomed the new arrivals, the Captain then introduced Mary to Andrew Jones, the ship's new doctor. The previous doctor had retired, intending to continue his practice in his home village. However, he had asked Dr Jones to give his best regards to Mary when seeing her. She was pleased and surprised as she hadn't expected him to remember her.

As they were talking Doctor Jones asked, "Pray tell me, do you know Miss Jayne Morgain."

Mary was hesitant. "Yes, I do. May I ask why?" She waited, hoping he was not a would-be suitor. She did not wish to tell him of unrequited affections, if such were the case.

As it turned out she need not have worried. "I have a message from her brother."

Mary became somewhat cautious at the news. "I do not think Jayne will be able to cope with any bad news at present. She is shortly due to give birth. May I ask you to give me the message?"

"Considering the circumstances, I think it might be better if I did." And he went on to explain about the Reverend. It seemed he had been thrown into prison, where he languished still and was looking to Miss Morgain for assistance. After Mary explained the situation Dr Jones realised Jayne was unable to assist her brother. "I would be most obliged Miss Watson if you would give the message to Miss Morgain?"

Mary thought for a moment. "Of course. However, I believe I will discuss the matter with Thomas, Jayne's husband, first. The Reverend left the island under a dark cloud. I believe he should be the one to make any decisions regarding him."

The doctor was relieved to have delivered his message, thanking Mary for her assistance before excusing himself.

After he had gone Dorothy, who had overheard the conversation asked, "What are you going to do about the Reverend?"

Mary looked at her. "Exactly what I said. I am going to speak to Thomas. I believe, with Jayne in her present condition, she should not be told of this just yet." Dorothy nodded her head in agreement as Mary concluded, "Whatever action Thomas decides is necessary, I will abide by." Satisfied the two ladies returned to Mary's home for coffee.

Later, after Dorothy had departed, Mary took out her unfinished letter, completed and sealed it. The Captain would take it back to England when he sailed on the morning tide.

*My Sweet Darling Lizzie*

*Oh, what joy I feel to have received a letter from you. But how I cried when I read the news. I so wish I was there to comfort and care for you. My heart is full of sadness for your loss but also full of joy for the safe arrival of your new son. When next I see Jayne, we will pray for dear James' soul, for you and the baby. I agree my sweet one, life is so cruel.*

*What a shock I got when I read of the behaviour of James sisters. Should I have been present, I surely could not have held my tongue. They appear to be such spiteful individuals. Do not let them get you down. Although I am pleased by your response towards them. You are coming into your own as a woman.*

*Your sadness makes me loath to give you my news? Yet, I am excited and delighted so I hope this will lift your spirits. At least a little. Jayne and Thomas are to be parents and they have bestowed a true honour by asking me to be Godmother to the child. I am not alone in this as they have also asked the Chief and Lord Falshaw. Both have readily agreed. I feel so privileged at their faith in me. I spend my time sewing clothes for the baby. And, Kuala and Chula are weaving a baby's sleeping basket.*

*The Johnstones left for England two days after Jayne's wedding. Laura is eagerly looking forward to meeting you. She bears a letter of introduction. Before leaving she gave me a small figurine as a token of our friendship. I felt a little embarrassed, having admired it while visiting her home. She insisted I take it because she knew how much I liked it. I believe she wanted me to have something to remember her by. As if I could forget her! She is such a delightful creature. One whom I am sure you will adore.*

*There is also some sad news about the Chief's daughter and her son. Sadly, the poor child has not fared well, passing away in his sleep some two weeks ago. The mother appears to have shown little distress at his loss. I believe she may be relieved as she never really wanted the child. I know you may find her attitude shocking but it is the way of the islanders. We cannot be overly concerned by what appears to be their lack of caring as they view life and death differently to us. Maybe because life can be hard here. Jayne has been allowed to bury the child in our church cemetery. Since then I have failed to see the mother around. Though I recently learnt she has gone back to His Lordships estate.*

*Captain Morrison's ship dropped anchor today. He kindly took the time to introduce me to a number of people who are now residents on our islands. We had not realised they were coming so it was a pleasant surprise. They hail from the Netherlands. There is Peter and Greta Van der Kerkoff, who have three children called Miela, Kurt and Baby Greta. They did not come alone, but have been joined by Mrs Van der Kerkoff's brother and wife, Etienne and Marta Beckoff, who have a daughter called Sareta. They too are a pleasant couple and I am sure you would like them. The two families will live on an estate on the other side of the main island on a plantation formally owned by Mr Van der Kerkoff's Uncle. It seems that poor gentleman passed away some time ago and, having no immediate heirs, Peter has inherited the estate. Their arrival means my school numbers have grown. All speak excellent English and Mrs Beckoff has agreed to teach me Dutch, as well as helping me improve my French. Dorothy and I spent a short time talking to them before they left for their new home. We are invited to join*

156

*them for tea once they are settled.*

*We had heard naught of Reverend Morgain since his departure. So, it was surprising to hear some unexpected news today, passed to me by the ship's new doctor. He is called Andrew Jones, alights from somewhere in Wales and appears to be a most personable young gentleman. I believe I shall like him very much. He asked after Jayne, telling me he had a message from her brother who, it seems wants her assistance. The Reverend is in gaol, having upset an important personage. It seems he was too outspoken, chaffing the man, even accusing him of being a debaser and a charlatan. This so incensed and infuriated the Governor, that he threw The Reverend in prison. Andrew says he languishes there still.*

*Oh, Lizzie, it took all my control not to laugh. I say it serves him right as he always was such an arrogant man. Anyway, I have decided it is not the right time to inform Jayne of the situation. My fear is she may, through a matter of unwarranted loyalty, feel she must venture abroad to save him. And so, I shall wait until after the ship sails before I inform Thomas, as I believe, it is he who should decide what to do.*

*On a different note. Since I last wrote, Lord Falshaw has called a number of times. He is most courteous, and often enquires how you are. He has requested I address him by his first name, but I am not sure it would be the correct behaviour for someone in my position. He tells me living on the island relieves us of the normal formalities of English society. Jayne believes he likes me and wants to know me better but I am unsure. I would appreciate your thoughts on the matter my dear as I have such mixed emotions and am unsure as to what I should do.*

*Night draws in so I will close. I am to give this letter to Andrew, Dr Jones, to take back to the ship with him. He is calling to take his leave of me and has promised to ensure it is despatched to you when he returns to England.*

*Strengthen your heart dearest Lizzie and write soon.*

*Your loving friend Mary*

With her letter finished Mary took out her journal: *What a day it has been. And what news I have received. I know it is unchristian to think ill of a man of the cloth but I can do no other for Reverend Morgain is a man waylaid by the devil. My heart goes out to Jayne. She should not suffer the sins of her brother. Sometimes I thank God I am an only child without siblings to disrupt my life. As for Doctor Jones, he seems a most personable young man and I am delighted by his demeanour. I hope to see more of him for I feel we will become good friends.*

# Twenty-three

Back in England Lizzie's health, and state of mind, slowly but surely, improved over the weeks. The baby was growing, getting stronger and more joyful each day, much to the delight of his Mother and Grandparents. It also seemed the new baby was causing quite a stir, and delighting all the household occupants. Lizzie slowly began venturing out more, visiting friends and acquaintances. She still wore black, being in mourning, but at least she was beginning to smile again, bringing much relief to her parents.

After their earlier visit, the Williamson sisters had not returned. Nor had they sent any missive or inquiry regarding their nephew's wellbeing. Lizzie had followed through with her threat of meeting with the family solicitor. And after much discussion between him and her parents, a letter was sent to the sisters informing them of her decision. For the present the sisters could remain at the country house. However, they were to give an accurate account of all expenses and costs incurred to her solicitor. Further, they were to ensure all income and debts were accounted for when he attended the estate to discuss these terms with them and the Estate Manager.

As regards the town house, they could not use it. Being informed that Lizzie would eventually be moving in there herself. How long before she actually did would depend on how she felt about living on her own. However, she had no intention of telling the ladies any of this. Aiming to keep the household staff, Lizzie attended the town house regularly. Thus, reassuring them she was very much the 'lady of the manor.' Had Mary been closer Lizzie would have moved her into the town house as her companion. The thought being that she would write to Mary and invite her to return to England. But it was merely a passing thought as Lizzie was not yet strong enough to leave her family home or the support of her parents. She would, however, write to Mary when the time was right an extend the invitation.

The initial mourning period passed and soon Lizzie was seen attending soirées and balls. Being young and attractive it wasn't long before she was meeting young gentlemen. Many of whom found her widow's demeanour entrancing and bewitching. With the memory of James still fresh in her heart and mind, Lizzie tended to treat these young men with some disdain and amusement. Secretly, however, she was flattered by their attentions.

With the festive season drawing closer Lizzie received a number of invitations. But, despite this she always put her young son first. Taking time to be with him and enjoying his development. Occasionally she felt some sadness, for when she looked at baby James, she could clearly see her late husband in his features, causing her to catch her breath. The only down side at present was the feelings of guilt she felt at her slowness in not having written to tell Mary of the recent events. Lizzie sincerely hoped she had not upset her friend by the delay. She also hoped to receive a letter in return to the one recently sent. In this she was not disappointed.

Sat in the library one day the maid informed her a young gentleman called Doctor Jones was requesting an interview. Lizzie was sure they were unacquainted but intrigued she agreed to receive him, something she would not normally have done prior to her marriage. As he entered the room Lizzie saw a good-looking, young man. As he introduced himself, she noted his sing-song accent.

Smiling she requested he take a seat. "Pray Sir, do we know each other?"

"I apologise. No, we have not had the privilege of meeting, Lady Williamson. However, we do have a mutual acquaintance. Miss Mary Watson."

Upon hearing her friends name, Lizzie smiled in such a way it made her face light up. And Andrew Jones was smitten. Unknowingly from that moment on he started falling in love.

Reaching into his coat pocket he passed Lizzie a letter. Mary hadn't asked him to personally deliver it. He had taken it upon himself to do so. And, if he were truly honest, Dr Jones was intrigued to learn more of Lady Williamson, having heard so much of her from Mary. Taking the letter Lizzie rang for refreshments, after which she began questioning Dr Jones about her friend and how she was doing. Andrew, a most obliging young man, extensively answered all her questions. Or maybe he just wanted to stretch out his visit for as long as possible? It was, upon their return that Lord and Lady Mountford, much to their surprise, found their daughter entertaining a young gentleman. After being introduced Andrew decided it was perhaps time for him to take his leave. Lizzie escorted him to the door, where he asked, "I wondered Lady Williamson if I could call on you again when I am next in town? I may have further news regarding your dear friend."

Lizzie readily agreed. "I would be delighted to receive you Doctor Jones. Thank you for your consideration." Standing by the window Lizzie watched him walk away and, for the first time since losing James, she felt an attraction towards another man. Much later in her room she sat reading Mary's letter, feeling more contented and happier than she had for some time.

Approximately a week later, while returning home from church, Lizzie was to meet James's eldest sister Edith, who politely requested an audience with her. While she was loath to have any conversation with her, Lizzie was too polite to refuse, so she invited Edith indoors. Going into the drawing room Lizzie was disappointed to note her Mother was out. Not about to let her feelings show she offered Edith a chair and instructed the maid to bring refreshments.

After the tray was brought, Lizzie poured the tea. "And what business brings you to town, Miss Williamson?"

Edith thought for a while before speaking. While polite in her speech, her manner was cold. "I wish to see my nephew." To Lizzie it sounded more like a demand than a request. But before she could respond Edith continued. "My sister and I are somewhat concerned about the baby's wellbeing. We feel it would perhaps be better if our brother's son were to live at the country estate. He is, after all, Lord of the Manor."

Astounded by the comments Lizzie was, for the moment speechless. Her silence encouraged Edith to continue. "We also understand your own health is not so good. Therefore, it might be more convenient if my sister and I took the baby to care for him. After all, we have great experience in nursing people, having looked after our father for many years."

Lizzie could not believe what she was hearing. Anger boiled up inside her, and it took all her strength not to jump up and lash out at Edith for her supercilious manner. Finally, she could tolerate it no longer. Straightening her back, Lizzie stood and spoke in a controlled voice. "Just who do you think you are? You come here, suggesting untruths about my health. Then you tell me what is best for my son. How... dare... you... enter my family's home and make such demands of me?" Taking a breath, she went on. "I do believe, as his Mother, it is my concern and mine alone to ensure my son is looked after properly. And as regards myself, you can be rest assured that I am in the best of health. Which means I am perfectly capable of bringing up my son without any assistance from you or your sister." Stopping, Lizzie took another breath. "I am astounded by your audacity."

Edith had turned white at Lizzie's outburst for she had not expected her young sister-in-law to react so vehemently. Being a woman of a certain age, she was more used to younger women adhering to her way of thinking. Yet here was this, this impertinent person, whom her brother had so foolishly married, speaking to her in such a manner. How dare she! With these thoughts in mind Edith stood up ready to say something. However, at this point Lord Mountford entered the room. His unexpected entrance causing both women to turn and look at him. Before he could speak Lizzie turned towards Edith. Her voice was polite but cold. "It appears there is nothing further to be said. I therefore presume this visit is ended? And as I have an appointment, I wish you good-day, Miss Williamson." Whereupon Lizzie left the room, much to her Father's surprise.

Her actions left Edith with little option but to say good-day to His Lordship and leave, which she hastily did. Later, when Lady Mountford discovered what had happened, she was extremely annoyed. However, she was pleased knowing her daughter had held her own against such a formidable person.

That evening, feeling restless and still disturbed by Edith's visit, Lizzie took out Mary's latest letter. Reading what her friend had written helped settle her mind. Then sitting at her writing slope, she began her reply.

*My Darling Mary*

*Your last letter raised my spirits, as all your previous ones have done. What news. Your island is growing in numbers and I am happy to hear your little school is flourishing. If you require anything for the children, please let me know. What an interesting life you appear to be leading. At this moment I wish I was by your side. I believe I would come and join you except Baby James is too young to undertake such a long journey, although he is well and grows daily. What a proud mother I am, for my son seems to have such a happy demeanour and a wonderful laugh.*

*And now to tell you what has happened here. As you can see, I still reside with my parents. As much as I love the Williamson town house I cannot live there alone at present. However, I am at last venturing out, spending time with my acquaintances and attending dinner parties. Of course, I still wear black which I find most unbecoming and quite depressing.*

*The Solicitor called recently to read James' Will and I discovered I am a woman of substance. My new status is most unusual but it means I have much more freedom and renewed strength. This has been born out when I tell you of today's unwanted visitor. Mary, you would have been so proud of me when I tell you how I handled a visit from Miss Edith Williamson. She was waiting upon my return from church and requested an audience. You can image my dismay. But I accommodated her. Edith behaved with such an air of superiority and condescension I found it quite shocking. She demanded to see her brother's son. The went on to infer my health was obviously not good so it would be better for the child if he went to live with them. I was astounded by her audacity. How I wish you had been here to support me.*

*And, it seems you were. For as my eyes passed over the chaise, I noticed the blanket you had sent Baby James. It somehow gave me a strength of spirit I did not know I possessed. It was as if you were sat next to me, giving me courage to speak. I was so angry I reproached Edith strongly for her outrageous comments. I stood up, saying her comments were unwarranted, and how my poor James would be turning in his grave at the manner in which she and her sister were treating me. I know not how or where the words came from. Luckily Father entered the room so I took the opportunity to end the visit. Leaving with my head held high. Both Edith and Father looked shocked but I didn't care. Mother was most annoyed over the visit. Father, however, congratulated me on having handled the confrontation so well. I am now calmer and at peace with my lot in life.*

*My dearest what a delightful young man your Dr Andrew Jones is? Now you will wonder how do I know this young man? Well My Sweet, he called a few days ago to deliver your letter. I was surprised but pleased for we spent a good hour talking about you. I did wonder if he had feelings for you? But, although he speaks of you well, I think it is as a friend, not a suitor. I trust you are not disappointed Darling Mary? He left promising to visit again when next in town.*

*Talking of gentlemen, I was most surprised by your mention of Lord Falshaw. At first, I thought he was being forward. Perhaps behaving in an improper manner. But, after giving the matter much thought I believe Jayne may be correct and he has some regard for you. I understand your concern dear one as to how you should address him. However, he is correct, you are not restricted by normal English society expectations. To be honest, if you feel comfortable referring to him by his given name, then do so and 'be damned' with the niceties of society. Oh, my dear, when I read this, even I think I am being forward. Am I wicked? Maybe, but it is quite amusing.*

*I must close now, for I hear Baby James calling for his Momma. He must need feeding. He has a huge appetite for one so small. I wish you could hold him as he would capture your heart.*

*Take care, my dearest.*

*Your loving, stronger Lizzie*


Having calmed herself, Lizzie left the room to feed her son, feeling more at peace with her world. Any worries soon vanished due to the happiness her son's welcome invoked in her. Being a mother was something Lizzie had quickly become accustomed to. In fact, she was enjoying it.

Returning to her room later she took out her diary to write: *I feel I am a different person. Today I found the strength to stand up to my sister-in-law; finding her demands and insinuations both offensive and unwelcome. Even though she is Aunt to Baby James I cannot, and will not, be talked to in such a way. I am only glad my darling husband is not around to witness such a display of arrogance and superciliousness.*

# Twenty-four

The days passed and life became busier for Mary. Jayne, growing heavier with the baby, was no longer able to help in the school. This meant Mary had more to do, especially since the new children had arrived. She found her daylight hours split between teaching Kuala and Chula to read and write, taking school lessons, and helping Mumna improve her writing. Weeks passed without her being aware of it. Yet she felt no remorse for the loss of time for she was enjoying her life. It was during this time that Mary saw more of the Chiefs daughter who had returned to the main island. She was being courted by a young man and whenever she saw them together, Mary thought how happy they looked. Always laughing together. She later learnt they were to be married.

It was during one of Lord Falshaw's visits that Mary confided in him. "Has Thomas told you about the Reverends misfortune?"

"Yes. We have discussed the matter, deciding we cannot leave the man to rot, even if he deserves such a fate." Mary was surprised by his comment but said nothing. "So, I have written to the Governor of the island where he is being held, requesting some leniency be shown. To-date there has been no news." Nothing further was said on the subject.

Within days the rainy season was once again upon them; although it soon passed without creating any major problems. This time Mary was ready, having managed to batten everything down in time. The winds were strong, with the hut losing only an odd large leaf from the roof, while the school room lost much of its roof. Luckily, Mary had stored the school's contents in a corner of the hut. Once the rains ceased, everyone rallied to repair the damage.

The newcomers to the islands proved to be friendly people, with all of them taking Mary to their hearts. As promised, Mrs Beckoff began teaching Mary Dutch and French. The lady's knowledge of European languages was excellent, being an intelligent woman. Her late father had been an Ambassador for the Dutch Court so she had travelled a great deal, with her wanderings only ceasing when she met her husband Etienne, the younger brother of a local dignitary. They had, as Marta put it, fallen head over heels in love the moment their eyes met.

It was during her language lesson Mary came to know much more about the two families and how they came to be on the islands. Unfortunately, their estate had fallen into a state of disrepair due to mis-management. Fortunately, Lord Falshaw had offered to lend them Peter, his new Estate Manager to show them what to do. Peter was extremely grateful for the kind offer, which had arisen due to the laziness of the old manager. Visiting one day, Mary had come across Peter arguing with the old manager. Having suffered enough of the man's complaining, Peter had sacked him. The man, not happy at being told to leave, had been left with little alternative but to remove himself to await the next ship. His Lordships offer of assistance had saved the day.

Over the next few weeks a number of ships visited the islands, allowing Mary the opportunity to obtain extra supplies for the school. With the festive season once again drawing near Mary asked Lord Falshaw to arrange delivery of some special items. She wished to create a special Nativity scene. Percy was only too willing to oblige, making sure she got all she required. Mary had approached a local carpenter, asking if he could carve a doll to represent the baby in the manager. As she was with him, she decided what to send Baby James for Christmas. A farmyard set. Carefully, having drawn the animals and the farmyard, Mary hoped the man would be able to carve them large enough for a baby's little hands. Although some of the animals were strange to the carpenter, he was happy to oblige her. A week later he delivered the finished results, much to Marys delight.

Deciding to paint the animals and farmyard in bright

colours, Mary knew the set would delight any young child. It was as she sat concentrating on the job in hand that Lord Falshaw came upon her. He stood watching her for five minutes or so before Mary realised, she was no longer alone. Looking up and catching sight of him leaning against the doorway, a strange smile on his face, she asked, "And what is so funny."

He pointed to his nose. She had paint on it. Stopping, Mary attempted to rub it away with a cloth she was holding. However, when she removed her hand His Lordship started laughing. "You've just made it worse." Looking at her reflection in a small glass mirror Mary started laughing as well, as she discovered she had spread the paint across her face. Rising she went indoors to wash.

Returning, His Lordship asked, "What are you doing?" Holding up one of the animals she explained about her friend's baby and the gift she was sending him for Christmas.

Admiring her handiwork, he said, "You're quite an artist." Blushing from the compliment Mary thanked him before asking if he would like some refreshment.

As they drank tea, the pair made small talk. Eventually Percy took the opportunity to ask, "I wondered if you care to visit my home during Christmas week." As she hesitated, he went on. "We won't be alone. My sister and her family are visiting and I would like you to meet them."

Mary was surprised. Not by the invitation, but by the fact Percy had a sister, for this was the first time he had ever mentioned having such a relative. Allowing curiosity to get the better of her she said, "Your sister? Why yes. I would be delighted to meet her and her family."

"Good. That's settled then," and he smiled, obviously pleased.

After some time, His Lordship departed, leaving Mary to return to her painting. She wanted to make sure the gift was ready to send on the next ship to England. As she sat, Mary marvelled at the thought that she had been living on the islands for over two years. It seemed Christmas was going to be a happy affair. She was happy to know she was accepted by those living here.

The following Sunday morning, feeling full of cheer Mary made her way towards the little church. After the service the congregation met to organise the celebrations for Christmas Day. It was decided they would have a large party after the morning service. They would meet in the centre of the village with each lady bringing a dish of food. After the feast, there would be music and Christmas Carols. The Chief and Mumna would be guests of honour. As she left, her day ended on a happy note, when Lord Falshaw asked her, "May I escort you back home." Agreeing, the pair strolled along making chit-chat. Just before leaving, Percy bent forward, lightly kissing Mary on the cheek who blushed at his forthrightness. Retiring that night, she felt delighted by his audacity.

Thinking of the forthcoming festivities Mary decided to give small Christmas gifts to each of her friends. The question though, was what? After much thought, she settled on making them a small keepsake each. From then on, she spent much of her spare time making things, such as place mats, shawls, embroidered handkerchiefs or floral paintings. Each gift was wrapped in special wrapping paper and completed with a small corsage of dried flowers. Mary was satisfied with the results of her labours.

A few days later Mary woke early, her intention being to complete her letter to Lizzie, and to finish wrapping the presents for her friends and Baby James. Sending them now meant they would arrive in plenty of time for Christmas Day. Sitting at the table her peace was disrupted when, surprised, Mary saw Mumna entering the hut holding a letter in her hand.

"Good-morning Mumna. Do you need me for something?"

Mumna sat down, holding out the letter. "I wish you to read and tell me if it is good."

Taking the missive Mary read it, surprised to discover

169

it was addressed to Queen Victoria and had been written by Mumna herself. Once she had finished, Mary looked up to find the Queen watching her. Coughing slightly to clear her throat, thus giving her a moment to think, Mary said, "It is a good letter Your Majesty. Pray tell me what you wish me to do with it."

"I want it sent to England. Send it with your parcel? It is for your Queen. It is a message of goodwill. I have also written to your Miss Lizzie explaining my request."

Mary, finding no reason to refuse, agreed to Mumna's request, deciding to add a small message at the bottom of her own letter in explanation of why it is in the parcel. She sincerely hoped Lizzie or her father would be able to get the letter to Her Majesty. Satisfied, Mumna left the hut leaving Mary to complete her own letter.

*Dearest Lizzie*

*My heart is full as I realise how you are coming into your own. The description of the way you dealt with James' sister made me smile. I felt so proud of you and would have been delighted to witness all as you left the room. I am sure your Father was pleased with you. Oh, what joy you must feel at having handled such a moment.*

*And what a surprise when you mentioned Doctor Jones. I assure you I did not request he call, so if his attentions are unwarranted, I apologise most sincerely. However, if you did not find his visit unpleasant then I am pleased. I too found him a most likeable young man. We sat and talked a great deal about England, James, the Baby and, of course, You my love. Maybe this is where the idea of paying you a visit came from. I will wait to hear further from you.*

*Life is much the same here, although I am busier with the school now Jayne cannot spend as much time with me. Travelling between the two islands is not easy for her and Thomas prefers she remains at the homestead with her birth time drawing near. Kuala and Chula have been a great help. Kuala is becoming more adept at her reading and writing which pleases me.*

*Tell me dearest, how does Baby James fare? I trust he is well and is growing stronger each day. As much as I like my life here on the island, I miss you and wish I was with you both. Of course, I adore him. After all, he is my dearest friend's son, so how could I not.*

*Since I wrote previously the Chief's daughter has become betrothed. Her future husband is a tall, good-looking man who shows no bad inclination regarding her having had Reverend Morgain's baby. It seems strange how the islanders are more relaxed, accepting life and death more readily than we do in England. When I see the young couple together, I am delighted she has found such happiness. They look to be so much in love. Mumna says there will be a 'joining ceremony' which I believe means they will be married. The ceremony will be conducted according to island traditions but Mumna has declared they will also be blessed in our little church. After the ceremony there will be a big feast, followed by dancing and music which will go on for four days. I may not get much sleep during this time. They are to live on Percy's estate in a new home the islanders are building for them. Plus, they will receive gifts from everyone. I am making them baskets which I will fill with fruit. This will be the first island wedding I will have attended so I am excited.*

*Jayne and Thomas are well. She grows more rotund as each day passes but is still feeling well. Of her brother we have heard naught else. Hopefully he will remain abroad. I told Thomas about the Reverends situation and after much consideration he agreed Jayne should not be told any more details at this stage of her pregnancy. Thomas spoke to Percy who has written a letter requesting the Governor show some leniency, perhaps even allowing him to return to England. We can only wait and see what the outcome will be.*

*The new residents to the island have settled in and the older three children have started attending school. All are bright young things who have brought new life to our school. As promised Marta, Mrs Beckoff, has been teaching me Dutch and improving my French. The two ladies have done*

*their best to make the homestead comfortable and habitable.
I do believe, as far as the estate is concerned, the two brothers
have their job cut out as the estate has deteriorated
somewhat. Needless to say, Percy has offered all assistance.
I am sure the two brothers will soon have the place back in
order for they are hard workers.*

*Earlier this week, Percy called asking me to visit his
home over Christmas to dine with him. I felt inclined to
refuse, for I do not believe it proper that a young woman dine
alone with a gentleman. Obviously aware of my predicament,
he reassured me we will not be alone for his sister and family
will be joining us and he wants me to meet them. You can
imagine my surprise. This is the first time he has ever
mentioned a sister. They are to sail direct to his island home
over the next few days. How could I refuse, for if nothing else
curiosity has ensnared me? I will tell all next time I write.*

*A ship arrived this morning which will bring my letter
back to you. Doctor Jones was not on board. When I asked
the Captain, he informed me Andrew had been called home
to see his father. The Captain believes his parent is ill. I was
disappointed for I wanted to talk to him about your meeting.
I know you tell me not to worry about you, that you are well
but I need to hear it from someone who has seen you.*

*It is my hope, by the time you receive this letter, Laura
will have called on you, for I believe the Colonel and she will
have arrived in England. Please let me know if she calls and
how she fares. Also, please remind her, she has promised to
write me at the earliest opportunity.*

*The weather here is good and the crops have survived
the hurricane season. The winds can be quite frightening
when they are at their highest. I suffered some damage to the
school this time which Mumna quickly had repaired. With
ships arriving regularly to the island and Percy's assistance,
I have been able to obtain supplies. Kuala and I are creating
a beautiful Nativity scene for the school and our little church.
And, I have also been making small Christmas gifts for
everyone.*

*Speaking of Christmas, you will see I have sent gifts for both you and Baby James which I trust you enjoy. I will be honest and say I did not make the gift for Baby James myself but I did paint it all. I pray he will be delighted. Your gift will, I hope, remind you of your dearest friend, who sends you her deepest regards and love at this festive time. Perhaps it will also give you a feeling of the islands too. I shall close now dearest for I must finish wrapping the gifts before I deliver them to the ship. May this season bring you much joy and peace? Please pass my felicitations on to your dear parents.*

*All my love Mary*

*P.S. My dearest I must tell you how Mumna progresses with her writing. She is so much improved she has requested I include a letter written by herself. Which I have done. You will see it is addressed to Her Majesty Queen Victoria. She has been so supportive of me I could not, in this request, refuse her. You may find this quite strange but I believe in her sincerity. So, if there is anything you can do to assist me, I will forever be in your debt.*

*Love Mary*


Here are the contents of Mumna's letter to Lizzie:

*Salutations Madam Lizzie*

*I am Mumna, wife of Chief Tonga and friend of Miss Mary.*

*Madam you will know your friend is in good cheer and I care for her as my own daughter.*

*I ask you please have this letter sent to your gracious Queen Victoria.*

*May your child grow to be a strong man who will take good care of his mother as all good sons should?*

*Mumna X*
*Queen of Barbuda Islands*


And the contents of the letter to Queen Victoria:

*To Her Most Gracious Majesty, Queen Victoria*
*I Mumna, Queen of Barbuda with my husband Chief*

*Tonga, do send you our best regards.*

*We hope to find you in the best of health.*

*Our islands are most blessed. Should you wish for some banana, sugar cane or other foods we have these here in great numbers. You are most welcome to receive them as gifts with no payment needed.*

*We also offer Your Majesty a place to stay should you wish to visit with us. Your Majesty would be most welcome. There would be a great feast in your honour.*

*We wish you good cheer and may all your feasts be merry ones.*

     *Mumna X        Tonga X*
     *Queen Mumna and Chief Tonga*


Happy with the contents Mary sealed her letter. Finishing wrapping her parcel, she took it down to the dockside to give to the Captain.

That night before retiring, she wrote in her journal: *It has been another strange day. It seems my days are often full of surprises. When Mumna called with the letter for Queen Victoria I was shocked, considering I wasn't aware she even knew of our Queen. In some way I am pleased she has written the letter herself, for it makes my teaching of her all the more worthwhile. My only wish, is that there will be a happy outcome.*

# Twenty-five

As time passed pleasantly for Mary, so it did for Lizzie. One day it dawned on her that she had been a widow for almost a year. Baby James was growing bigger each day, looking more like his father, as well as taking after him in manner. His character was placid and happy, also like his Fathers, which pleased Lizzie greatly.

Since Edith's last visit, Lizzie had heard nothing more from the sisters, having instructed the solicitor to act on her behalf. It was agreed he would handle the affairs of the estate, thus relieving any pressure on her Father. They all agreed a non-family member was perhaps better in handling her affairs. Lizzie had been surprised to discover her financial circumstances. Already a young woman of status this was, in reality, of little interest to her. In fact, she was bored by the whole process.

A few short weeks later, Lizzie returned home to discover her Mother in the drawing room, talking to a lady and gentleman. He was dressed in a uniform while the lady was attired in what was obviously new winter clothing. Going forward the lady placed a small letter in her hand. Recognising the handwriting, Lizzie realised it was from Mary. It being a letter of introduction for Colonel and Laura Johnstone. She was delighted to meet Mary's island friends, being eager to question them about Mary. The remainder of the afternoon was spent chatting together. It was as if they had known each other forever. And, in some way they had, both being close to Mary, who discussed in her letter's details of each of them with the other.

It was during the course of the conversation that the Colonel mentioned he was looking for a town house to rent. At his comment Lizzie said, "I happen to own a town house which is empty. It is furnished and has servants. If it suits, you may rent it." Laura was delighted, with arrangements being made for them to visit the house the following day.

As Christmas approached Dr Jones became a regular visitor to Mountford House. Fortunately, Lizzie's parents did not object for they found Andrew to be a most personable young man. Whether they thought he had an interest in their daughter is only to be guessed at. What mattered most to them was that Lizzie should have someone to look after her and Baby James. Not that they were wanting her to move away but, being ever practical, they understood the necessity of ensuring their daughter and Grandson were cared for after they were gone. As Lizzie appeared to like the doctor more than any other young gentleman, Lord Mountford asked, "Andrew, my wife and I wondered if you would like to join us on Christmas Day?"

Without hesitation Andrew eagerly replied. "I would be most delighted Sir and thank you for your kind invitation. Earlier in the morning I will have to attend my father who is still unwell but I will join you after the church service if that is agreeable." It was.

Lizzie asked if Laura and the Colonel could also join them, being their first Christmas since returning to England. She felt the couple might be lost, not being close to their island friends at this festive time. Her father readily agreed to her request.

In the days leading up to Christmas Lizzie threw herself into the excitement of buying gifts for everyone. As well as helping the servants decorate the house and tree. Occasionally Andrew would join her in these endeavours, causing the house to be filled with the sound of happy laughter. The sound pleased her parents, especially after the sadness of the previous year.

A few days before Christmas Day, Lizzie was surprised to receive a visit from Captain Morrison. He too had become a regular caller, always taking time out to ensure Lizzie received her young friends' letters at the earliest opportunity. This Christmas was one such visit. "I have called to offer my seasonal greetings and to deliver a parcel entrusted to me by Miss Watson." Not long afterwards, Andrew arrived. He of course, was delighted to meet the Captain again, which meant both men spent more time on the visit than each had originally planned. Shortly afterwards Lord Mountford, entering the drawing room, was surprised to find all three gaily laughing. The sight of his daughter in such high spirits pleased him greatly. It was perhaps at this point that he began to understand and appreciate the relevance of his daughter's friendship with the young woman on the islands. Greeting the Captain warmly, Lord Mountford enquired, "Pray Sir, tell me how does Miss Watson fare."

The Captain smiled. "When last I saw her, she was well and in fine spirits."

"Please extend my sincere felicitations to her the next time you meet." Her father's response surprised Lizzie. Yet she was happy, as it seemed at long last, he was accepting her friendship with Mary.

Later, after the two gentlemen had departed, Lizzie retired to her room to read her letter. She was pleasantly surprised by the contents of the parcel Mary had sent. After reading the letter from Mumna she requested an immediate audience with her father, whereupon she showed him the missive for the Queen. He in turn expressed his surprise at the content. After giving the matter some thought, His Lordship decided to pass the letter on to an acquaintance at the Foreign Office. Satisfied her father would do all he could, Lizzie retired to her room to finish reading Mary's letter?

Having read it through a couple of times Lizzie decided to write to tell her about the last few weeks and her visitors. She wanted her friend to know she was thinking of her at this special time of the year.

*My Dearest Mary*

*Once again, I feel the warmth of your affection coming through your letter, which pleases me. Baby James is well and growing bigger daily. He is crawling and is such a delight to both his Grandparents and his Mother. Soon it will* be Christmas and Baby James' first birthday.

Dr Jones has now called a number of times. I find him a most amusing and considerate person. He is also very attentive to Baby James, willingly taking him on his knee when he cries. This pleases me greatly. Father appears to have some regard for him for they have spent much time together discussing politics. Apparently, he remains on dry land due to his father's ill health. Sadly, that gentleman may not have long for this world. I know Andrew worries about his father deeply as he is all alone since his wife passed some two years ago. I understand his feelings for it has now been almost a year since I lost my poor James. But I will not let these sad memories spoil the festive season. As for me, my own health and state of mind have vastly improved, and I am feeling more like my old self.

I admit to being a little shocked upon discovering the additional letters enclosed in your package. Please tell Mumna I thank her for her well wishes. As for father, he was more surprised to discover that Mumna is a Queen and she has written to our Queen. Under the circumstances he decided to take her letter to the Foreign Affairs Minister, who happens to be a good friend of his. We now await a response. Father says the Minister will probably share the letter with Her Majesty. It makes me smile in amazement, that you and I, may be the instigators of diplomatic relationships between our two Queens!

How glad I am to learn you are progressing well with your languages, and look forward to the time when we speak French together. When that time will be, I know not, but I pray and hope it will be some time soon. Oh, Mary do you realise it is now almost three years since we last set eyes upon each other. How we must both have changed from the silly young women we were back then.

There is still so much to tell you my dearest but where to start. First, I have met your friend Laura. What a delightful creature she is. And, of course the Colonel is a gentleman. We both felt an immediate connection. As if we had known

178

*each for years and in a way, we have because of you my sweet friend. We sat and talked together for over two hours. Laura has told me about the islands and in such a way that I feel as if I know them well. She has promised to write to you as soon as she is settled. The Colonel mentioned they were looking for somewhere to live so I have offered them the Williamson town house. To be honest, I do not believe I will ever reside there, at least not for the foreseeable future for there are too many memories for me. Laura is delighted with the idea. They will take up residence shortly. Although the Colonel returned to his regiment Laura says he has been disappointed as the Ministry will not send him overseas. He remains in the Ministry of Defence offices conducting operations from a desk, much to his frustration but Laura's thankfulness.*

*Of the Williamson sisters I have heard naught else. All dealings with them are now handled by our Solicitor who calls each month to give his report. So far, I have let Father handle the affair but Andrew tells me I am more than capable of taking care of my son's inheritance. As such, I now sit in the meetings with them. To be honest Mary I find the whole thing quite boring but at least I know a little more of how the estate works.*

*This year we have decorated the house. We did not do it last year due to the sad circumstances. Father says we are to have a New Year's Eve party to which we have invited many friends. Laura, the Colonel and Andrew will join us as I feel their presence will bring me closer to you. Over the last few days I have been buying small gifts for each of them as a surprise. I have put your gifts under the tree in readiness for Christmas morning. I find myself quite excited as this will be Baby James' first real Christmas. You will understand why I do not count last year.*

*I see from your letter you have resolved your dilemma regarding the manner in which you address Lord Falshaw. I am so glad. You tell me he has a sister coming to stay on a private yacht, how intriguing. I would not concern yourself about meeting her for I know she will love you my Dear One, as much as I do.*

*Tomorrow evening I shall be attending a ball at the palace and for the first time in a year I will be wearing a gown which is not black. Of course, it will not be as pretty or as gay as the ones I normally wear. But, Mama says, as I am coming out of mourning, it is okay to wear a dress more acceptable to a woman my age. Whatever that is supposed to mean? I am so excited as I haven't been to a ball in ages. I will tell you all about it when next I write.*

*Anyway, my dear I will close now as the footman is waiting to take the letter to the post.*

*Take care of yourself my Dear One. Enjoy your stay on His Lordship's estate and have a peaceful, pleasant and joyous Christmas time.*

*With all my good wishes and love for a festive season.*

*Your loving Lizzie and Baby James*

# Twenty-six

Christmas Day turned out to be much the way Mary had described it would be in her letter to Lizzie. The morning service was taken by the new Chaplain. A young man from Scotland who had arrived a few weeks previously. His name was Gordon Scott, he was 30 years old and the youngest son of seven children. It was not long after being ordained that he had met and married his young wife Sally. Having worked as an aide, the Bishop had sponsored him, allowing him to progress in his calling. When the vacancy of Chaplain to the islands had become available, it was agreed he should accept the post. He was most observant of Mumna and the Chief and was therefore warmly welcomed by the pair.

Initially, Mary was a little concerned by what Jayne's reaction might be. However, she need not have worried for Jayne took them to her heart. Gordon's wife, Sally, was an experienced midwife which Mary considered might have helped Jayne make up her mind. It certainly did for Mary, as she knew her friend would be in good hands when the time came for her to give birth.

She wrote in her diary: *I am delighted by the new Chaplain's wife. She is a lovely warm-hearted person. Her husband Gordon seems such an energetic man who gets on well with everyone. I like them both exceedingly well and am looking forward to the Christmas morning service.*

On Christmas morning, Mary left her home, meeting up with Jayne, Thomas and Percy. A radiant looking Jayne greeted her with a large smile and a thickened figure. Her friend looked the picture of health and Mary was happy for her. As the four strolled into the little church they were greeted by a number of people. The place was full, making the Christmas service a joyous one. Once the service was over the whole congregation made their way outside amid much excited chatter. Heading towards the village centre they were delighted to see the islanders had prepared a large area ready for their festivities. Taking their places on the mats spread on the ground the refreshments were passed around. Throughout the day there was much laughter and merriment. When everyone had eaten, gifts were passed out.

Mary had made something extra special for Mumna. A cape, which she had embroidered with tiny colourful flowers and feathers. It looked grand, and it was obvious Mumna was delighted by the gift. Choosing for Percy had been a harder task. Finally, Mary had settled on a new quill pen, making it from a large feather she had found. Passing the gift to him, she held her breath, hoping he would like it. She need not have worried, for he was delighted. He in return gave Mary a bolt of silk of the most gorgeous pale lilac, a colour he knew suited her well. She was delighted with the exquisite gift. Afterwards she gave out the remainder of her other gifts.

Percy sat watching Mary receiving presents in return. Surprise was clearly written on her face, being close to tears at the thoughtfulness of the givers. It dawned on Percy that she was unaware of her standing within the community. Later she told him, "It has been the best Christmas Day ever. I am overwhelmed by people's generosity." Percy smiled at her girlish enjoyment, and he couldn't help but think how lovely she looked.

After the party everyone sang Christmas Carols, much to the amusement and delight of the island people. As day moved into night and the evening drew to a close Percy escorted Mary back to her home, helping her carry her numerous presents. Reaching the hut, she turned towards him. "Thank you for your assistance. Would you care to come inside and have a drink? I have some sherry I keep for special occasions. I think this is one."

Whether it was she or Percy who was most surprised by the request, after all it was late in the evening, neither was sure. But both were delighted at her forthrightness. Taking a seat inside he thanked her for the drink. As they sat sipping the sherry, they made small talk. And, for some reason Mary couldn't explain she began telling Percy about her past life. Sitting still he quietly listened, not wanting to stop her mid-flow. This was the closest they had ever been. Besides, he was trying to understand the emotions currently flowing through him.

Looking up, Mary suddenly realised she had been talking for some time without Percy speaking. Seeing him watching her, she blushed and instantly closed her mouth. Not wanting to spoil the moment he realised maybe it would be a good time to leave, before the silence became too uncomfortable. Smiling he stood. "Thank you for the drink, and the conversation. I appreciate and am honoured to have been given your confidence. But I had better leave, so you can get some sleep ready for your visit tomorrow."

Mary followed him out of the hut. "Thank you for escorting me home." Turning he took her hand in his. Slowly raising it to his mouth he kissed it before reluctantly letting go. Then, just as quickly, he leant forward and brushed her lips with his, lingering for a mere second before pulling back. "Goodnight my dear. Sleep well."

Before she could respond he was gone, heading for the docks where his yacht was anchored. As she watched him walk away, Mary tenderly caressed her mouth. Once he was out of sight she went back inside the hut, a small smile playing on her face. That night Mary slept soundly, dreaming of that brief kiss again and again and again.

Up early the next morning Mary was filled with excited anticipation. Today she was going to Percy's home to meet his sister. She wondered how he would behave after last night and whether or not he regretted the kiss. Only time would tell.

Taking out her journal she began to write: *What a joyous and delightful Christmas Day I have had. The morning started in good cheer and continued throughout the day. Everyone has been so generous to me. I have received so many gifts, it feels as if all the Christmas Days of my life have been rolled into one. Percy kissing me goodnight has left me*

*feeling confused for I am unsure of his intentions. I hope he*
*does not think ill of me for not pushing him away. I must be*
*truthful, if only here in my journal, and say how much I*
*enjoyed his kiss. Am I wicked for doing so? I hope not.*

Two hours later Lord Falshaw presented himself at the hut ready to escort Mary to his yacht. As Kuala and Chula watched the couple walk off to the dockside, they turned to look at each other. A knowing smile passed between them. Both agreed His Lordship was taken with Miss, and unbeknown to her, Miss was taken with His Lordship.

As the yacht sailed across the blue waters to Percy's island home, Mary felt herself relax. She had become a little tense at the thought of the forthcoming visit. Despite herself Mary was still aware of her social status. She was beneath Percy and therefore his sister. Although she was accepted by most of the island residents, they were predominately American and therefore more tolerant. But she wondered if Percy's sister would accept her as readily as he did.

The island was drawing closer so Mary prepared herself for some rejection. Had she been aware of the welcome she was about to receive she would not have fretted so much. Especially as when landing she was met by the most welcoming, adorable creature she had ever met. Alighting from the yacht, Mary was surprised when a young woman literally threw herself at Percy, being so excited at seeing him. She was followed closely by two young boys, Percy's nephews, who in turn threw themselves at their Uncle. Mary smiled as Percy laughed out loud, taking his sister's and the boy's onslaught in good humour.

Extricating himself from the clinging arms, he turned to draw Mary forward to meet his sister Amelia and her two sons, Richard and Martin. Introductions over they were suddenly hailed by a large booming voice. It was Jackson Stanton, Amelia's husband. With the greetings over Amelia took charge. Taking hold of Mary's arm, she escorted her towards the house. As they walked, she declared in her southern American drawl, "I want you to know how pleased

I am to meet you. I am sure we will become the best of friends." The warmth of her greeting left Mary feeling totally at ease. Smiling back, Mary agreed they would.

Over the next few days, time passed in a whirl of laughter and excitement, and when the moment came for Mary to return home, she felt sad. The ride back to her island home passed all too quickly and it was not long before Percy was escorting her to the hut. As they arrived, she turned towards him. "I want to thank you for a most enjoyable stay. I cannot tell you how delightful I found your sister."

Percy smiled. "I am happy you like her. I wish you two to be good friends." Whereupon he kissed her hand and then her cheek before departing.

Watching him leave, Mary felt a loss and for a moment she didn't know what to do.

That evening she wrote in her journal: *What a delightful person Amelia is. She was most welcoming. Greeting me as if we had been friends for years. Little does she realise how relaxing her presence made me feel. Percy's home was a wonderful surprise. I am amazed at how easily I felt at home and the few days I have spent there have left me feeling most refreshed. What a marvellous, delightful Christmas it has been. My only disappointment is my not having seen my dear Lizzie or Laura.*

A few days later Mary went to visit the Van der Kerkoff's, taking Kuala with her so the young girl could visit her cousin who worked for the family. Mary thought their house was exceedingly comfortable and pleasant. Being shown around she exclaimed, "What a delight everything is, and what a great job you two ladies have done, in making the house feel so welcoming." Her comment caused them to beam as they thanked Mary for her kind words.

The evening was a great success with Mary eating food she had never tasted before. Marta explained they were traditional recipes from their homeland. Strange or different they may have been but Mary still found them delicious. The two young women stayed overnight, with Mary being delighted by the hospitality shown them, proving the Van der Kerkoff's and the Beckoffs were two wonderful families. The following day Peter escorted them back home, taking great care to express his gratitude to Mary for her friendship to his wife and sister-in-law. He admitted it was not something they had expected. "However, I am most happy for your consideration."

His compliment made Mary blush. "How could I not like two such delightful ladies. And I thank you for your generous hospitality."

It was a couple of weeks later that a ship struck anchor in the harbour and at long last Mary received a letter from Laura. As she sat reading, Kuala came in to say, "Miss you are to come to the main hut at once."

Putting the letter in her pocket Mary quickly made her way to the village centre. Arriving at the Chief's hut Mary wondered what the problem was, as there were a large number of islanders standing around. Catching sight of her, Mumna brought Mary forward, whereupon the Queen introduced her to a Major Philip Smithson of Her Majesty's Army. Mary discovered the officer had come from England on a special mission. To deliver a reply from Queen Victoria. Pleased and delighted that Mumna had received such a formal response, Mary smiled. When requested to, she took a place between Mumna and the Major on a mat outside the hut. Once settled Mumna instructed Mary to read the contents of the letter out loud. She wanted everyone present to hear what the great Queen of England had written to her.

Clearing her throat Mary began reading:

*"To Your Most Gracious Majesties, King Tonga and Queen Mumna.*

*I am instructed by her Britannic Majesty Queen Victoria Regina to extend her heartfelt wishes and greetings to Chief Tonga and Queen Mumna.*

*Her Britannic Majesty takes this opportunity to thank your gracious Majesties for their kind offer and asks me to reassure you that the Royal Family are well provided for. Her*

*Majesty would not wish to deprive the island nor its residents
of any of its fine produce.*

*Her Britannic Majesty further instructs me to extend
her grateful appreciation for the consideration of a residence
should their Majesties care to visit the islands.
Disappointingly, her Royal duties prevent Her Gracious
Majesty from making such a journey at this time.*

*I am also instructed by Her Majesty's Government to
say they would be pleased to offer their hospitability to your
good selves should you care to visit Great Britain.*

*Her Majesty, Her Husband and Her Government are
delighted to extend the warm hand of friendship to Chief
Tonga and his lady wife Queen Mumna at this festive season.*

*I am your humble servant.*
*Lord Montague Charles Short,*
*Minister for Foreign Affairs*

Everyone was amazed at the contents of the letter.
Whilst Mary had read the letter out loud, Mumna had sat
regally with a big smile on her face. Once she finished
reading Mary solemnly handed the letter back to Mumna,
who pretended to read it herself. Mary hid a small smile at
her action. Whilst Mumna could write fairly well she still had
some difficulty with her reading. Particularly when the
writing was as flowery as this was. However, the importance
of the visitor and the letter was not lost on Mary. She hoped
Mumna and the Chief would make every effort to
accommodate the Major while he stayed on the island.

Later, while the Chief escorted the Major around the
village Mary took the opportunity to speak to Mumna. "I feel
it most important, that when the Major leaves, he goes with a
good impression of the islands and its residents."

Looking at Mary, Mumna nodded her head. "But of
course. You are right. We will make every effort to make him
welcome. Is there anything we should do?" The pair then sat
and discussed what should be done to ensure the correct
impression was given.

The Major intended remaining on the island for only a short period of time before returning to England. In the meantime, Mary was appointed to act as his guide. It was while talking to him she discovered he had been a Royal Equerry to Her Majesty for five years. She liked him, taking the job of escort seriously, and making every effort to ensure he met all the island residents.

# Twenty-seven

Over the next few days Mary escorted the Major everywhere. He visited the various plantations and while at the Van der Kerkoff's they bumped into Percy. Introducing the two men, she was unaware of Percy watching how the young man looked at Mary. Suddenly he felt some strange sensations in him and began to wonder if this man was competing for Mary's affections? Did she like him? The thought disturbed him and, for the first time in his life, he was actually jealous. A feeling which took him totally by surprise. It was only after learning the young man wouldn't be on the island long that Percy breathed a sigh of relief. Making his excuses he left as he needed to investigate the feelings raging inside him.

Unbeknown to Mary it seemed the Major was having similar feelings of his own. He was wishing he didn't have to leave so soon as he found Mary most attractive. As the end of his stay approached, the Major approached her. "Miss Watson, Mary. I wondered if it would be an imposition if I were to write to you once I am back to England? Also, if I were to return to the island sometime in the future would you object to my calling on you."

Although surprised, Mary could find no reason to object to his request so she readily agreed. If she were honest, she was flattered by his attentions. Besides, she didn't really expect him to return. However, had she known what the Major thought of her, she might not have been so eager to say yes! In reality he had been trying to think of a way to extend his stay. Or, at the very least, return to the islands soon. Having completed her duties as guide Mary made her excuses, explaining she must write a letter to her dear friend. The Major was due to leave in a few days and, even though they would part friends, Mary would be relieved.

Back in her home she took up her pen.

Dearest Lizzie,

What a delight to receive your mail. Not only your letter but also one from Laura. Most surprising however, is that we have received a formal response from the Ministry of Foreign Affairs. A letter addressed to Mumna and the Chief was delivered by a most delightful young officer called Major Philip Smithson. I have to say Mumna was exceedingly pleased and proud. She called a meeting and once all were present instructed me to read the contents of the letter aloud. Kuala repeated my words in the islands own tongue. There was much rejoicing. I was given the task of escorting the young officer around the plantations to meet all the residents. He proved to be a most personable young man. Please extend my sincere appreciation to your Father for taking the trouble to approach the Minister. The response has made Mumna and the Chief extremely happy indeed.

The letter from Laura gave all the news of her travels through America. Then she described her meeting with you. She sounds to be pleased with her stay in England. And has, of course, fallen in love with Baby James, telling me what an adorable child he is. I am therefore reassured you are all happy which pleases me greatly. I am truly delighted you and she like each other and will, I hope, become good friends.

Poor Doctor Jones. We are all sorry to hear about his Father. Please tell him our thoughts and prayers are with him. He has been sorely missed. The replacement ship's doctor does not appear to be as friendly or as caring towards his patients as Andrew. I also know the Captain misses his company but I am grateful you have offered him support and comfort at this difficult time.

And now my dear I have a great deal to tell you. As promised, I will start with my visit to Percy's home. The house is large and stylish but obviously very much a bachelor's home. When we arrived, there was a large yacht in the harbour which belonged to Percy's brother-in-law. He is called Jackson and is American. Percy's sister is called Amelia. Their accents have a most peculiar drawl but nothing *like Dorothy's. I find them both exceedingly pleasant. Amelia has a delightful smile and obviously loves her husband deeply. They have two boys, Richard and Martin. Normally they would have been at naval school in Boston but were allowed home to visit their favourite Uncle over Christmas.*

*The first evening we four dined alone, giving me a chance to learn more about Amelia and her life in South Carolina. The following evening Percy invited some of the other island residents to join us. There was quite a party atmosphere. The last evening, we four dined on Jackson's yacht. Lizzie, I have never felt more at ease or as relaxed as I did during my stay there. Everyone treated me as an equal and I admit to feeling sad when it was time to leave.*

*Oh! I must tell you, while at Percy's I saw the Chiefs daughter with her new husband. Both are glowing with such happiness. And no wonder as they are expecting their first child. I feel such envy for their contentment.*

*A few days after I returned home, I spent the evening with the Van der Kerkoff's, remaining overnight. The bedroom I used contained some delightful pieces of furniture. It appears they brought a number of items with them. Greta has hung beautiful lace curtains at the windows which she says are a speciality of their homeland. Both families welcomed me warmly, making me feel at home. Kuala went with me, thus taking the opportunity to visit her cousin who works at the house. Mumna's family is quite large. When I mentioned this to Dorothy, she told me it is because the islanders are all related to one another. Something to do with inter-breeding?*

*Dorothy is doing well and sends you her best regards. Our sewing circle has grown in numbers as more ladies have joined us. This year we held our pre-Christmas gathering at Jayne's house which Mrs Conway, Beatrice organised. Beatrice and her husband live on one of the north islands. She and her husband Roland are jolly people. They often make me smile, lifting one's spirits when around.*

*The gift you sent me was wonderful and has been*

*admired by everyone. Thank you, my dearest, for thinking of me. I am hopeful that both you and Baby James enjoyed your gifts.*

*My days are busy with the school, my hobbies or with visiting the various residents. Our community has become so extensive I find I have an active and enjoyable social life. The most amazing aspect of it all is how I am held in such regard which I still find a little strange. Only Mrs Maberley, and you dear Lizzie, ever behaved this way towards me. Percy continues to call regularly and I find myself looking forward to our conversations. As each day passes, I discover more and more about him, so my initial impression of him being aloof is totally dispelled.*

*I will close My Sweet as I hear Major Smithson calling. By the time you receive this letter the festive season will be upon you and as such I hope you have a joyous time.*

*Please give Baby James a big hug and a kiss from his Aunt Mary.*

*Take care, my dear,*
*All my love Mary*


Sealing the letter Mary welcomed the young Major, who was in reality sorry to be leaving. Although Mary found him personable, she did not reciprocate any emotions he may have for her. She offered her goodbyes with no deep sorrow.

Later she wrote in her journal: *I am pleased and delighted by the response received from Her Majesty. A letter alone would have been wonderful but to have it personally delivered by a Royal Equerry shows a great honour to Mumna and the Chief. I admit I liked Major Smithson and if my affections were not placed elsewhere, I might have found his departure upsetting. But I feel no regret, for I realise I am becoming more and more attracted to Percy. I do not believe anything will come of it but I know I cannot commit my heart elsewhere if there is a chance, he feels the same.*

# Twenty-eight

Christmas Day in England proved to be one of great joy in the Mountford House. Just as Mary enjoyed her festive season so did Lizzie and Baby James. Surrounded by her family and friends, the day proved to be an enjoyable and entertaining one. Following the Church service, a number of the guests returned to the house for Christmas Lunch. Later, His Lordship, being a generous employer, gave each staff member a cash bonus, which they thought a fortune. Plus, a gift chosen by his wife and daughter. Afterwards everyone toasted the Royal Family before the guests and family sat down to a delightful meal of many courses. With lunch over the guests and family watched Baby James open his presents before they too were presented with a gift.

Lizzie had become more excited as Christmas drew nearer, wanting to see Baby James' reaction to Mary's gift. She was not disappointed. As soon as her son caught sight of the farmyard, he laughed out loud, delighted with the brightly coloured animals. Following the gift opening everyone gathered around the piano to sing Christmas Carols or tell Xmas stories. The day was filled with lots of laughter, which carried on into the evening when a light supper was served.

Later, as Lizzie lay in bed, she felt happier and more contented than she had since her husband's passing. Of course, the euphoria may have been partly due to Andrew taking the opportunity to kiss her under the mistletoe!

Before retiring she wrote in her diary: *What a glorious, happy day. I am pleased Baby James is delighted with Mary's gift. I think her most clever to have designed and painted all the items herself. Island life must be bringing the creative spirit out in her. The party was full of cheer and merriment. And when Andrew caught me under the mistletoe, I offered no resistance to him kissing me. He is a handsome man and I find myself more attracted to him each day.*

Andrew was now calling at the house regularly. As Lizzie found talking to him easy, one day she began telling him about the problems with the Williamson estate. Apparently, the sisters were once again being difficult by not complying to the terms set them. The Solicitor had been left with no choice but to ask her father to intervene. Andrew encouraged her to take charge, telling her she was perfectly capable of sorting the matter out. Lizzie was grateful for his support but still, she fretted over facing the sisters. However, perhaps it was time for her to take a stand.

Thus, a few days into the New Year, Lizzie, her parents and the Solicitor left for the Williamson estate. Although she wasn't looking forward to the visit, Lizzie realised she should be present. Fortunately, having the support of her father made her feel confident enough to face the sisters. But Lizzie's worries were not unfounded. When Edith was confronted, she behaved in a most supercilious manner, believing she could say whatever she wished. But, the longer the discussions went on the angrier Lizzie got. As did her parents. Finally, Lizzie could take no more, reacting in a way which shocked all those present.

Standing up, so Edith was forced to look up at her, Lizzie spoke in a quiet but strong voice. "Enough! You will be quiet, and you will cease your distasteful behaviour. You have already said far too much for someone of your supposed sensibilities." At this outburst Edith went white, as did her sister. Lizzie's parents and the Solicitor sat staring, surprised by the unexpected turn of events.

Taking a deep breath Lizzie continued. "I will tell you exactly what is going to happen. Unless you comply with everything as previously agreed, there will be no option but for you to remove yourselves from the estate. You have only been allowed to stay here, due to my generosity, in memory of my dear darling James." Pausing, she took a breath. "Now, if I hear one more complaint from my Solicitor regarding your behaviour then I will come back and I... will...

personally... throw... you... out."

Edith began to rise ready to respond. But before she could speak Lizzie, held up her hand, "Stop. Please remain seated and silent. I haven't finished speaking." She then went on to berate both ladies. "I am extremely angry with you. My poor James will be turning in his grave at your unladylike behaviour, especially towards his widow and his son. It is unbecoming in women of your mature years and I will no longer tolerate it. Do you understand me?"

While Lizzie had spoken, her mother and father had sat in silent wonder, amazed by their daughter's demeanour. Never had she been known to speak in such a way and they were shocked. The Solicitor, however, wanted to grab Lizzie's hand and shake it warmly for achieving what he had, so far not done. As for the sisters, both were white, too shocked to say anything, remaining seated, heads bowed. Eventually they reluctantly agreed to what Lizzie had said.

Two days later the party returned to town where Lizzie told Andrew what had happened. Smiling, he congratulated her warmly, telling her how proud he was of her. Even Laura, who had been looking after Baby James whilst the family were in the country, applauded her actions. "How proud Mary will be when she hears." The thought made Lizzie smile.

That evening Lizzie wrote in her diary: *I am in a most happy frame of mind. The problem with the sisters is, hopefully resolved. Yet, I feel this will not be the last time we hear from them. Laura has become such a dear friend that I find myself spending more time with her. She brings me closer to Mary. As for my feelings for Andrew they grow daily. As I believe his do for me. Baby James has taken such a liking to him, going to sit with him whenever he visits. I feel my life is good.*

Lizzie's life settled into a normal happy routine. Andrew continued to call often, as did Laura, meaning Lizzie found herself fully occupied. With her mourning period over she was now attending soirées and parties. The relationship with Laura was growing, which helped both ladies cope with missing Mary. As for Andrew, Lizzie was delighted to see how her son loved him. With the arrival of better weather, the three of them were often seen walking in the park together. Love was certainly blossoming.

It was about three weeks later that Lizzie received an unexpected visitor. Major Philip Smithson, Equerry to Her Majesty Queen Victoria. Entering the room, the young man discovered the most adorable creature he had ever set eyes on. Sitting alongside her was a young gentleman holding a child on his knees. It was, he thought, a picture of happy family bliss. Watching them, the Major realised the pair were deeply in love, and for a moment, he felt pangs of envy as his thoughts flitted to Mary. Pulling himself together, he bowed and formally introduced himself. "Lady Williamson, Major Philip Smithson at your service. Forgive my uninvited interruption but I have recently returned from the islands where I gave my solemn promise to deliver this to you." And he proffered a letter.

Recognising the handwriting Lizzie knew it was from Mary. "You are most welcome, Sir. I thank you for your thoughtfulness. Please, take a seat. I will have some refreshments brought."

Once the Major was sat Lizzie asked, "Please, tell me about your recent visit and how my dear friend fares?" The Major was happy to tell all, regaling them with details of his journey. Andrew was, for a moment, slightly taken aback at how personally the Major spoke of Mary. Lizzie however, found nothing wrong with the young man's manner.

After the Major departed Lizzie and Andrew discussed the visitor? Taking the opportunity Andrew expressed his concerns. "It appears to me the Major seemed most familiar when speaking of Mary."

Lizzie laughed. "Do you think so. Does it matter? I am sure if Mary feels anything for the Major, she will write to tell me, so please do not worry." Andrew said no more on the subject.

Looking at her it dawned on him how much he loved

her and Baby James. Without a moment's hesitation or thought, he leant forward and kissed her gently. Although taken by surprise Lizzie found herself enjoying his kiss. She was loath to stop him. Moving apart at last, Andrew apologised. Placing her fingers on his mouth, Lizzie whispered, "Shush." Stopping him from speaking further she smiled, leaned forward and kissed him back. Later, the pair sat looking into each other's eyes, amazed at their feelings. No more was said of Mary or the Major, although Andrew hoped she was safe. He loved Lizzie, but was concerned for Mary, a dear friend, not wishing to see her hurt.

That evening Lizzie retired early and wrote in her journal: *I never realised it was possible to love more than one person in a lifetime. Am I right to think of Andrew in this way so soon after James' passing? And yet, I am sure my dear James would not want me to be alone for ever. I will ask Mary what she thinks.*

Taking up Mary's letter, she began to read it through. But lying on her bed her thoughts wandered to Andrew, remembering the feel of his kisses, which left her with a warm glow. Thinking of him made her smile and on this thought she fell into a dreamless sleep.

The following morning Lizzie woke early. Finishing reading Mary's letter, she sat at the desk and wrote her reply.

*Dearest Mary*

*I am so pleased you liked my gift. It delights me to know you will think of me whenever you wear it. Christmas Day here was such a joyous occasion. Baby James adored the little animals you sent him. He plays with them often. And the basket is a delight. I have placed it on my dressing table and shall keep my handkerchiefs inside. When I walk past, I find the aroma wafting from it, reminds me instantly of you my dear one.*

*There were many visitors over the holiday season including Laura and the Colonel and of course, Andrew Jones. The time has left me in a most happy and settled state of mind.*

*I know this will surprise you, but since I last wrote, I have visited the Williamson estate. I did so because the Solicitor reported some problems with the sisters. They were being most difficult. I must be honest dearest I felt some trepidation about meeting Edith again. But, by the time we left they understood if they want to stay, they will have to comply with the terms laid down. To be truthful, I vented my anger against their horrible behaviour. I did not believe I could ever behave in such a way but I feel I have honoured my husband's memory.*

*Whilst away Baby James stayed with Laura, who was delighted to look after him. I think she was secretly sad at having to give him back having enjoyed looking after him. Needless to say, even though he was obviously happy to see me I believe he was sorry to leave her for she spoils him. Too much, I think. The Colonel is still working at the Ministry, leaving Laura feeling fairly contented since he has not been sent overseas. She visits me often and I am delighted with her company. Thank you so much my sweet one for sending her to me. She has confided in me that she would love to return to their island home but cannot foresee when that will be.*

*And now I have a confession to make. Andrew has kissed me. The first time was under the mistletoe at Christmas, but more recently too. I confess at neither time did I find it unpleasant. Although it has left me feeling confused. You know I loved James dearly so it concerns me how I can feel so affected by Andrew's attentions. What do you think Mary? Am I wicked for liking the touch of Andrew's lips against mine? Can I allow him to come closer or should I keep him at arm's length? Oh dear, I so need your guidance. You are the only person I can confide in. I know Father and Mamma like him and he is wonderful with Baby James. Please advise me Dear One?*

*Apart from all I have written life here continues much as before yet my days are fulfilled. Baby James grows bigger and stronger each day and is now doing his best to crawl and talk. He is trying to walk as well which causes us much laughter. I feel my life is settled. I am so lucky to have such supportive parents and friends. Being a young widow is not easy but I believe I am coping well.*

*I must close now my dearest. This evening I am to have dinner with Laura, the Colonel and their guests. Going out to dinner is something I am starting to enjoy again. I also enjoy not having to wear black anymore so feel much more cheerful when in company.*

*Think often of Baby James and Me.*

*All My Love Lizzie*

# Twenty-nine

Not many days after returning from Percy's home Mary received an unexpected visitor. Amelia. Although pleasantly surprised, she wondered what the lady wanted. Despite that Mary made her welcome. Sitting Amelia began. "I wanted to come to let you know we are returning home but before leaving I came to extend an invitation to you. Perhaps, sometime soon you might come and visit our family home in Georgetown."

Mary was delighted by the invitation. "I am honoured and will most certainly visit you, should the opportunity arise." Mary couldn't see when or if such an event would ever take place as she had no plans to leave the islands in the foreseeable future. However, she chose not to disappoint Amelia by saying this out loud.

After Amelia had departed, Mary felt some sadness at the loss of her new friend, although her spirits soon rose when Percy arrived. He was in a good mood. "Tell me did my sister call to see you?"

"Oh yes. She came to say goodbye. She has invited me to visit her. I think her a delightful person." Lord Falshaw was happy Mary liked his sister, and feeling satisfied by her comments he left.

Two weeks later, Mary was woken in the early hours of the morning. Thomas had sent one of the islanders to fetch her to his wife's bedside. Jayne was in labour and was begging for her friend to attend without delay. Hurrying to get dressed Mary rushed down to the dockside, surprised to discover Lord Falshaw's yacht waiting for her. Standing onboard was Sally, the vicar's wife. Within fifteen minutes they had landed at the Johnstones. Calling out thanks to Percy, the two ladies quickly ran up the hillside towards a very agitated Thomas. Entering the house, the two young

200

women went straight to Jayne's room, finding her lying on the bed in a state of distress. Without hesitation Sally took charge. Firstly, by shooing Thomas from the room. Then by organising the servants into fetching everything she needed.

"What can I do to help," Mary asked?

"You look after Jayne while I finish getting things ready." Mary gave her a questioning look? "Talk to her. Soothe her mind."

Following Sally's instructions Mary sat down near her friend. Then taking hold of Jayne's hand, she began stroking it, talking soothingly to her. Soon organised, the midwife made sure Jayne was comfortable by helping her relax and easing her stress.

Poor Jayne's labour appeared to go on for hours. In reality it was less than five. As the time to give birth came closer Sally told Jayne what would happen and how she was to breathe to lessen the pain. Approximately one hour later Jayne gave birth to a bouncing baby girl. One tired but exceedingly happy mother lay back against the pillows totally exhausted.

As soon as baby and mother were cleaned and dressed, Mary fetched Thomas. Entering the room, a look of love passed between the happy parents. It was so wonderful Mary was filled with envy. The tenderness making her turn her head away at such a private moment? Looking on his daughter for the first time Thomas was filled with pride at what his wife had just achieved. Tears filled his eyes which he quickly wiped away.

Not long afterwards Percy entered the room. As Mary and Percy looked at the new Baby Thomas, after a slight nod from Jayne, asked, "We hope you will honour your promise to become our baby daughters' Godparents?"

The watching couple happily replied in unison. "Yes, of course. We are honoured to."

Returning to the room Sally shooed everyone out, saying Jayne needed her rest. Thomas took his time, before being urged to pull himself away from his wife and new daughter. Causing much amusement to everyone.

After Jayne was settled Sally joined the others on the veranda. Thomas insisted, "We must toast the new baby's health." Raising their glasses of champagne, they congratulated Thomas and Jayne, on their new daughter. Shortly afterwards breakfast was served on the veranda. During the meal there was much laughter and cheer. Later, Sally went to check her patient and once she was happy Jayne would be okay with the maids watching over her, the two young women returned to the main island.

Arriving back on shore, Sally called goodbye before dashing away to tell her husband the good news. Percy insisted on escorting Mary back to her hut. Still being full of joy over the birth she asked, "Would you care to join me in some refreshments?"

"I would be delighted."

Entering her hut Mary made them coffee which they took outside to drink. Sitting in the sun they made small talk about the previous night's event. Leaving the couple in peace Kuala went off to open the school, while Chula went to tell Mumna the happy news of the new baby. As she sat Mary felt settled and at ease. She found she always enjoyed the time spent talking to Percy.

Finishing his coffee Percy rose to take his leave. Before going he held his hand out to Mary. Pulling her to her feet he bent down and kissed her fervently on the lips. The kiss seemed to last an age, yet it was only a matter of seconds. As they moved apart, Percy apologised. "I am sorry for being so forward. It was ungentlemanly of me."

Without knowing why, some devil took hold of Mary. "Why? I'm not upset. In fact, I quite enjoyed the experience." Then realising what she had just said, Mary blushed profusely, begging his forgiveness for being so forward.

Percy laughed. "I do not think you are in the least bit forward. And I am in fact, quite pleased you enjoyed my kiss." Then taking her in his arms again, he kissed her once more, before bowing, bidding her good-day and leaving. As he headed towards his yacht, he was heard whistling. Mary stood watching him. Climbing aboard his yacht, he turned, waving once before disappearing below decks. Mary went inside the hut, a smile on her face.

Four days later a ship anchored in the harbour and Mary received a visit from the Captain. He was to impart some important news. Listening, she was surprised to learn that Percy's intervention with the Governor meant Reverend Morgain had now been set free. Luckily, he would not be returning to the island, having been instructed instead, to return direct to England where he was to report to the Bishop. Mary was relieved. She would tell Thomas of the situation once she was alone with him. She was sure he still wanted Jayne to remain unaware of the matter whilst recovering from the birth of their new daughter. One could only imagine what the Bishop would say to the Reverend.

With the passing days, Mary found her life settling back into a routine. Wanting to learn more of the other islands she spent much of her spare time visiting the various plantations. She discovered a great deal about the produce grown on the various estates. With the plantations expanding so the number of ships calling at the islands likewise increased. Which wasn't necessarily a bad thing as it meant the islanders were kept busy. It did, however, mean there were more strangers on the islands. The only downside being, that occasionally there was some minor trouble from some of the seamen onboard.

Percy had finally taken action. Mainly due to Mary having been accosted one day by a drunken crewman. Expressing his deep concern to Mumna about Mary's safety they agreed a new residence was to be built for her, only placed closer to the centre of the village. That way Mumna could watch over her more closely. He had initially wanted Mary to move to his island home but she had told him, "It just isn't possible when the school is on the main island. I would find it difficult to continue teaching, which is the reason I came to the islands in the first place."

After much deliberation it was agreed she would move closer to the village centre. Mary was now an integral part of island life, which was why the Chief was more than happy to accommodate Lord Falshaw in his request. Over the following weeks there was a lot of activity as the new building slowly developed. In the meantime, Mumna arranged for someone to watch over Mary whenever a ship was in harbour. Jayne, visiting with the new baby a few weeks later, was surprised by the changes taking place. She was also pleased that Percy was looking after her dear friend. If she was honest, Jayne felt guilty at deserting Mary. At not spending as much time with her, but the baby came first.

Two weeks later the islands little church was packed as Jayne and Thomas christened their daughter. Apart from Percy and Mary, the happy couple had also asked Mumna and the Chief to be Godparents. What made the event more special was the baby being dressed in a Christening robe designed and sewn by the ladies of the sewing circle. After the service a large party was held with Mumna taking great delight in being a new Godmother.

Mary later wrote in her journal: *I feel most honoured at being Godmother to Jayne's new baby. This is a new experience for me. But one I shall endeavour to carry out with great energy. The child is a happy mite, who appear to be constantly smiling. I admit to feeling slight pangs of jealousy whenever I hold her in my arms. It makes me wonder when and if I will ever become a mother and if so, will I be a good one.*

Over the next few weeks Mary was kept quite busy. She spent her time teaching, meeting with Percy or visiting the families on the islands. Her knowledge of languages was fast improving under Marta's tutorage. Having mastered French, she was now developing her Dutch. Greta was also taking time to teach her how to weave the cotton which grew on the islands. So far, she had made some placemats. Her intention was to send some to Lizzie, to show her friend how improved her sewing had become. She had even embroidered some little flowers, similar to those growing in the forest, onto each one.

*My days pass quickly and pleasurably.* Wrote Mary in her journal that evening: *I find myself well occupied. I cannot remember a time when I have felt so happy and contented. My skills improve daily. I am grateful for Marta's patience in teaching me the languages. My dear Lizzie will be most surprised at my expertise in French. The day for my moving into my new home draws ever closer and I find myself becoming excited. I am grateful to Mumna and the Chief for their consideration. I feel this will be a place I can call my own. I never dreamed I could be so fortunate.*

It was just before she was due to move into her new home that Mary received a visit from Captain Morrison, who was delivering a letter from Lizzie. When shown the new buildings he was surprised. "What a delightful place. Who is it for?"

"Me."

He exclaimed, "I see you will be most secure and safe there. I am glad." And he was. The Captain liked Mary, having told his wife all about her and the adventure she had undertaken. After taking some refreshments he left her to read her letter, promising to return the following day to collect a reply.

Mary sat thinking about the Captain's kindness. She was honoured by his concern for her safety. Unbeknown to him Mary looked upon the Captain as the father she had lost. Watching him leave, she smiled to herself. 'What a good man he is.'

Then taking up Lizzies letter she began to read. Once finished, she fetched her writing implements and penned a reply.

*Dearest Darling Lizzie*

*How delighted I was to receive your last letter. I was surprised at the news of Andrew kissing you. But my darling, why shouldn't he kiss you for you are a delightful creature. One whom any young man would find easy to kiss. As for your*

205

*feelings? Darling Lizzie, you are still a young woman so why shouldn't you be attracted to Andrew. Or any other young man whom you may like. There is nothing to prevent you from falling in love more than once. God works in mysterious ways, so you enjoy the feelings Andrew gives you without feeling any guilt.*

*Talking of kisses, I too have now experienced my first proper kiss. You will never guess with whom but maybe you will? It was Percy. We had no excuse of being under the mistletoe for such does not grow here on the islands. His kiss was deep and done with such fervour. I was taken by surprise although he apologised most profusely afterwards. He said, he hoped I was not offended, and I was not. Am I wicked Lizzie? It is not the first time he has been familiar in this way. Over the last few months he has often brushed his lips against mine whenever we meet or part. For some reason I found his familiarity comforting but I confess I do blush. We have also met a few times for dinner. Either at his home, my little hut, on his yacht or at the home of one of the other residents. I find his company exceedingly enjoyable.*

*And now for some wonderful news. Jayne has given birth to a beautiful baby girl. They have called her Sarah after Jayne's Mother and Rose after Thomas's. Her labour was long and hard but she fared well and is now fully recovered. The Christening took place on Sunday last with the whole island joining in the celebrations. I am honoured and delighted to be a Godmother. Being a mother certainly suits Jayne. We are all so pleased for them. They both look absolutely full of happiness.*

*There has also been news of The Reverend Morgain. It appears Percy's letter to the Governor has worked for The Reverend has been set free. However, he has returned directly to England. Jayne remains ignorant of his dilemma but I am sure she will hear from him in due course.*

*The island continues to provide me with an abundance of delights, including an assortment of exotic foods. Some of these I like while others I find strange. I wish I could send you some fruit for I am sure you too would find them enjoyable. The island estates send much of what they produce to the America's but some of the cotton and coffee goes to England.*

*Kuala spends much of her time working in the school with the younger children. I believe she has all the makings of being a good teacher one day. As she is doing so well it leaves me time to spend doing other things. I am learning to cook like the islanders. Mumna has decided I must be able to cook otherwise I won't, as she puts it, 'get me a good husband.' Percy laughs at her comments, telling me Mumna is trying to make me more native every day. He does not mean anything bad as he laughs at such comments, which I find endearing. Oh, Lizzie dear, I believe I am becoming more attracted to him but cannot seriously see any future in the relationship. Perhaps, I should distance myself before it is too late. I would appreciate your comments and advice my sweet one.*

*With my new-found freedom I am able to spend more time with Marta, so my languages have vastly improved. Marta and Greta are two of the most delightful ladies. They both have such a wonderful sense of humour. Greta has been teaching me to weave using the raw cotton grown here on the islands. You will find one of my attempts enclosed which I hope you will like. It is a small set of mats for your dressing table. I am sure you will get much pleasure from looking at them.*

*And now I will tell you about a forthcoming event. You will be surprised to learn I am moving homes. But I will not be going far away. Just closer to the centre of the village. There will also be a new school attached to the house. Once the place is finished, I will tell you more about it. As yet I have no access to the buildings but I wait in eager anticipation for them to be finished.*

*I will close now. I send a big hug and a kiss for Baby James.*

*Keep enjoying your life.*
*With much affection your loving Mary*

Having finished writing her letter Mary placed the mats inside and sealed the packet. Thinking of the Captain, Mary also decided to send a small gift for his wife. Taking two more of the small mats she wrapped them carefully, completing the package with a small decoration.

The following day when the Captain called, Mary presented him with the small package. "This is for your dear lady wife. I would be pleased if you could present the gift to her with my best regards."

The Captain was deeply moved by Mary's thoughtfulness. As he stood Mary noted a small tear in the corner of his eye which he quickly wiped away. "Thank you so much. I am sure she will like it very much." He paused before going on. "May I say Miss Watson that should you ever need assistance you must not hesitate to ask me as it would be my honour to serve you." With that he bowed, and took his leave, holding the precious packets close to his chest. A few hours later the ship left the harbour.

Sailing across the ocean the Captain would often visit his cabin to look at the small package for his wife. The more he thought about Mary the more he was drawn to her, finding he wanted to offer her his protection. The next time he sailed to the island he vowed to speak to Lord Falshaw to ensure she was being well looked after. He also decided he would speak to his wife as a thought had entered his head. He would, with his wife's agreement, like to offer Miss Watson a home.

# Thirty

Back in England, Lizzie and Andrew's relationship slowly progressed. Finally, the day arrived when Andrew plucked up the courage and declared his true feelings by asking Lizzie to marry him. She was delighted by his proposal, accepting without a moment's hesitation. Pleased with her response, Andrew left the room to formally ask her Father for Lizzie's hand in marriage. Not that he needed to as, being a widow, she no longer required her parents' permission to remarry. However, being a most exacting young man, and certainly knowledgeable of good etiquette, Andrew felt it only correct to do so.

Lord and Lady Mountford were overjoyed by the proposal. After giving his agreement to their marriage His Lordship called for champagne, with the whole household joining in a toast to the happy couple. Lizzie had never felt as happy as she now did, for as much as she had loved James, her love for Andrew was deep and strong. She knew what a good husband and wonderful father to Baby James Andrew would be. It was a few days later that the forthcoming marriage was announced in The Times, followed by a betrothal party at the house.

When Laura called later in the day, she was delighted to hear the joyous news. Joining Lizzie and Andrew in a celebration toast, she willingly accepted an invitation to attend the forthcoming wedding service. Once Lizzie's many friends read of the announcement, Laura was not the only one calling at the house to offer congratulations.

Approximately two weeks later, Lizzie prepared for her betrothal party. Baby James, seeming to pick up on the excitement of the evening's event, took some time to settle. Fortunately, Andrew arrived early and was able to soothe him. His actions further convincing Lizzie what a good father he would make. That night Lizzie, full of joy and happiness, danced the night away in the arms of her fiancée. It wasn't until the early hours of the following morning that she climbed into her bed feeling the happiest of women.

As the summer progressed the weather in town became oppressive so the family adjourned to the coast for the summer months. On the way there, they took the opportunity to visit Andrew's family home, where Lizzie was presented to the young man's father, Lord Weston. Being too ill to travel to town he had missed the betrothal celebrations. The only downside for Lizzie, during this time, was that her dear friend Mary was absent yet again. She made the decision to write to Mary on her return to town, to tell her all the news. She knew Mary would be happy for her.

Three days later, after returning from the coast, Lizzie received a visit from Captain Morrison, delivering a package from Mary. Upon hearing the good news of their forthcoming marriage, he chose to spend more time with the happy couple, being most profuse with his congratulations. After a warming glass of wine, the Captain left for home where he informed his lady wife of all he had recently become acquainted with. As he strolled along, he walked with a light step, feeling as proud as if he had been Lizzie's father. Something he felt a small right to feel having come to know, and grow close, to both young ladies. Lizzie was always happy to receive the Captain for he was yet another link to Mary.

Much later, as Lizzie read Mary's letter, she smiled to herself at the news within. The small mats enclosed delighted her. She placed them on the dresser next to the other gifts from Mary. Looking at the items sent she thought of her dear, dear friend, remembering how much their lives had changed. That night Lizzie prayed God would keep Mary safe and happy.

Waking early the following morning Lizzie dwelt once more on all that had happened to her and Mary. Both their lives were different now from the day they had parted. Taking up her pen she began to write a letter.

*My Dearest Mary*

*What wonderful news about Jayne and Thomas's new daughter? They must both be so happy. Feeling no doubt, the same as I did after having Baby James. What a wonderful honour for you to be a Godparent. Had you been here then I too would have chosen you to be Godmother to Baby James. Please send them my best regards and wishes. You will find I have enclosed a small gift for the baby and ask you to please pass this on to Jayne for me. Laura called this week and I have told her about the new baby. She too is highly delighted and is going to write to Jayne and Thomas direct to send them her good wishes.*

*The Colonel is due to cease working at the Ministry within the next two months as the war has ceased. I do believe they are looking forward to returning to the islands. I shall miss dear Laura greatly when they leave, but will be pleased, as she is returning to you.*

*You tell me your heart has felt the first stirrings of love. My dear Mary you should forget all the nonsense of what you think is or is not proper. Follow your heart. If you have any regard for Percy and are sure of his for you, then it matters not a jot about social correctness. Forget what others think. Just be happy and contented.*

*Now my dear I have some exciting news. I hope you are sat down Dear Heart for what I am about to say will come as a big shock, I am sure. Over the past few months I have spent a great deal of time with Andrew Jones. Following the kiss at Christmas we have drawn ever closer until now, when Andrew has proposed to me. I was surprised at his asking, as you may well imagine, but I am delighted for I find I love him dearly. Of course, I was a little concerned it might not be the correct thing to do. I mean, to marry again so soon after losing James. But Father tells me not to concern myself with such stuff and nonsense. The mourning period has passed, and proprietary has been met.*

*Mother and Father are delighted, having no objection to the marriage. I am so very happy. We had a betrothal party*

211

this week and have set the wedding day for August. I am so excited. It will not be as grand an affair as when I married James as it would not be proper. Perhaps a smaller family affair with a few friends as guests. If Laura is still here, then I hope she and the Colonel will join us. My only sorrow is that you will not be here to attend me on the day.

One good side of my betrothal is that Andrew has agreed to take over control of the Williamson estate. The idea of this greatly relieves me. He will look after the estate as Baby James' guardian until my son comes of age, when James will inherit the estate as Lord of the Manor. He will control the estate as James' stepfather until he is old enough to come into his fortune. Andrew and I have agreed that we will make sure Baby James grows up knowing all about his own father.

Once we are married, we shall live in the Weston house here in town. It is a delightful place and is not far from my parent's home. Andrew is hoping his Father's health will improve enough to attend the wedding but if not, then we will all travel to his family home and have a blessing in the family church.

Father has spent a great deal of time with Andrew and is satisfied with his financial position which is far better than he realised. Not that such things concern me. He is a second son, which is the reason why he trained as a doctor and went to sea. It seems his older brother was killed in an accident, meaning Andrew will inherit the family estate when his father passes. Which we pray will not be for some time yet. I admit to being most surprised when I was told all this. Andrew said the shock of losing her eldest son caused his Mother to take to her bed. She too passed away. Seemingly from a broken heart. I believe I understand what sorrow she must have suffered and my heart goes out to Andrew, having lost both his mother and brother at so young an age. Not that his financial position matters for I am well-off enough for us both.

The summer this year has so far been pleasant enough.

*Although it did become unbearable at one point so Father took the whole household to the south coast. He rented a house overlooking the sea where the fresh air was most invigorating for us all. We took many strolls along the promenade. Oh, I must tell you about Baby James wetting his nurse. One day she took him paddling in the sea. He got so excited by the way the waves licked his legs that he started kicking them. So hard did he kick he splashed and wet the poor nurse through. We found it so amusing; even nurse laughed. The time away did us all some good. We felt invigorated by the sea air, returning to town but a few days ago, feeling fully refreshed. Happily, the weather has now cooled.*

*Well my dear this is all my news. I will close now as James wants his Mommy. He is such a joy to me; changing day by day. Being a mother is my greatest happiness.*

*I hope you are happy and still think of us often.*

*Sent with all our Love, Lizzie and Baby James*

*PS. Andrew sends his best regards and thanks you for introducing me to him.*

# Thirty-one

The new house and school building were soon finished and before long, Mary found herself moving into her new home. During the building process it had been decided the school room would be extended. The number of children attending school had increased dramatically since Mary's arrival on the islands. Kuala and Chula, quick learners, were improving daily and were now able to aid Mary full time. Sally also volunteered to teach some of the younger children. While her husband, Pastor Gordon, took on the mantle of spiritual advisor. This left Mary with more free time, which she often spent with Percy on his yacht or plantation.

*My life is settled and most satisfactory.* Mary wrote in her journal. *I am moving into my new home soon and am pleased with it. Kuala and Chula will share one bedroom while I have the other. The attached schoolroom is well proportioned which allows us to separate the younger children from the older ones. I am satisfied and most grateful by all that has been done for me.*

Over time Mary and Percy's love grew, though neither was yet able to acknowledge how they felt. Finally, it was Percy who declared his feelings when, one day, taking Mary's hand in his he looked deeply into her eyes. "I have a confession to make. I have deep affection for you, Mary. And, I am wondering if you would do me the honour of becoming my wife."

Mary, while pleased and delighted, was a little taken aback. After a short silence she asked, "Are you sure? Perhaps you should think about it. You are aware I am a common school teacher, whilst you are a gentleman."

Eyes widening, Percy snorted at her comment. "Don't be so snobbish." Mary without speaking, looked at him aghast. "If I thought for one minute you were not good enough for me do you think I would have asked you to marry me? Or, is it that perhaps you don't think I am good enough for you to marry?" The shock of his response shook Mary leaving her unsure as to what to say.

"Anyway," Percy continued, "If polite society doesn't like us being married then they can be damned," and he stopped, again looking deep into her eyes. "I love you and I want you for my wife."

It was the love showing on his face which proved to Mary how truly he cared for her and how genuinely he wanted to marry her. Slowly smiling and without any hesitation, Mary stepped into his outstretched arms, breathlessly saying, "Oh yes. Yes. I accept. I would love to marry you."

As Mary moved from his embrace, the couple sat discussing how amazed they were to find they loved each other. Later Percy said, "I must write to Amelia to tell her the news."

"She will not be angry, will she?"

Now it was Percy's turn to be surprised. "Of course not. She will be delighted. And so pleased that I have finally managed to pluck up the courage to ask you to marry me." Whereupon he kissed her soundly before leaving to see the Chief. After which he was to return to his estate to write a letter to his sister. While loath to leave he went away smiling.

Sometime later Jayne called. Looking at her, Mary perceived her friend was highly distressed and angry. When questioned as to what was wrong, Jayne took a moment before speaking. "I have received a letter from my brother. It is not of a nice nature." And Mary sat, quietly listening to Jayne rant and rave about the whole affair of the Reverend. She even blamed poor Thomas for keeping secrets from her.

Once she had finished Mary felt free to speak. "Now, I want you to calm down and listen to me." Jayne started to speak, but Mary held up her hand. "Shush, be quite." Then taking a deep breath, she said, "I already know about your brother and what has happened to him." Jayne gasped, but before she could say anything Mary went on. "I was told by Doctor Jones. Considering your condition at the time we weren't sure if it was right to upset you with the news or not. I asked Thomas what he thought. Reluctantly he agreed it would be better, under the circumstances, not to tell you. Besides, what could you have done. Nothing?"

When Jayne again tried to object Mary stopped her. "Please, be quiet, listen and think about it. You were close to giving birth. The Doctor said our not telling you was the correct thing to do as he didn't want you, or the baby, becoming distressed." Pausing a moment to take another breath she went on. "It was agreed we would all remain silent until after the birth. Which we did. You shouldn't be angry with Thomas. He did what he thought was best for you and your daughter. Besides, had your brother returned, you would not be as happy as you now are?"

Thinking over all Mary had told her, Jayne reluctantly agreed. "Oh, I am such a wicked person. I have been so cruel towards poor Thomas. Blaming him for keeping secrets when I know he would do nothing to harm me." She looked at Mary calmly. "I am sure any action he or you took was for my benefit. If I am truly honest, I agree with the decision."

After discussing the matter further, Jayne left shortly afterwards to find Thomas. She realised what a big apology she owed her husband for shouting at him over her brother's letter. She hoped he would forgive her. Which of course he did for he loved her deeply.

A few days later Mary was called to attend Mumna and the Chief. Surprised by the summons she removed her apron, ran her fingers through her hair and made her way to the main hut. To her surprise she found everyone in high spirits, being relieved to learn the Chief's daughter had given birth to a baby boy. Mary took delight in offering her sincere congratulations at the birth. She would have returned home if not for Mumna insisting she stay to join in the celebrations. The festivities went on for some time and it was only as Mary started to nod-off that Mumna allowed her to leave. Before she left Mumna insisted Mary return the following day for a special ceremony. Being too tired to enquire what ceremony she left. Back home Mary retired for the night, sleeping soundly despite the noise made by the celebrating islanders.

The following morning, unsure as to what was happening Mary dressed with care. She wanted to look her best for the Chief and Mumna. Approaching the big hut, she was met by Percy who was likewise dressed in his best clothes. Taking her hand, he smiled at her with a deep look of love. "Good-morning, my love."

Mary, blushed slightly at the compliment. "Good-morning, Percy."

As they walked along, she asked, "What is happening?"

"We are going to a Christening."

Taken aback she exclaimed, "Whose?"

"It's the Chief's new Grandson. Mumna has decided he is to be the first island baby to be christened." The news delighted Mary.

Percy went on. "And we two are to be Godparents." Mary was astounded for it was not what she had expected to hear. Entering the church, Percy leaned towards Mary, whispering in her ear, "Soon we'll be coming here to get married." Smiling she looked up at him.

After the service everyone returned to the big hut where a second ceremony took place. This one being carried out by the islander's Holy Man. Attending such a ceremony was a new experience for Mary. So far, she had not witnessed any such events so felt most honoured to do so now. Once this was over there followed another big feast. The day was full of joy and laughter. Watching the young parents Mary was pleased to see how happy they were.

Much later Percy escorted Mary back to her home, remaining to take tea. As she placed a cake on the table he asked, "Have you made this?"

A smile on her face, Mary said, "Yes, I have."

Tasting it, Percy declared, "It is delicious. I see I am going to have a very clever wife, aren't I." His compliment caused her to blush and smile with satisfaction.

Noting Mary's eyes starting to droop, Percy left her to retire for the night. As she got into bed, she realised how safe she felt in her new home. Having a bar on the door kept any unwanted intruders out, helping to settle her mind. 'It feels like a proper house,' she thought, and closing her eyes she drifted off into a deep, dream filled sleep.

Six days later Mary watched a ship drop anchor in the harbour. Recognising the vessel, she went down to the dockside. Standing onshore the Captain appeared overjoyed to see his young friend, delighted to be bringing her welcome news. He also wished to express his wife's sincere thanks for the gift sent to her. "Miss Watson, I must tell you Mrs Morrison was most delighted with your gift."

Mary smiled warmly. "I am so glad. Thank you, Sir."

While in England the Captain had spoken to his wife about Miss Watson's situation. He had suggested a way of offering her the opportunity to leave the island. His dear wife had listened carefully and, loving her husband dearly, realised he was concerned for the young woman's welfare. Though not wealthy they were comfortable and had room to accommodate one other person. It was settled that the Captain would, when he next saw Mary, broach the subject of her returning to England, if she so desired.

"Miss Watson, I wondered if I could possibly call on you after I have met with the Chief? There is something I wish to discuss with you."

Although a little surprised Mary was happy to oblige. "But of course, Captain. I will ensure there is some hot tea ready for when you return."

It was some time later in the day when the Captain returned.

"Please, be seated Captain Morrison."

Sitting he gratefully accepted the tea offered, making small talk until he felt able to broach the subject of England. Taking a steadying breath, the Captain began. "I have discussed a small matter with my dear wife and we are both in agreement. Miss Watson, I am concerned for your continued presence here on the islands."

Surprised, Mary declared, "I am most grateful Captain Morrison for your kind thoughts, but there is no need to worry."

"What I really wanted to say is, should you care to return to England, at any time, you would find a warm welcome in my home, as a member of my family."

There was a short silence as Mary absorbed the Captains offer. She was astounded. Finding her emotions disturbed by such thoughtfulness. Shaking her head, such was her gratitude for his generosity that she burst into tears. This caused the poor Captain to be alarmed, wondering if he had been wrong in making the offer.

Unfortunately, it was at this very moment that Percy arrived. And, seeing Mary distressed, demanded, "What is happening here?" The Captain, still upset by her reaction sat stunned as Percy stood over him, demanding an answer.

Seeing Percy's behaviour made Mary start laughing. Quickly standing she prevented him from behaving foolishly. The Captain also stood to face His Lordship so Mary stepped between the two men quickly explaining. "The Captain has been most honourable and I feel such humility at his generosity. You see dear, he and his wife have kindly offered me a home should I wish to return to England. It is this kindness which caused my emotional state."

Percy, stunned by the offer, was left lost for words.

In the silence which followed, the Captain said, "I am so sorry for upsetting you Miss Watson. It was not my intention to cause any distress."

Wanting to reassure him, she said, "Pray please do not concern yourself Sir, for it is I who have been foolish. I allowed my emotions to overtake my sensibilities." And as Percy finally understood what the Captain was offering Mary, he apologised profusely for his ungentlemanly behaviour.

As Mary looked at Percy, an unspoken agreement passed between them. Then she expressed her deep appreciation to the Captain, and his good lady wife, at such an honour. "It is, however, with regret I am unable to accept your kind and generous offer Sir. I am in fact betrothed to be married. Therefore, at this moment in time I have no intention of leaving the islands."

Upon hearing the news, the Captain expressed his joy and delight at the happy tidings. "Why, congratulations Miss Watson. May I ask if I am acquainted with the lucky gentleman?"

Mary looked at Percy who, turning to the Captain, announced, "Yes Sir you are, for I am the lucky man and we would both be honoured if you could return to attend our nuptials."

Captain Morrison was so taken aback he sat down with a thump. However, having taken in the delightful news he heartily declared, "I would indeed be honoured to attend your wedding ceremony."

Rising again, he declared, "I must say Miss Watson, I know my wife will be delighted by the news. Congratulations. I will leave you now. But I am sure there are many questions I should be asking you that my wife will want answers to. Perhaps, next time we meet you will be able to satisfy her needs?"

Mary went towards him. "Captain Morrison, does your previous offer of assistance still apply?"

"Why of course Miss Watson. How may I help?"

Looking once more at Percy, who nodded his head, she turned back to face the Captain. "As you are aware, I have no parents. And so, I wondered if you would do me the great honour of giving me away when we marry?"

The Captain, looking first at Mary, then at Percy who was smiling, then back at Mary, smiled. "I would indeed be most honoured and delighted to do so." And before taking his leave, he offered his hand, first to Percy, then to Mary. She in turn, kissed him on his cheek whispering, "Thank you."

After the Captain had gone Percy took Mary in his arms, kissing her with a fervour which left her breathless. "I think we must set our wedding date. And, soon. Don't you?" Mary agreed and they decided to announce details of their betrothal at the harvest ball to be held at the end of the month.

Left alone Mary sat at the table mulling over all she had learnt during the last few hours. She replayed the scene of the Captain's kind offer over and over in her mind. Finally, taking up Lizzies letter she read it, astounded by the news. Tears of joy and delight running down her face.

'*What news she sends me,*' she thought. *"And what news I shall send her in return.*' Fetching her writing materials Mary took up her pen to begin her letter.

*My Darling, Darling Lizzie*

*What wonderful news you send. How I wish I could be there with you on your Wedding Day. I am so happy that Andrew brings you such joy. I am sure he will make a wonderful husband and a delightful father also. You must write and tell me all about your day and what Andrew's family home is like. I trust his family will be nicer to you than James' sisters have been.*

*Lots of things have happened here since I last wrote so I will bring you up-to-date. Firstly, Jayne has at last heard from her brother. She was surprised by the content of his letter as he was most caustic in his comments. He has of course, blamed her for all his misfortunes and for deserting him in his hour of need. Jayne was aghast at his outburst and quite upset. Venting her anger on poor Thomas. He was so taken aback he had to confess all. Jayne told me she felt betrayed by him but I reassured her he, and we, acted in her best interests. She later admitted, that if she were honest, she was glad her brother had not been allowed back to the island. Otherwise she would never have married Thomas whom she loves with all her heart. She left to write a letter in response, intending to tell him a few home truths. As well as instructing him to leave her alone as she is now happy in her new life. I swear I never thought to see the day when Jayne stood up to her brother in this fashion.*

*The next good news is the Chief's daughter has been*

*delivered of a baby boy. Mumna and the Chief are pleased with the new addition to their extensive family. I have discovered Mumna has five sons and four daughters plus twelve, no, thirteen grandchildren. Mumna agreed to the baby being christened in our little church. Percy and I are the Godparents. The child is the first island baby to be christened so. I realise I didn't tell you about our island's new pastor. He arrived some weeks ago. He hails from Scotland and is called Gordon Scott. His wife is called Sally and she is practiced in midwifery. They are a delightful couple, having readily been accepted by everyone.*

*I have some more good news. I have taken up residence in my new home. Because of the increase in school children the new school built next door is larger than planned. It looks impressive and I am highly pleased with both buildings. My two young girls help me in the school. As does Sally, when she can, so I do not see us requiring a new teacher for some time yet. Pastor Gordon comes to teach scriptures three times a week whilst Sally looks after the younger children. We shall be closing school in a few of weeks' time ready to gather the harvest. I shall join the women in helping to prepare and cook the meals for the pickers. It will be a busy time for everyone.*

*Today I received the most unexpected of news. Captain Morrison, who has become such a good friend called today and extended a most generous offer to me. It appears he and his wife, being concerned for my safety, have offered me a home should I care to leave the island. I am overwhelmed by their generosity, as is Percy. I was so taken aback, I burst into tears.*

*And now for the most important of news. I know you asked me to sit down when you told me your happy news so I must request you do the same for I am sure to shock you.*

*Percy has asked me to marry him!*

*I was most surprised for I wasn't sure of his feelings towards me. I did ask him to consider his question carefully. Particularly as I am only a humble school teacher and he is, of course, a titled gentleman. I have to be sure he wants to marry me for the right reasons. Do you know Lizzie he actually snorted with laughter? Accusing me of being snobbish? Me! How silly is that? But I need him to understand and appreciate that for a man it is easy, but for a woman it is much harder. Especially for one with my upbringing. I did ask what would happen if we returned to England. How would society react to our marriage? He told me if polite society didn't like it, they could all go to hell and be damned. I think it was at this point I realised just how much he really does love me.*

*And so, my dear one, by the time you read this I will be betrothed to Lord Percival Edward Montague Falshaw, Eighth Lord of Wentworth.*

*I shall await your response and hope you will be pleased and will wish us both well?*

*Your loving friend, Mary*


Happy with her letter Mary took out her journal: *What joy I feel. My heart is full to breaking point. I am so very, very happy. Percy has declared his love for me and we are to be married. Could I have ever dreamed of such an alliance? I think not. We are to set our Wedding Day soon for Percy says there is no reason for us to wait. Besides, I have no parents to whom I need ask permission. My one desire would be to have Lizzie at my wedding but this will not be possible.*

# Thirty-two

The marriage of Andrew and Lizzie occurred with great joy and happiness. Even Baby James had fun. The bride, who wore a beautiful dress of pale blue with a short veil to match, was seen smiling throughout the whole proceedings. The day was completed with a celebration dinner. Afterwards the happy couple left for a short honeymoon at the coast, where they spent much of their time ensconced in their own little world. Lizzie had never been as happy.

Prior to the wedding Lizzie had spoken to her parents about Andrew adopting young James as his son. She felt if he did it would be of benefit to the child, even though he was already well provided for through the Williamson property, when reaching his majority. At that time, he will take control of the estate in accordance with his late father's will. Andrew's property will go to his and Lizzie's eldest male child, if she has one, which they hope she will. If there are no children, then young James will inherit everything. Both parents felt this was only fair. Her Father readily agreeing, as once he passed away his property would initially go to Lizzie's Mother and would thereafter be jointly shared by all their grandchildren. As for the Mountford title that would pass to James Junior being the eldest Grandson.

Lizzie had confided in Andrew how she found managing the Williamson estate a problem. But Andrew was to come to her rescue. "You mustn't worry yourself about any of it my Darling. From now on I will take care of everything." Upon hearing this Lizzie was relieved, thanking her husband for his consideration as she still expected problems from the sisters. This was borne out when they learnt she was to remarry.

As if to prove a point it was but a few days later that the solicitor called to see them. "I am, unfortunately, the bearer of bad news." After listening to him Lizzie became distressed.

However, Andrew, reassured his young wife. "I think Sir, you and I should handle this problem from now on." The Solicitor willingly agreed as he was loath to put Lizzie under any further pressure.

Thus, it was a few days later, that Andrew and the Solicitor left for the Williamson country estate. So incensed was Andrew, at the ladies' behaviour, he decided to resolve the matter once and for all. Once there, he took no pleasure in telling the ladies they were to remove themselves from the house without any further delay. Which they did. Despite their attempts to argue the point they were left with no choice. Andrew and the solicitor remained in the country until the ladies had departed, wanting to ensure they only took what they were entitled to. During this time the two gentlemen also took it upon themselves to interview a new Estate Manager, finding a trusting man in Jack Brandon. He was a good honest man with a number of years' experience in running larger estates.

Lizzie would later write in her diary: *I am the happiest of women, finding married life quite satisfying. Andrew has proven to be the best of husbands, taking over the problem of the Williamson sisters. I knew they would not remain quiet for long. But he has resolved the matter.*

Baby James had stayed with Laura whilst the couple were away on their honeymoon, which delighted her. The Johnstones were not overly bothered by the lack of youngsters in their lives, as they both enjoyed their lifestyle, accepting children would hinder them. But it was nice every now and then to be able to look after a child. It was also probably the last time for Laura as the Colonel had made the decision to return to the islands. There was nothing further to keep him and his wife in England so their intention was to leave before winter set in.

After much thought the Colonel had decided upon their return, he would take Thomas into the business as a partner.

Having no other relatives of their own there was no-one else to inherit the estate. Laura agreed with him wholeheartedly in the decision. And so, at the end of September they took leave of their new friends. Lizzie was filled with disappointment and sadness to be losing her new friend so soon. However, a few days before the Johnstones departure Lizzie held a farewell party for the couple. The event was a great success, being enjoyed by one and all. Leaving Laura and her husband feeling delighted by the honour shown them.

After the Johnstones had departed Lizzie settled back into a normal routine of soirées, parties and dinners. Life was good. She found herself feeling happy and contented. Lizzies Mother called to see her and young James quite often. Her Ladyship was pleased to see her daughter settled in her new life. Her only concern was the continuing relationship between Lizzie and Mary. When, she quietly mentioned this to Andrew one day, he was surprised. He had no inclination to stop Lizzie's friendship, explaining to his mother-in-law, "If it wasn't for Mary, I would never have met my Darling Lizzie." Understanding his reasoning Lady Mountford said no more. Maybe finally realising she would have to accept the relationship between the two young women which would continue regardless.

Two weeks later Lizzie received a visit from Captain Morrison who was calling to extend his heartfelt congratulations to the newlyweds. He wanted to tell Lizzie the good news of Mary's engagement but realised it was not his place to do so. At least when he returned to his own home, he would have much to share with his wife. Including the fact, he was to give the bride away. He knew she would be delighted with the news.

After the Captain left Lizzie sat in the drawing room reading the letter from Lizzie. Suddenly she cried out. Hearing his wife Andrew rushed in to discover what had distressed her. Entering the room, he was distraught to discover Lizzie sat with tears rolling down her face. Concerned, he took her in his arms. "What has happened?

Who has made you cry?"

Raising her head from his shoulder, he watched as a large smile crossed her face, and holding up the letter she declared, "It is Mary. She is betrothed."

Andrew was shocked. "What. Who, where, when?"

Once he stopped speaking, Lizzie, calmer, managed to read the letter to him. As she did Andrew smiled. "Bravo. Well done Mary," insisting they toast the happy couple. Afterwards he left her to continue reading the letter, whilst he went to write a missive of congratulations to Lord Falshaw and his future bride.

The following day when her parents called Lizzie took great delight in sharing some of Mary's letter. In particular, the good news of her forthcoming marriage. Both of Lizzie's parents were taken aback by the news, especially her Father when he realised to whom she was betrothed. "Surely there must be some mistake. Such a thing cannot be true?" Lizzie was astounded by her father's comments. Then she noticed a glancing look from Lady Mountford which prevented His Lordship from saying anything further on the subject.

After they had left, Lizzie said. "I cannot believe why father was unhappy about the news. There is no reason why Mary cannot marry someone like Percy, is there?"

Andrew took her hand. "Do not worry about it my dear. I am sure he was just shocked. It was a little unexpected. He will come around to the idea in time." Lizzie was not so sure, thinking, 'What a snob my father is.'

"The only thing you need to remember Lizzie dear that should Mary and Percy return to England, then they are to be made most welcome in our home." Lizzie found her husband gracious in his comments. Leaning over she placed a gentle kiss upon her his face, telling him how much she cared for him. Andrew smiled in return. "You must write a letter of congratulations to Mary. Tell her we are both extremely happy and pleased with the news."

Returning to his study Andrew thought how much he loved his wife, finding her innocence totally endearing. She

227

could see nothing wrong in the marriage, as in her mind Mary was an equal. Not that he disagreed with her for he liked Mary and was, as he told Lizzie, happy about the betrothal. He just hoped Percy was strong enough to cushion his future wife from those in society who might think differently.

Back in the drawing room Lizzie picked up her pen and sat thinking excitedly about what to put in her letter. Eventually she started with their congratulations.

*My Dear, Sweet Mary*

*What wonderful, delightful news I have from you. Both Andrew and I send you and Percy our heartfelt congratulations. I am so pleased and delighted by your betrothal. Andrew has a great regard for Lord Falshaw and believes he will suit you well indeed.*

*I shared the news of your engagement with Mama and Father. You should have seen the look of surprise on their faces. They did not believe me and thought I was teasing, until Andrew confirmed how happy we are for you. You say Percy called you snobbish but I really think it is my father who is so. All he could do was say I had obviously misunderstood your news. Anyway, Andrew and I say well done. We have raised a glass of champagne to your future happiness. And Andrew instructs me to tell you we will be delighted and honoured to receive Lord and LADY Falshaw, should they care to pay us a call when next in town. Oh, how wonderful that sounds. I do hope we can be together sometime soon.*

*Perhaps by the time you receive my letter harvest time will have finished and you will be back in the comfort of your new home. You have not told me much about your house so I am looking forward to reading all about it the next time you write. And your school sounds to be developing well. Tell me, once you become Lady Falshaw will you give up teaching? Perhaps Kuala can take over the role of school mistress.*

*My dear friend I have a most delightful surprise for you. You are about to receive visitors for Laura and the Colonel left England at the beginning of September. They wished to depart before winter set in otherwise, they would not have been able to sail until next spring. Laura seems pleased they are returning, although a little sad at leaving us. I also believe by the time you receive this letter they may have arrived.*

*I am delighted to hear about Mumna's new grandchild. Yet another new life to the island. How pleased everyone must be. Please send our greetings and felicitations to the happy parents. I have enclosed a small present for the baby. Please give it to them on our behalf.*

*As for Reverend Morgain, he certainly seems to have no regard or humility for his fellow man. I am so glad Jayne has at last found some sense in her dealings with him. Oh, does that sound bad?*

*And now for some more news which I hope you may find enlightening and perhaps slightly amusing? Andrew has been to the Williamson estate with the Solicitor. His reception was most unwelcoming and cold to say the least. After the sisters affected a tirade of nasty comments towards him, Andrew told them to go pack their belongings and leave. When they tried to involve the Solicitor, informing him Andrew had no right to interfere he, quite rightly, told them they were wrong. As Andrew is now James' legal guardian, he is in charge which allows him to make all the decisions regarding the estate. The outcome is, the sisters begged to stay but Andrew told them they were not being honest and must leave. And so, they have gone. To stay with their Aunt and Uncle. I understand, that the couple are not overly pleased to have them as they do not find them at all pleasant. Anyway, my dear, Andrew has employed a wonderful new Estate Manager. The matter is resolved and I do not have to worry about it anymore.*

*Oh, dear how remiss I am. I almost forgot to tell you about my wedding. It was wonderful albeit a small affair. The sun shone brightly all day. I wore a beautiful dress of pale blue with a short veil to match. Baby James was dressed in a lovely outfit which matched my own and Laura acted as my attendant. After the service we all returned to the house for dinner before Andrew and I left for the coast via his country estate. His father was most effusive in his welcome, managing to attend the blessing of our union in their little church. We stayed away a few days before returning to Andrew's town house. Now my new home, as you will see from the address on my letterhead. Baby James stayed with Laura whilst we were away as it was the last time, she was able to look after him before leaving. My Wedding day was truly marvellous and I am so very, very happy.*

*You must let me know what is happening with regards your forthcoming marriage. I want to know all the details. In the meantime, please give my best regards to Laura when you see her.*

*Your loving friends, Lizzie, Andrew and Baby James*

# Thirty-three

Being engaged created a myriad of confusing emotions in Mary, causing her to doubt her decision in accepting Percy's offer of marriage. It wasn't that she didn't care for Percy as she knew she was deeply in love with him. But their different social backgrounds still concerned her. She knew she couldn't discuss it with Percy as he obviously saw no reason for her worries. Normally she would have turned to Lizzie to talk about such personal matters. However, this wasn't possible, so for the moment she had to put the thoughts to the back of her mind.

'Perhaps, when Laura returns to the island, she may be able to advise me,' thought Mary?

School life was busy; Mary being delighted by the progress of the children. Kuala and Chula, were doing well with their teaching skills. This meant Mary found more time to spend with Jayne, Greta, Marta and Dorothy, as well as the other ladies on the islands. Her life was settled and, for the first time since arriving, she felt the happiest she had done since leaving England.

Sitting outside her new home one day, thinking about everything she had experienced, Mary found she was content. Dorothy appeared around the corner, hailing her, "How are you my dear? Tell me is it true you are engaged to Lord Falshaw?"

Mary blushed, as smiling she tentatively replied, "Err yes, it is true, but how do you know about it?"

At her response Dorothy rushed forward, took Mary in her arms and swirled her around, all the while congratulating her. "What delightful, wonderful news." Then she began inundating Mary with questions. "When did you know you were in love? How did he ask you? Come on Mary tell me everything?" All without allowing Mary a chance to answer.

"When are you planning to marry? Are you happy?"

So overwhelmed was she by the exuberance and warmth of Dorothy's reaction to the news Mary began laughing. Encouraging Dorothy to sit Mary went inside to make tea. "After which," she promised, "I will tell you all."

As she made the tea Mary found herself smiling and humming. Laying some cakes on a plate she took the tea tray outside. Pouring the tea Dorothy said, "You do know that everyone is so delighted by the news." The fact Mary and Percy had been circumspect about their relationship meant the news of the forthcoming nuptials was a shock to everyone but still, a happy one. For all it was a secret, it was not a very well-kept one. As the two ladies sat drinking their tea, Mary told Dorothy all she felt able to about Percy and her falling in love. When she had finished, they sat in companionable silence until she felt able to broach the one subject bothering her. Before Mary realised what was happening, she was pouring out her fears. Dorothy sat listening, bemused. When Mary stopped speaking, there followed a long silence.

At first Dorothy did not respond. Leaving Mary thinking she had said too much and feeling embarrassed by her indiscretion. She need not have worried though. "Tush. What utter nonsense. Nobody thinks there is anything wrong with the relationship, especially as they realise how much in love you two are. Tell me does Percy know all this?"

Mary nodded yes, so Dorothy asked, "Well. Has he said or done anything which makes you think it is wrong for you two to be together?" As Mary shook her head no, Dorothy said, "Then I think you should put such silly thoughts from your head. I also think we must have a party to celebrate the engagement. And I am going to start organising one as soon as I return home."

"But we aren't going to make the announcement until the ball at the end of the month."

"Too late. The news is out." And, after finishing her tea Dorothy stood ready to leave. "I'll let you know when the party is, ok." Then with a quick peck on Mary's cheek she

232

left, waving and smiling gaily.

Continuing to sit in the sunshine a little longer, Mary began to feel that maybe she was being foolish about her concerns over Percy being a titled gentleman. 'Still, it was easy for Dorothy to say it was nonsense, after all she is an American. And they tend to look at life a lot differently than the people in England.'

It was the ringing of the school bell to mark the end of lessons which brought Mary out of her reverie. Deciding to follow Dorothy's advice she put the thoughts from her mind. She would write to Lizzie and ask her advice on the subject. With her mind more settled Mary left to say goodbye to the children before making the school ready for the following day. She never did find out who had let the secret of their engagement slip.

A few days later Mumna sent for Mary. Leaving the house, she strolled towards the Chiefs' hut, meeting Percy along the way. Taking her hand, he bent to kiss her.

"I have been summoned by Mumna."

Much to her surprise, Percy said, "Me too. I have been requested to attend the Chief and his wife."

"Do you know what they want?"

"I think perhaps we are to be honoured. It seems our secret engagement is no longer a secret. I believe it has become public knowledge."

Mary looked up surprised. "Yes, Dorothy was here two days ago congratulating me."

"Ah, I see."

"Do you think I am suitably dressed?"

Percy laughed. "Don't worry. You look beautiful." At his response Mary blushed, causing him to smile even more. He realised how much in love he was with this delightful young woman, making him feel the luckiest man in the world.

Holding hands, the pair approached the Chief's hut just as Mumna and her husband came outside to greet them. Standing in front of Mumna, Mary saw her looking at both of them. Smiling she took hold of each of their hands. Then looking at the people gathered around Mumna began making an announcement in her own language. Bending towards her, Percy started translating. Having spent so much time on the islands, Mary found she could actually understand most of what was being said. However, she enjoyed listening to Percy's voice so pretended otherwise.

The Queen told the islanders. "I am the proud mother of these two young people who are now given to each other." Mary found herself smiling at the kind words being used to explain the Chief & Queen's feelings of pleasure at the news of their betrothal. When both had spoken, Mumna declared. "There is to be a big celebration feast tomorrow. Everyone must come and make merry."

At the end of the speech Mary was allowed to return home. Entering her house, she told Percy, "I am overawed by the generosity of Mumna's comments. And amazed at people's reactions and the warmth they have shown me"

Percy questioned, "But why should you expect them to be any different?" When Mary shrugged her shoulders, Percy went on. "Don't you realise how esteemed you are by everyone? The residents and the islanders have all taken you to their hearts." His comment stunned Mary. Being modest the thought had never entered her head that she could be so well thought of.

Feeling confident Mary decided to broach once more the subject of their different social backgrounds. After making coffee, she sat opposite him. For a short while they sat in companionable silence. However, being an astute man, Percy soon realised she needed to say something but was obviously finding it difficult to start. Leaning over he took hold of her hand. "Tell me, what is the problem?"

Taking a breath Mary spoke. As she did the flood gates opened and she began pouring forth all her doubts and worries. Percy sat quietly listening, allowing her to 'get her concerns out of her system.' As she stopped speaking Mary sat with her head bowed, not daring to look at him.

After a short silence, he asked, "Have you perhaps

changed your mind. Are you finding that perhaps you do not love me after all? Do you want to break our engagement?"

This was the last thing she had expected him to say. Looking up, shock written over her face she burst into tears. "No, no, no!" she repeated over and over.

At her reaction Percy swore and rising he took her in his arms. Holding her tight and stroking her head, he made soothing, calming noises. Once settled, Mary looked up to see him smiling down at her. Looking deep into his eyes, she realised what a foolish girl she was. As far as Percy was concerned, there was no difference between them. Swallowing hard she started. "I am so sorry. I am being foolish, I know." But she could go no further for Percy was kissing her. Long and deep.

Finally, he raised his head. "Do you know how much I love you? Now let this be the end of the matter. We are to be married, regardless of whether anyone else likes it or not."

All Mary could do was smile at him. "Yes, it is the end. But you do understand, don't you?" And he reassured her he understood perfectly. Having finished their drinks, he bade Mary goodnight, leaving her to retire. She still felt foolish but was now happy and contented.

The following evening Percy arrived to escort Mary to attend the celebration of their engagement organised by Mumna. She had dressed with great care and as they walked to the village centre he asked, "Are you more settled in your mind about our betrothal?"

She reassured him she was. "I know I'm being foolish but I hope you understand it is my upbringing which has affected my thoughts. Please forgive me."

"I understand perfectly. But we will say no more about it."

Arriving at the large hut they found everyone waiting to greet them. After many cheerful congratulations those gathered sat on the mats to enjoy the luscious feast and entertainment arranged by Mumna. The celebrations went on late into the night with everyone retiring fully content. Later,

Percy walked her home, leaving her only after thoroughly and solidly kissing her goodnight. That night Mary floated to bed. Lying in the dark she went over the day's events, smiling to herself, thinking how fortunate she was. Over the following days Mary walked around in a cocoon of happiness, feeling totally satisfied with her lot in life.

It would be about a week or so later after the monthly ball, that Dorothy held the official celebration party for the engaged couple. All those attending brought a gift and after the meal, which was excellent, there was music and dancing. Mary was again surprised by the warmth of the congratulations and the gifts they received. Being engaged made her feel special.

Three weeks later, just as school was closing for the day, Mary heard shouting. Going outside she watched as the islanders raced down to the seashore. Looking she saw a large ship anchored in the bay, and being lowered into the water was a small skiff. Knowing the ships arrival would cause too much excitement in the children she closed the school quickly, telling everyone they could leave. Noisily they scrambled out through the doorway. Some raced down to the shore to watch the small boat arrive, while others set off home, happy at being allowed out early. Leaving Chula to finish tidying up Mary took off her apron and set off down to the dockside.

Watching the small boat gliding across the water Mary suddenly realised there were two people sitting in it who seemed familiar. Starting to run as fast as she could, she began waving her scarf in the air. At the water's edge she jumped up and down, waving and calling. In response the people in the small boat began waving back. It was Laura and the Colonel returned home.

As soon as the boat pulled alongside Mary went forward, eagerly waiting for her dear friend to alight. Once on dry land the two women literally threw themselves into each other's arms, laughing gaily. Staring into each other's face, the ladies were amazed at the changes having taken

236

place in such a short period of time. Then, laughing, they hugged each other again. Even the Colonel hugged Mary before quickly stepping back a little embarrassed, but with a huge smile spread across his face.

Just then the Captain came forward, extending his hand in greeting. Once the pleasantries were over Mary insisted Laura and the Colonel go to her house for refreshments. However, the Colonel excused himself, leaving to see the Chief and his wife. Laura was surprised by Mary's new house spending some time looking around it whilst Mary made the tea. As the two women settled down Laura expressed her delight at the place and how glad she was to be home. Both ladies were soon lost in a world of their own. Of course, Mary's betrothal was the most surprising news of all and occupied much of the ladies' attention.

Sometime later when the Colonel returned, he was surprised to discover the two ladies still merrily chatting away. Smiling to himself, he wondered how it was that women always had so much to talk about. Eventually he managed to pry Laura away. "Come along my dear we need to get home before the evening draws in." As they left Mary promised to visit them as soon as she could.

After the Johnstones had gone home Mary gave thought to all Laura had told her. For the first time in weeks, she felt homesick for England and Lizzie. That night she slept fitfully, dreaming of returning to her own land. Once again this raised the worries of the difference between her and Percy. It was therefore a slightly depressed Mary who left two days later to visit Laura's island home.

Arriving at the Johnstone estate Mary's state of mind was soon obvious to both Laura and Jayne. Sitting her down, they demanded an explanation for her poor demeanour. Their insistence forced Mary to tell all. Which she did. Having stopped talking Mary sat still looking at them. To her surprise the two women burst out laughing, totally throwing her off guard. As they didn't appear to be stopping, she began to get annoyed. But so infectious was their laughter, she soon found herself starting to snigger and then giggle. Before long she was sitting back in the chair literately rolling with laughter, tears flowing down her face.

Ten minutes later all three had calmed down, whereupon Jayne told her, "You are a silly girl and should not be letting such stupid thoughts enter your head."

"Besides," said Laura, "If you can't ignore anyone who has any doubts about your right to be the future Lady Falshaw, then you are not the Mary Watson we think you are." At Laura's comments Jayne agreed.

"You are right." Accepting finally that perhaps she really was being foolish, Mary decided it was time lay the idea to rest. That evening there was much joy and laughter in the Johnstone household.

Arriving home, the following day Mary found Percy sitting drinking tea and talking to Captain Morrison. For a moment she stood unseen, watching the two men, thinking how well they got on together. Looking up Percy saw her and, as he smiled, her love for him intensified. Rising from his chair he greeted her warmly, the Captain following his example when he realised she was there.

Greeting them both, the Captain said, "I have a letter from your friend which I am most pleased to deliver." Thanking him profusely the three sat making small talk until the Captain took his leave. He told her he would call the following day to collect any missive she might have for England.

Rising from her chair, Mary took hold of the Captain's hands. "Please, won't you call me Mary. I feel it only right, as we are such good friends. Besides if you are going to give me away on my wedding day it seems only fitting you should address me so."

The Captain, touched by her request, smiled warmly. "I would be most honoured to do so, Mary!"

Once they were alone Percy asked her about her visit to Laura's. Smiling she told him all about it. With the exception of her confessing her worries as she felt he should not be bothered with her girlish foolishness. After he departed Mary took her letter inside, eager to read all her friend had written. Sometime later, happy with the news Mary took up her pen to write a reply.

*My Dearest Lizzie*

*I was so delighted to read your letter and to learn you are now a happily married woman. You sound to have had a wonderful Wedding Day. I am sure you will be very happy and contented in your new life, and young James will find pleasure in his new father.*

*I too have been getting used to the idea of my forthcoming marriage. Although I have been troubled slightly with the difference between our social status. But Percy says I am being silly and he is probably right. I know I will accept the situation. But, perhaps not until after we are married.*

*Laura has arrived home and I have spent time with her and Jayne. I did mention to them my concerns but they just laughed at me. At first, I was quite cross for they were not taking me seriously. But so infectious was their laughter I soon found myself giggling. You should have seen the three of us sitting in the lounge rolling with laughter and tears coursing down our cheeks. Their reaction has finally made me realise how strong I am. I will, with Percy's support, be able to cope with anything or anyone who has a problem regarding my position as Lady Falshaw. I realise if Percy is happy with me then so should other people be. With this new-found feeling your parent's reaction to the news does not distress or surprise me. I am content and very much in love with a wonderful man. Are you not pleased for me my dear one?*

*How surprised I was to read about the Williamson sisters leaving the estate. I say well done Andrew as I am sure it was the right thing to do. What a wonderful, caring, strong man you are married to. I am so happy for you.*

*The return of Laura has cheered me up and her description of Baby James is a delight. I do believe she misses him. Although she now has Jayne's baby to coo over. Laura*

239

has told me how much she enjoyed staying in your house and was sorry to leave. But I do feel she is glad to be back here in her island home. Jayne and Thomas were a little concerned about their return but the Colonel has assured them they are welcome to stay in the house. It is so big there is plenty of room for all of them. I believe they have both got used to having a young child around. Besides, the Colonel has now offered Thomas a partnership which has pleased and delighted them.

My dear, I realise I have told you little of my new home. It is delightful and I think you would love it. There is a large central room which houses a small kitchen, as well as dining and living areas. Plus, two bedrooms. One for Kuala and Chula to share and one for me. I have a bar on the outside door ensuring we are always secure at night. And there are proper windows with shutters that can be locked. I feel secure and am comfortable.

The school is next door. There are three areas for teaching as we have quite a number of children now and need the space. Mumna comes once a week for writing and reading lessons. She is progressing well and I am pleased with her.

Over the last few weeks I have reflected on all that has happened in my life. I finally accept where I am now, on these islands, is where I should be. That may sound peculiar to you dear Lizzie but for the first time in a long while I feel as if I actually belong somewhere. Not that I wouldn't be happier if you lived near me. But it is not to be. At least not just yet. Hopefully, however, we will see each again in the near future.

After Percy and I marry I am not sure where we will reside. We shall be returning to England for a short period of time to visit his estate there but I have a feeling he will wish to return to the islands. I will tell you more once I discover what is to be.

It seems the future, while unknown, may prove to be an interesting and exciting one for me. But no matter where I go, I shall always keep in touch with you my dearest friend.

Well, night draws in so I will close and be away to my

*bed as it is a school day tomorrow.*

*Take great care my dear one. Give my love to James and Andrew*

*Your loving friend Mary*

Closing the letter Mary took out her journal to write: *I am a foolish woman. Jayne and Laura have convinced me my concerns about my position are stupid and should not be tolerated. Laura says Percy must love me deeply to have asked me to marry him. I believe she is right, so I will endeavour to stop my girlish foolery.*

# Thirty-four

Back in England married life for Lizzie and Andrew was wonderful. They were extremely happy and Lizzie felt life couldn't get any better. The only event to mar their ideal life was the passing of Andrew's father. In some respects, it had been a blessing as Lord Weston's health had been deteriorating for some time. Unfortunately, his passing left Andrew feeling somewhat guilty as he hadn't expected to inherit the title or the lands. Lizzie while comforting, also reassured him that it must have been meant to be. Reluctantly he had agreed. Young James was growing fast. He was often seen running around the house causing mayhem. Not that anyone minded for he was such a loveable child. Even the staff adored him. Within days of their marriage he began calling Andrew, 'Daddy' delighting both parents. Lizzie smiled each time she heard him. They soon became a happy family unit.

Returning home after taking James to the park one day, the butler informed Lizzie, "There is a visitor for you Madam. A Miss Williamson." The news made Lizzie sigh in dismay. "Have I not done the right thing Madam in allowing the lady in?"

Lizzie shook her head. "Not really but you were not to know so do not worry about it."

"Oh dear. She told me she was Madam's sister-in-law so I thought it would be acceptable to allow her to wait for Madam's return. Should I ask her to leave and say you are unavailable?"

Lizzie thought for a moment before responding. "No. I will see the lady but, if His Lordship returns please ask him to join us immediately."

Passing Baby James to his nurse Lizzie instructed her to keep him until sent for. Then taking off her outer garments she went towards the drawing room. Placing her hand on the door-knob she took a deep breath, straightened her back and entered the room. Edith was just as she remembered, appearing not to have changed in the slightest. Even her greeting was the same. Cold and aloof. Asking Edith to be seated Lizzie ventured, "May I ask why you have called?"

Swallowing hard Edith then proceeded to explain. "My sister and I wish to return to our home."

When Lizzie questioned, "To which home do you refer?"

"The family home in the country."

Astounded by the effrontery of the woman Lizzie took a moment to calm herself, refraining from responding as she didn't really know what to say. The silence stretched. Lizzie knew she would have to say something, and soon. Just as she was about to speak the door opened and Andrew entered the room. Feeling great relief at seeing her husband Lizzie rose from her seat. Turning towards Edith, she said, "As the country estate is now under my husband's management, I am afraid you will have to discuss any such matters with him." On that note she turned, smiled an apology at Andrew, wished Edith a good-day and quickly left the room.

It was about fifteen minutes later before Andrew, looking for his wife, found her sitting in the study. As he entered, she stood up and ran into his arms. "I am so sorry leaving you to handle the situation. I just couldn't cope with her."

Andrew held her close. "Don't worry my Darling. I have sorted the whole affair out. Besides, you put me in charge of managing the estate so you did the right thing by leaving."

Feeling relieved Lizzie kissed his cheek. Looking at her husband she realised how very much she loved him. As the couple parted from their embrace Andrew said, "I have in fact refused Edith's request. I have told her we cannot trust either of them to behave correctly where the estate management is concerned. Needless to say, Edith was somewhat vitriolic in her response to my decision. So much so, I was forced into the unhappy position of requesting she leave the house."

"What happened next," whispered a pale Lizzie?

"She stormed out of the house, cursing the lot of us but me in particular."

Shocked by her sister-in-law's behaviour Lizzie became indignant. "They have plenty of money of their own so they can afford to rent a small house in the country or even a town house if they so wish. I just don't understand what I have ever done wrong that they would treat me this way?"

Andrew, did not like seeing his wife upset. "Do not worry about them my dear. They will not be made welcome here again. I shall instruct the butler not to allow either of them entry. And I will send a legal notice preventing them from bothering you again. I will also send instructions to the Estate Manager to turn them away should they attempt to enter the country house."

That night Lizzie wrote in her diary: *What a day it has been and how shocked I was to find Edith waiting for me when I returned home. She has changed little and is still the same austere, demanding person she has always been. Not once did she enquire how little James fared. Fortunately, Andrew arrived home at just the right moment, allowing me to make a quick escape. I felt so guilty at springing her on him but I knew he would resolve the situation. He is my hero. I am the most fortunate of women to have such a husband.*

With Andrew inheriting the family's large estate it was decided the Weston family would split their time between the two country estates and their own town house. As for the Williamson town house, they decided to rent it out, perhaps with a view to selling it, should a good offer be received. Both knew they would never reside there. Lizzie was also determined never to allow the two sisters access to it. Besides, if Mary returned to England then it would be made available to her. When or if that would ever take place neither was really sure, but Lizzie felt confident that one day her dear friend would return.

It was about two weeks later that Lord and Lady Weston received an invitation to attend Marlborough House. The Prince and Princess of Wales were holding a dinner party and wished to meet Andrew's new wife. The news sent Lizzie into a panic. Having attended more than one ball at the palace Lizzie had never been formally introduced to Their Royal Highnesses. Sending a note to her Mother for advice, Lizzie began checking her wardrobe. She needed to know if she had anything suitable to wear to such a prestigious event. Within the hour Lady Mountford was seen entering the Weston house full of excitement. Of course, her Ladyship insisted Lizzie should have a brand-new dress. However, when she objected, her Mother went to see Andrew. When he discovered the reason for the upheaval in his normally placid household, he laughed, finding the whole thing most amusing.

When Lizzie declared, "But, it is too extravagant to buy a new dress just because we are to have dinner with the Prince," he laughed even louder. With a serious face he told her, "It is no problem for you to have a new outfit. In fact, you can have six if you wish. We can easily afford them."

At his announcement Lady Mountford clapped her hands, "Wonderful. I will arrange for the seamstress to call tomorrow. Come Lizzie we can start deciding which style will be more suitable." And soon the two ladies were immersed in their task. Quietly Andrew left the room smiling, thinking what a wonderful, innocent person his lovely wife was.

It was some two weeks later that Lord and Lady Weston took their carriage to Marlborough House. Arriving, they had expected to see many other carriages. They were surprised to note there were only six or seven other vehicles drawing up at the same time as theirs. Upon entering the drawing room, the young couple were further surprised to see only fourteen people gathered inside. Passing through the door a well-dressed man stepped forward to greet them. Both Lizzie and Andrew recognised the Prince immediately. By his side was his wife Princess Alexandra. The warmth of their greeting was relaxing.

Taking Lizzie's arm, the Prince led her into the centre of the room. "My Lords and Ladies please welcome the new Lady Weston."

Andrew followed closely behind with the Princess. Although Lizzie had been apprehensive about attending the dinner, she actually found the evening enjoyable. The Prince spent a great deal of time talking to her. However, had she been aware of the Princes' reputation she might not have felt so relaxed. Unfortunately, the Prince was reputed to be quite a womaniser, having a number of mistresses! Andrew, fortunately, was very much aware of the Prince's reputation and being a dutiful husband, he kept a watchful eye on his wife throughout the evening. Later, riding home in the carriage Lizzie expressed her delight, stating how much she had enjoyed the evening but also how glad she was it was all over.

Andrew thought no more of the evening until a few days later, when, much to his surprise, Lizzie received a letter from the Prince. Going to show it to her husband she was surprised to see how put out by the missive he was. When she questioned him why, he found himself having to explain. "It appears the Prince has a reputation where the ladies are concerned. I feel you should be careful as to how you respond to his letter."

Being an innocent person, Lizzie at first couldn't believe what she was hearing. But she accepted what her husband told her to be true, recalling some gossip she had read in one of the tabloids. So shocked was she her immediate reaction was to destroy the letter.

"I don't think tearing up the letter and ignoring the His Highness will resolve the situation. We need to think what to do to avert his advances."

Andrew knew if the Prince had his eye on Lizzie then they would need to ensure he lost that interest, and quickly. They decided it might be better to discuss the matter with

Lizzie's parents. Perhaps between them they could come up with the best solution for diverting the Prince's attention away from her. And so, two days later, while they were dining with her parents, the matter of the Prince's letter was raised. His Lordship was distressed and annoyed over the matter but Lady Mountford soon soothed her husband's anger, "I am sure we can find a solution if we all remain calm."

After much discussion it was decided Lizzie would reply to the letter, which was an invitation to meet with the Royal personage. Lady Mountford told Lizzie she was to write to say how delighted both she and her husband would be to receive a visit from His Highness. Should the Prince not take the hint she was not interested in him then a meeting would have to be arranged? The idea of meeting the Prince shocked Lizzie.

"But I do not want to meet him."

Her Mother replied, "I know my dear. But don't worry, you won't be alone with him for I shall be present." Reluctantly and despite her reservations, Lizzie wrote the reply as instructed. Sealing the envelope, she prayed it would be the end of the matter.

Nothing was heard from His Highness for the next few days. As such Lizzie started to feel relief by the lack of a response. That is until she arrived home one day to find yet another letter from Marlborough House. She began to panic and when Andrew returned home later that day, he was met by one very agitated wife pacing the room in distress. As soon as he entered the room, Lizzie flew into his arms begging him. "Oh, please my darling, don't let the Prince come near me."

Her demands threw him slightly off balance. "What, has he replied to you?" Secretly he had hoped the Prince would have taken the hint his wife wasn't interested.

Lizzie showed him the response. Reading the letter Andrew knew there was no way Lizzie could cope on her own in a meeting with the Prince. He also knew it would be better if she was fully chaperoned all the time. Managing to calm

247

his wife, he decided to take the letter to his mother-in-law. Returning sometime later, he explained to Lizzie what she was to do, whereupon a letter in response was despatched to His Highness.

Three days later, as planned, a carriage pulled up outside Weston house. As the Prince alighted from the carriage, the house door was duly opened allowing him entry. He was shown into the drawing room where Lizzie sat, nervously sewing. Upon his entry she rose from her seat and curtsying greeted him. "Welcome Your Highness, please take a seat."

The Prince in doing so enquired, "Is Lord Weston not at home?"

Lizzie swallowed hard. "He is not. He is currently away from home on business and has been delayed."

The Prince stood and took a seat closer to Lizzie. Then taking hold of her hand he began showering her with compliments. "You must appreciate how much I admire you Lady Weston? Or may I call you Elizabeth?"

Lizzie shaking, played her part well. Being by nature a shy and bashful person. "I am most honoured by Your Highness's compliments."

Slowly the Prince inched closer to Lizzie, who in turn did her best to move further away, until such time as she could go no further. The Prince took Lizzie's failure not to move any further as a sign that his attentions were not unwelcome. Leaning forward he was about to kiss her when the door suddenly opened and in walked Lady Mountford. She stopped and studied the scene. "And what is going on here? Oh, it is you Your Highness. What a pleasure to meet you again."

Lizzie jumped to her feet, as did the Prince. A guilty look spread across his face as he turned and bowing acknowledged Her Ladyship's presence. At her Mother's entrance Lizzie took the opportunity to escape, leaving the room as fast as possible, explaining she must go see to her son.

Without any outward sign of having noticed anything untoward Lady Mountford requested His Highness sit down. Then joining him she began making small talk. As she spoke, she took the opportunity to tell him, "I have to say how delighted my husband and I are with our daughter's new marriage. Never Your Highness, have you seen a couple so much in love. We are so fortunate to have such an honourable daughter. Do you not agree Sir?" From the tone and words used by Her Ladyship the Prince was left in no doubt that he had intruded where he was not wanted. After a suitable passing of time, he rose to take his leave. Once he had departed, Lady Mountford smiled warmly, believing the Prince had now finally come to understand the position. Which he had.

As for His Highness? Well, he may have been a little frustrated at being thwarted in his intentions but he was not overly put out by the rejection. As he later told one of his confidants, "You see my dear Count, there are 'plenty more fish in the sea' who will not baulk at my advances."

From that moment on there were no more invitations to private dinners at Marlborough House. But, more importantly, no more unwanted correspondence. Lizzie was relieved, knowing she could relax and continue enjoying her married life without fear. Andrew too was relieved. Telling his mother-in-law, "I am deeply in your debt for resolving the situation so easily." Her Ladyship merely smiled in response. After all what was a mother for if not to protect her daughter's honour!

The following week as Lizzie was taking breakfast the butler brought in the mail. Amongst the pile Lizzie was delighted to see a letter from Mary. Rising from her chair she took it into the drawing room. Entering the room, she discovered Andrew playing on the floor with James. Looking up he smiled at his wife, noticing she looked relaxed and the happiest she had for some time. He knew the problem with the Prince had really upset her, so it was good to see her smiling again. 'Besides,' he thought, 'it would not have been the 'done thing' to call out the Prince of Wales in a duel. No matter how slighted a husband he was, one just did not do such a thing to Royalty.'

Rising from the floor Andrew kissed his wife warmly as she told him of having received a letter from Mary. Knowing the pleasure these letters gave her, Andrew said he would leave her to read it in peace. The maid was called to remove young James, whilst Andrew departed for business in town. Smiling at how thoughtful her husband was, Lizzie sat and began reading, delighting in the news it contained. Much later she took the opportunity to pen her friend a reply.

*My Dearest Mary*

*What delightful news. I am so happy Laura has returned safe and is well. I must confess to missing her as she always made me feel close to you whilst she was here. I think even Baby James misses her.*

*You will be pleased to know we are all well and I am truly happy. Although for the last few weeks I have been living under a cloud, which at times has made me somewhat distraught. The reason you will not believe, but I will endeavour to tell all. The whole incident started after our attendance at Marlborough House for a small private dinner. You can imagine how I felt being shown such an honour by Their Royal Highnesses. The evening was most delightful but how I wish we had declined the invitation. It appears I unintentionally caught the eye of the Prince of Wales and he attempted to pursue me.*

*I am most fortunate to have a husband who loves me dearly and cares about what happens to me. It seems I am not the first lady upon whom the Prince has cast his eye. You see dear one he has developed quite a reputation for chasing women of all characters. It shocks me deeply. Andrew was quite annoyed about the Princes' attentions but Mama took control and it was she who managed to resolve the whole affair. I now realise how naïve I am for I did not suspect such matters occurred between ladies and gentlemen of standing but, according to Mama it is quite common. My sympathies go out to the Princess who is an admirable lady and who should not have to suffer such indignities. I must say I felt most uncomfortable about the whole affair. Anyway, the matter is now finished with, thank God.*

*Now on to happier news. James grows bigger each day. He adores Andrew and has taken to calling him Daddy, which delights us both. You will be surprised to hear how domesticated I am becoming, even enjoying running my own household. Something I never thought I would be capable of doing. How fortunate I am that Andrew has surrounded me with the best of household staff.*

*Sadly, Andrew's father, Lord Weston recently passed away. And so, now I am called Lady Weston which I find most strange. Because of these changes we spend our time between the two country properties and our town house.*

*We had heard naught of the Williamson sisters for some time after they moved. But recently Edith paid us an unexpected visit. She requested, no demanded, they be allowed to return to their home? She meant the country estate. I was astounded. Fortunately, Andrew arrived home at just the right moment. He handled the situation admirably, leaving Edith dissatisfied. Having discussed the matter, we have decided we shall sell the Williamson town house if a good buyer can be found. In the meantime, we will continue renting it. At the moment there is a new family in residence. They are genteel people so I am contented the house is in good hands.*

*Thank goodness you are no longer tormented with those feelings of inadequacy. Just think of your time spent with Mrs Maberley. Did she not teach you how to behave like a lady? I am sure she would be distressed were she here and knew of your unrest. Be content in your mind my dear, for you are worthy of all you have received and gained in your life.*

*The social season has started but, with the recent experience of His Highness still fresh in my mind, I have been loath to be involved. We shall not miss out but will only go where we feel comfortable and welcome. Not that we are out*

251

*often as we are both happy with our family lifestyle. And of course, we entertain at home.*

*Tell me my dear, have you made the decision as to when you will marry? If so, please send me all the details of the event. I want to know how your day goes, what you will wear and who will attend you? Laura and Jayne, I am sure will be amongst your choices. If you do return to England, we will be delighted to see you again.*

*And now I have some rather special, secret news which only you will know about as I have yet to tell Andrew. Although by the time you receive this letter the news will be known to all. My Dear One, I am so delighted for I believe I am with child again. I wait but a few days more before breaking the news to my dear husband and parents. I hope you are happy for me. This time I shall not be afraid as my love will be by my side. I shall also pray for another son. Even though Andrew loves James as dearly as he does, I am sure he would wish to have a son and heir of his own.*

*There is little more to tell you as I am now very much a lady of leisure, spending my time between tending James, running the household and being a dutiful wife. I shall close so my letter is ready for when the post is collected.*

*Take care my dear one and write to me soon. I so enjoy reading your news.*

*Give my love to Laura and Jayne.*

*Your Loving Friend, Lizzie*

# Thirty-five

Mary's life had continued much the same as usual. But, by the time Lizzie's letter arrived on the island she was in the middle of her wedding preparations. Having asked Captain Morrison on his previous visit to give her away, the happy couple set a date for their wedding to take place. Much to Percy's delight it was agreed it would happen when the Captain returned to the island.

In the meantime, the ladies of the sewing circle, who were delighted with the news, vowed Mary would have the best wedding day they could possibly arrange. Unbeknownst to Mary, Dorothy had already begun organising things. Having sent away for some silk and lace, the ladies intended making her a beautiful wedding trousseau. Kuala, Chula, Laura and Jayne happily agreed to be maids of honour meaning they too would have new dresses sewn for them. It was agreed with Mumna that the island women would collect flowers for Mary's headdress, her bouquet and to decorate the church. As for the wedding feast, everyone on the islands was going to contribute something. While Laura's cook was to bake the Wedding Cake. So it was that Mary soon discovered there was nothing for her to do regarding her wedding plans. Surprisingly, she also discovered, she had somehow acquired a family of people whose only wish was to make her wedding day a most glorious affair.

This had come to light a few days after the betrothal announcement, when Mary had been talking to Dorothy. "I am a little worried about my wedding as I haven't started organising anything yet."

Unable to remain silent a moment longer, Dorothy announced, "Well my dear, you can stop worrying. It's all in hand."

Mary looked aghast. "What do you mean it's all in hand?"

253

"Well. Everyone on the islands wants to be involved in making your day special. So, we've all got together and so... it's been organised." Dorothy then went on to explain exactly what had been arranged, and who was involved in doing what.

Mary was dumbfounded. She couldn't take umbrage at their effrontery for it made her realise how much they loved and cared for her. Expressing her heartfelt thanks, she sat smiling and quietly crying at the same time. "Oh, Dorothy, you are all so good to me. Thank you so much. I feel... I feel... so special." It was the sign of tears which caused Dorothy to become concerned. Although, she soon realised they were in fact tears of happiness.

Once calmer, Mary said, "I want to thank everyone. You are all being so kind and considerate but it is too much to ask? Them doing all this for me."

Dorothy smiled warmly. "No, it isn't. Don't be so silly. They want to show you how much they care, so please Mary, accept their help."

"Oh, I will. I do. Thank you so very, very much," she whispered.

Dorothy took the opportunity there and then to take Mary's measurements for her wedding dress, insisting she was to have no part in creating the outfit, as all the ladies wanted the dress to be a surprise. "Besides, you have done so much for other people, this is their way of returning your generosity."

Feeling the matter was out of her hands Mary gracefully acquiesced. In some ways she was relieved as it helped her enormously. 'What wonderful people they all are,' she thought to herself later.

The following day when Percy arrived, she said, "Did you know what was happening with the ladies and the wedding plans?"

Sheepishly, he grinned. "Yes. I hope you're not angry with me for keeping it a secret?"

Being so much in love with him, Mary knew she could

not have been upset even if she had wanted to be. "No; of course not." And smiling she went on to tell him all that was being done for her; for them. And how surprised and delighted she was.

Percy smiled. "It is just what you deserve. I am so happy, and hope you will accept their thoughtfulness with good grace."

"Oh, I will. I am. It's just that I am not used to such generosity." The more Percy heard of Mary's past life, the more he found his love for her deepening. He truly believed she was the love of his life.

Later, the happy couple went to speak to Chaplain Gordon to arrange the wedding service. This had been the one area the ladies felt it only right and proper they should leave to the happy couple. A wedding ceremony is such a personal affair and the ladies believed the bride and groom should make their own choice of music and service.

With her wedding organised Mary found life easy. She spent as much time as possible with Percy on his yacht, at his home or in her little house. Chula and Kuala were developing into good teachers so she felt the pair might soon take over the running of the school. Perhaps with help from Sally and occasional assistance from Jayne, should it be needed. Percy had made the decision that they would return to England after their wedding. He was determined to show Mary his English home. And to introduce his new wife to his estate workers and his friends.

Despite herself Mary could still not resist expressing a concern over her suitability for such a grand estate? But Percy merely brushed her fears aside. "That may be but you are as much of an aristocrat as any other person I have met."

When, laughingly, she told him, "Maybe but, I think you are biased." He wholeheartedly agreed, still insisting he was correct.

Thinking of England, Percy realised it was perhaps time to explain more about his life and how he came to be living on the islands. With Mary having confided details of her past, he felt duty bound to reciprocate. Sitting her down he began explaining his history.

"I am the second son of a Marquis. However, I inherited the title and lands of Lord Falshaw from my maternal Grandfather. The estate was not worth very much at that time. My Grandfather was a philanthropist. Spending much of his fortune on good causes."

Percy laughed at the memory before continuing. "He was often heard to say he would reap the benefits in heaven. Although there was a little money left, he still owned a decent sized estate in the country which has proven to be self-sufficient. He also owned the property and plantation on these islands. During the eight years since I arrived on the islands, I have managed to build up a successful business. The plantation is the largest on the islands and is quite prosperous. Over those years I have invested the profits wisely."

Pausing, he allowed Mary to digest his comments. "This means; we will be quite comfortable in our married life. We can travel or spend our time wherever you would care to. You will have a choice of places to live. All this, I give to you Mary, along with my heart."

Overwhelmed by his gesture, it took Mary a moment to respond. "I do not care where we live. As long as we are together, that is all that matters to me. Of course, I would like to see Lizzie again if possible?"

Understanding how much her friend meant to her, Percy declared, he was more than happy to bring the two young women together once more. "As such, I have started making plans to find someone capable of taking charge of the estate during our absence."

Mary was delighted to discover they would travel back to England through America. "Besides, if I don't take you to visit Amelia after we are married, she will never forgive me." Secretly, Percy felt his sister would also be able to help Mary adjust to her new life as Lady Falshaw. Hopefully helping to make it easier for her when they arrived back in England. Even though he was confident when telling her that society could be damned, he was aware there could still be some problems, however minor. For the moment he wasn't going to worry her with these thoughts. Hence the visit to his sister's home.

With Mary aware that she would be leaving the island soon she decided it might be better if a new school teacher was found. Despite her confidence in the two young girls being capable of running the school, they only knew so much. And, there was still much more for them to learn. So, it was, with Mumna's agreement, that a missive was sent to England advertising the position of school mistress or master. The post to take effect at the earliest opportunity. With the decision to find a replacement having been made Mary knew there was no turning back. Her destiny was sealed. Becoming Lady Falshaw was the start of another new chapter in her life. But, one she was looking forward to; albeit with some slight trepidation.

Three weeks later, Mary returned from school to find Dorothy waiting for her. The lady appeared quite excited, insisting Mary follow her to the church house. Approaching the building Mary was surprised to discover a number of the ladies waiting there. Looking to Dorothy she questioned, "What is happening?" But Dorothy just placed her fingers against her lips. As if to say it's a secret, wait and see. Then she beckoned Mary to follow her into the church house.

Once inside, there was much twittering and giggling. Before Mary realised what was happening some of the ladies started to undo her dress. As she began protesting, she was quickly silenced. Standing in her under shift, she watched as Sally and Jayne entered the room. They were carrying, what could only be described, as a wonderful creation. Mary, suddenly realised she was being presented with her wedding dress, and stood waiting in eager anticipation.

With care the two ladies placed the dress over Mary's head, proceeding to carefully button the back. Once fastened Jayne and Dorothy pinned a headdress to her head before attaching a beautifully embroidered veil to it. "On the day there will be fresh flowers attached to the headband," she was told.

Satisfied with the result Jayne carefully removed the cover from the long, looking glass. Then, turning Mary around to face the glass, everyone waited with bated breath. Mary was amazed at the image staring back at her. In fact, she was awestruck and dumbfounded. The ladies waited, eager for her reaction. They had worked so hard to prepare the dress, needing to know she approved of it. For a moment Mary couldn't speak, so amazed was she at how lovely she looked. Then turning to look at the ladies she smiled. "Oh, thank you so much. It's... beautiful. I'm overwhelmed by your generosity and kindness." And tears of joy welled in her eyes.

Just as they were about to fall Jayne rushed forward with a handkerchief. "Stop that, you mustn't spoil the dress with tears."

Controlling herself Mary dabbed her eyes with the proffered handkerchief, before allowing the ladies to remove the dress and veil. These were then taken away to be wrapped and hung away, until her wedding day. After redressing, Mary turned to look at all the ladies. "Thank you to each one of you for your part in making me such a beautiful dress." With Mary happy, the ladies were pleased with their efforts and began chattering, feeling relieved that this, the most important of jobs was complete. Returning to her little home Mary literally walked on air and, for the first time in her life, she felt very important. Never had she been happier.

Ten days later a ship docked in the harbour, and venturing ashore Captain Morrison called to see how things progressed with Mary. Answering the door of her little house Mary was pleasantly surprised to find, not just the Captain, but standing beside him a lady she had never met before. The visitor, small in stature, was smiling warmly at her. Mary realised who it was. Inviting the couple inside the Captain said, "Mary, I would like you to meet my wife, Molly."

Delighted she had guessed correctly, Mary greeted Mrs

Morrison warmly. "Welcome. What a lovely surprise. I am so pleased and delighted to meet you and so happy you have come for my Wedding."

When she asked about Molly's decision to visit the islands she was told, "Well, I thought if William was going to act as Father of the Bride and give you away; then it seemed only proper Miss Watson you should also have a Mother-of-the-Bride. And so, here I am."

Taken aback by Molly's thoughtfulness, Mary smiled. "Oh, you must call me Mary. And, what a superb idea. I shall be most honoured to have you act as my mother, for my own is no longer living. However, I must warn you," she said seriously, "You will have competition from the Chief's wife Mumna for I believe she has decided to take the same role as she treats me like a daughter."

At this comment they all laughed. It seemed even Molly was aware who Mumna was. No doubt having heard all about the lady from her husband. However, both the Captain and his lovely wife were pleased, and delighted by Mary's response. Knowing Mary would agree to the idea, the Captain was satisfied. His wife, however, had been unsure, even though he had done his best to tell her she had no need to worry.

Suddenly realising she was not being a good hostess, Mary said, "My apologies would you like some tea. Please sit and I will make some."

"Thank you." replied the Captain, "Sadly however, we have to decline, for we are expected by Mumna and the Chief."

"But we would be honoured if you would join us on board ship tomorrow for afternoon tea?" said Molly.

"I would be delighted, thank you." Once the arrangements were made as to what time she should be ready for the little boat to collect her, the Captain and his wife bade Mary good-day and left.

A couple of hours later when Percy called to see her, Mary told him the good news. Although surprised, he too was

259

delighted by the good Captain and his wife. He liked the Captain a great deal. Pleased by the caring manner he always showed Mary when visiting the island. Percy felt him to be a most honourable gentleman.

The following day at the appointed time, Mary stood waiting at the dockside for the small boat which was to take her across the harbour to the ship. Climbing aboard the large ship it felt as if she was somehow coming home. Silently she remembered how it had been over three years since she took those first steps aboard this ship towards her big adventure. This caused her to remember, that in three days' time, she would board Percy's yacht on the start of yet another new adventure. That of being a married woman.

For just a moment, a sense of fear spread through her as she realised, she would once more be facing the unknown. However, this time she would not be alone but under the protection of a loving, caring husband. Husband, how nice that sounded to her. Shaking her head to clear the thoughts Mary stepped forward to where Molly was waiting to greet her. Taking hold of Mary's hand Molly leant forward to kiss her lightly on the cheek. Then she gently drew her towards the table and chairs set upon the deck. Sitting under an awning stretched above the table, it offered them protection from the heat of the day's sun.

As they settled Molly enquired, "Do you have a wedding dress?"

"Oh yes," replied Mary, almost breathlessly, as she recalled the beautiful creation made for her. "The ladies of our sewing circle have made me one. It includes a veil and a headdress and is very beautiful."

"That is good. I am so pleased. Although, I confess I did bring my own wedding dress and veil just in case you needed one. Of course, it is quite old so may not have suited you."

Mary was delighted by the lady's forethought. Leaning over she whispered, "Thank you. How kind you are to think of me."

Before she could say anything further the ship's cook appeared, carrying a tray with a plate of sandwiches and a beautiful silver tea service. Mary was delighted by the tea service causing Molly to explain. "It belonged to my Mother. I take it with me wherever I travel."

Captain Morrison, arriving a short time later, joined the ladies and the three of them spent the next couple of hours chatting amicably whilst enjoying the refreshments. Mary explained all the plans for her wedding day. "If it suits you, Molly, could you come to the house a little earlier and help me prepare for the day?"

Delighted by the request, she declared, "I would be honoured to do so. I must say how excited I am at the forthcoming event."

Three hours later Mary returned to her home where she began writing her last letter to Lizzie as a single woman. There was much to tell her dear friend for Mary wanted to be sure she missed nothing out. Time passed, until she placed the letter to one side, knowing she would finish it after the wedding yet before the ship left the island.

*My Dearest Lizzie*

*I was most delighted to receive your last letter and, as expected, both surprised and amazed by its contents. If the news is as you have stated, then I send you my heartiest congratulations and well wishes for your health and the future addition.*

*But what surprise and shock I got when I read of the unwanted attentions of the Prince of Wales. I told Laura all about the incident. She confirmed His Highness is well known for his philandering ways. You must have been most distraught. I am glad the situation has now been resolved. Laura says some husbands turn a blind eye to the Prince's approaches as they are probably looking for favours from the Royal household. How fortunate Andrew is so honourable, cares so deeply for you and will not tolerate such a situation. And how clever in allowing your mother to represent you.*

*I mentioned the matter to Percy who likewise was*

261

annoyed. He agrees with Andrew that such an occurrence should not take place. Especially if a man loves his wife and takes their marriage vows seriously. I confess to being concerned for you. I know I could not tolerate a husband who would not protect me, even from such a notable personage. Anyway, the matter is finished with and thankfully need never be mentioned again.

The plans for my Wedding Day have progressed with great ease on my part. Mainly due to the fortitude of the ladies of the islands as they have organised everything. Apart from the actual church service. Anyway, two weeks ago, Dorothy took me to the church house where the ladies presented me with my wedding gown. Oh Lizzie, it is so beautiful and fits me perfectly. I am so very grateful to them for they have worked hard in preparing the whole trousseau. I was close to tears at the wonderment of it all. It seems everyone is involved in the preparations, meaning I have done little. I am most blessed to have such wonderful friends who are like sisters towards me.

My two young girls have cleaned my little house as there is to be a new School Mistress arriving soon. They have also washed and sorted my clothes ready for my leaving the island. For yes, my dear, we are to return to England after the wedding. We will go stay with Amelia and her family first, remaining there for a period of time. Percy wants to show me something of America so I am unsure as to when we will arrive in England. I will let you know as soon as I am able. If I am honest, I am getting more and more excited. Not just at my forthcoming nuptials, but at the prospect of seeing my dearest Lizzie once more.

With only a few days to go before the wedding I received yet another wonderful surprise. Captain Morrison and his wife Molly have arrived on the islands. You will not believe me when I tell you, she has travelled all the way from England, especially to act as 'Mother-of-the-Bride.' She told me she felt it only proper since her husband is to give me away. She even brought her own wedding dress and veil in *case I needed one. What a wonderful, charming lady she is to be so considerate of my situation. Their generosity has left me feeling most humbled. Today I spent the afternoon on board ship having tea with them. I felt so comfortable talking to her, as if with my own mother. It was a wonderful time. Although, for just a moment, I suffered a small amount of sorrow as I remembered my dear departed parents. Remembering they will not be here to see me on my special day.*

*Queen Mumna too has been most kind and motherly towards me as well. She appears to be enjoying organising the island ladies into making new mats and decorations for the day.*

*And so, I write this, my last letter, as a single woman. I know your thoughts will be with me. My one sadness is you will not be alongside me but my consolation is that we will soon be together once more.*

*I will break now as I intend completing this letter before we leave the island. I shall give it to the Captain to bring back to England with him as he will arrive before we do...*

# *Thirty-six*

On the morning of her wedding day, Mary lay awake in bed, thinking of the momentous event she was about to undergo. If she was honest, she must admit to feeling a little nervous. This was a big step for any young woman. However, more so for her, as this marriage would change her life forever.

A small knock at the door brought her out of her reveries. "Enter."

Mary was expecting to see Kuala, so was surprised when Molly entered carrying a breakfast tray. About to jump out of bed, she was told. "No, stay where you are a little while longer. The two young girls have already left for the church house. I believe Jayne and Sally are to help them get ready. Dorothy is sitting in the kitchen having a cup of tea."

"Oh! Thank you but shouldn't I get up?"

"No, you take it easy for another ten minutes, and when you are ready there will be a hot bath waiting for you."

Mary was delighted. "I think I am being made a fuss of, aren't I?" Molly nodded yes. "Well, then I think I will take full advantage of the situation, thank you so much." And lying back against the pillows she relaxed, endeavouring to make the most of being spoiled.

Finishing her tea, Mary got up and going through into the next room found the bath ready for her to step into. Stripping out of her nightclothes she slipped into the luxuriant warmth of the water. Settling down into the bath Mary watched as Dorothy entered the room. Carrying some warm towels. "I have come to help you wash your hair."

Fifteen minutes later Mary was out of the bath and dry. As she sat in her under shift Dorothy rubbed her hair dry and brushed it until it shone. Next, Molly lightly rouged Mary's cheeks before colouring her lips, after which the two ladies carefully helped her into her wedding dress. To complete the outfit, Dorothy pinned Mary's hair ready for the veil. Then she fitted the headband which now contained some fresh flowers, followed by the veil itself. Turning to look in the mirror Mary was astounded at the image staring back at her. Happy with the results of their work the two ladies declared her ready for church.

As they waited for the Captain to arrive the three ladies sat drinking a small glass of fortified wine. Mary had at first refused until Molly insisted. "It's only a small glass and besides, it will settle your nerves."

Mary had laughed. "What makes you think I am nervous?"

Molly and Dorothy had looked at each other with a knowing smile. "Well, if you aren't then we should perhaps be worried about you, as all young brides are nervous on their wedding day. I know I was."

"Me too," piped in Dorothy.

Looking at them Mary smiled. "You are of course right. I am shaking with nerves." After which she slowly drank the wine. By the time the Captain arrived to escort her to church, Mary was calm and ready for her big day.

Upon entering the house, the Captain stood stock still. He was taken aback and amazed at how beautiful she looked. "I have never seen a more beautiful bride since I married my sweet Molly." Both Mary and Molly blushed at his compliment.

Feeling happy, Mary lifted the hem of her dress in one hand, placed her other on the Captain's arm and allowed him to escort her from the house. The small procession of Mary, The Captain, Dorothy and Molly made their way across the village towards the church. As they passed the islanders stopped and watched, taken with Mary's beauty. Besides, the day's events were also a novelty to them as this was only the second Christian wedding ever to take place on the island.

Arriving at the church, Mary was met by Jayne holding a bouquet of wild flowers for her. Leaning forward, she kissed Mary's cheek before carefully lifting the veil forward over her face. Asking if she was ready the bridal party silently waited until everyone else had entered the little church. Peeking through the door Mary saw how full the church was. From wall to wall. It seemed no-one wanted to miss this event. Once everyone was quiet the organist began playing the bridal march and as the congregation rose, the wedding party entered the church. Slowly Mary walked down the short aisle towards her husband-to-be and her future life. A warm smile covered her face, but her eyes were focused ahead.

To Mary the wedding passed in a haze as all she could do was concentrate on Percy. He likewise stood looking down at her throughout most of the service, his eyes overflowing with love. Once the service was over the newlyweds left the church amid much laughter and cheerfulness. Outside the congregation threw fresh flower petals over the happy couple. And everyone offered their heartfelt congratulations to the newlyweds. Slowly, the wedding party moved towards the village centre where there followed a wonderful celebration feast, amid much laughter and good cheer. Percy was ribbed about no longer being a bachelor, and the ladies teased Mary on now being Lady Falshaw. The Chief gave a wonderful speech on how he was going to miss Mary and Mumna had a small tear in her eye as she too expressed the loss of her 'daughter.' Although she agreed with the Chief that Mary would be in safe hands with His Lordship.

Later, returning to the celebrations after changing her dress, Mary took the opportunity to ask the Captain if he would be available in the morning to receive a letter for Lizzie. "But of course," he said smiling.

"Also, I wish to thank you and Molly for all your support. Your presence here has made my day a special one."

The Captain smiled at her, before gently taking her in his arms to whisper, "God bless you. And remember, there is always a place with us if you ever need one."

As he released her Mary, looked up at him and smiled. "Thank you so much."

Once the evening started to draw in the newlyweds left for the yacht where they were to spend the night. Mary had been a little concerned about saying her goodbyes. But Percy had reassured her there would be plenty of time in the morning before they sailed. Arriving at the yacht Mary was shown into the master bedroom. Percy left, allowing her time to prepare for bed. He was a man of the world and knew she would be nervous. Yet, he was also a caring and considerate person as she would soon find out. That night Mary learnt what it was to be loved and caressed by a man deeply devoted to a woman he loved.

The following morning when she woke, Mary found herself alone. Lying in bed she relived the previous day and night. The latter causing her to blush as she recalled Percy's delicate exploration of her body, and the feelings he had invoked in her.

There was a knock at the door. Calling, "Enter," Mary was surprised when a young woman entered carrying a tray with a cup of tea on it.

"Good-morning, Your Ladyship, I'm Jessie. My husband is Captain of the yacht."

"Oh, good-morning. I didn't realise there would be another lady on board. Please, call me Mary. I'm not used to being addressed as Her Ladyship, just yet."

Jessie smiled. "I'd be honoured to. But only when we are alone. And you must call me Jessie. Breakfast will be served shortly. Do you need help in dressing?"

"No thank you," said Mary smiling. "I think I can manage." After Jessie left Mary got washed and dressed then went up on deck to join her husband for breakfast.

They sat for some time making small chit-chat until Percy asked, "Did you sleep well?" Blushing, Mary nodded yes.

"Good. When you are ready shall we go and say our goodbyes to everyone on the island. Once that's done, we will set sail."

"Oh yes please. Although I must warn you, there will

probably be lots of tears."

Percy laughed. "I wouldn't expect anything else. Come, let us go"

With all her goodbyes having been made Mary returned one last time to her little house. She had deliberately left her adieus to Kuala and Chula until last. Kuala having packed Mary's wedding outfit into the trunk had ensured Percy's man had taken it to the yacht. Before packing away her writing implements Mary took the opportunity to complete her letter to Lizzie. Kuala was going to deliver it to Captain Morrison after they left. Picking up the letter she completed it.

*Well, it is done. I am now Lady Falshaw! What a day it was, full of happiness and joy. I am so very, very happy and contented. My husband is the best of men, and I feel honoured he has chosen me to be his wife.*

*Dorothy and Molly came to help me prepare for the day. What a lovely relaxing time they made the morning. Before I knew it, I was ready. To be honest, I was slightly nervous but they insisted I drank a small glass of wine to help settle my nerves. Once Captain Morrison arrived, we all made our way across the village towards the church. As I passed, the islanders stopped to watch and smile at me. I felt like royalty.*

*At the church we were met by my maids in waiting, and before I realised it, I was walking down the aisle. The little church was packed. But all I could see was Percy, waiting at the other end of the aisle, watching and smiling at me, his eyes full of love. Any nerves I had were completely dispelled. The service was wonderful, with everyone singing out loudly and heartily. Afterwards we made our way towards the village centre for the most sumptuous of feasts. My Darling Lizzie it was a glorious, glorious day. Percy and I spent our wedding night on his yacht. Like you my dear, I too felt some trepidation at what was to happen. But I need not have concerned myself. Percy proved to be the most caring of husbands.*

*And so here I sit, having said my last goodbyes to my little island home. I shall be sad to leave the island and all my new friends as I now realise how much I have come to love my life here. But I hold no regrets for I know that from today I start another new adventure. One I look forward to with all my heart. I am sure Percy and I will return here in the near future, and it is my hope that Andrew, James and You will return with us.*

*Well my dear, Percy has arrived to collect me so it is time to close my letter. As I do, I close another chapter of my life. The Captain and Molly are due to sail for England and I want to ensure he receives this letter before he leaves.*

*Be well my dear one and know we will see each other soon.*

*All my love and devotion*
*Your dearest friend Mary, Lady Falshaw*


Sealing the letter, Mary took up the journal, Lizzie had given her one more time. Turning to the last entry she saw the pages were almost full. Picking up her pen she began to write:
*This will be the last day I will make an entry in this journal. Yesterday I married Percy and today, as we get ready to leave the islands, I know I am about to start a new part of my life. All my island friends are waiting to wish us bon-voyage. I shall miss them all dearly. My life here on the islands has been a happy one. Although I leave with sadness, the memories I take with me will stay in my mind forever. Jayne has given me a new journal and I shall start recording my future adventures in that. How many more journeys I will travel during my life I do not know? But in the years to come I will always have these journals to look back on. I know the journey I am about to undertake does not cause me fear for this time I will not be alone, but under the protection of my husband. And of course, always in the heart and mind of my dearest friend, Lizzie.*